Nothing Left but Silence

# Nothing Left but Silence

Laura Lo Sapio

First published in Great Britain in 2026 by
The Book Guild Ltd
Unit E2 Airfield Business Park,
Harrison Road, Market Harborough,
Leicestershire. LE16 7UL
Tel: 0116 2792299
www.bookguild.co.uk
Email: info@bookguild.co.uk

The manufacturer's authorised representative in the EU
for product safety is Authorised Rep Compliance Ltd,
71 Lower Baggot Street, Dublin D02 P593 Ireland (www.arccompliance.com)

This work is entirely fictitious and bears no resemblance to any persons living or dead.

Typeset in 11pt Minion Pro

Printed and bound in Great Britain by 4edge Limited

ISBN 978 1835743 485

British Library Cataloguing in Publication Data.
A catalogue record for this book is available from the British Library.

*To everyone who dares to dream*

*So I'm still and I am silent, because if I open my mouth, I may never stop screaming.*

*(attributed to) Franz Kafka*

# Prologue

"Well, for what it's worth, I think you should go. It's not like you have anything to lose." There is an arrogant smirk on Alex's face as he lies on his bed, his arms folded under his head and his long legs stretched across the mattress.

"Of course you'd say that." I shake my head. Alex has always been the impulsive one. As twins, we were similar in most things but utterly different in others. While Alex's head was permanently in the clouds, I needed solid plans. Plans I could count on. But if life has taught me something, it's that you can plan all you want, but there is only so much you can do when things decide to take a different turn. A turn that crushes both your dreams and your plans. "You know how crazy it is, don't you? I'll never be able to do this without you."

A tiny wrinkle appears between my brother's eyebrows as he tilts his head to me. "That's where you're wrong, Sabrina."

I shut my eyes, trying to hold on to the sound of his voice a little longer. Will I always be able to remember it?

Will it ever fade away? "You know this whole conversation would make much more sense if you were actually here, right?"

His pained burst of laughter hits my eardrums. "You know what they say: only children, drunks, lunatics, and the dead tell the truth."

"I'm pretty sure it doesn't include the dead, Alex," I whisper back, hoping my brother can hear me wherever he is. "The dead can't speak."

He shifts on his elbow, his eyes locking on me, and a sad, haunting smile spreads across his face. "They can. They do. You just have to listen."

*

"Are you out of your mind, Sabrina?"

Mom nervously paces the room, reminding me of a small, caged animal. A terrified one. She pivots to Dad, pointing her index finger at me. "Is she out of her mind? Are you listening to her? Why don't you say something?"

An urge to laugh builds in my throat, but I suppress it. Because it's not a joke. It's a decision. One that I should have made a long time ago.

"I'm going," I repeat, my jaw firmly pressed and my eyes locked on both of them. I can tell how much they've aged these past two years, but so have I. What was it that my therapist said? We all needed to move forward. Right. It sounds so damn easy, except it isn't.

"You know we won't pay for that," Dad finally says. He isn't screaming or trying to talk me out of my decision, only stating a fact. Expecting him to help when I know he doesn't care would be foolish, and I'm not about to make that same mistake twice. I can't help but wonder, though… Does he ever wake up in the middle of the night wishing he'd done things differently? Does he wish Alex were still alive?

"I got a full scholarship, and I'll get a job."

"Can you even get a job with a student visa?" Mom asks, slowly massaging her temples.

"What kind of job?" Dad frowns, a look of doubt flashing across his face. He almost makes it sound like he actually cares.

"I don't know. A job. One that pays money." I'm not good with words, the spoken ones, anyway. But when it comes to writing my words on paper and turning them into a song, it's a whole different story. Songs can bear so much more weight than real life. They can deal with all the pain you throw into them, and then some, and still hold together. People can't. They break.

"I'll find something. The scholarship covers accommodation and food, so I shouldn't need much else. And yes, I'm allowed to work on a student visa as long as it doesn't interfere with my class schedule and it's on campus." I don't add that, as a part of my scholarship agreement, I already have to work for free at the university bookstore. I'm sure I can always add another paid on-campus job in my free time. Other free time, that is, assuming there is any. No idea when studying and practice are going to happen, but I don't mention that either. Because really, what's the point?

Alex must be laughing at me right now, but I also know he'd have wanted me to go. So here I am. I'm going, no matter what.

"Boston is far away," Mom says. "Too far away."

I cringe at the reproachful tone in her voice, not wanting to say that the very fact that Boston is on the other side of the world, as far away from Prague as it gets, is kind of the point. So I don't say anything. For a brief moment, we just silently look at each other.

"You know that going to Boston Music College has always been my dream." I gather my last bit of strength, but my voice still comes out as a whisper. At first, I'm not even sure they heard me, not until Dad answers.

"I thought it was your brother's dream," he says in a dry, distant voice that cuts right through me like the sharpest of knives. I keep my tears from spilling over. He won't see me cry. I've cried way too much, and I'm not even sure I've anything left. "For God's sake, Sabrina! When will you stop wasting your time with this silly hobby of yours and start preparing for real life? Do you even know what that is?" Dad angrily shakes his head, red expanding across his face and reaching his neck.

*Music is not our fucking hobby*, Alex's voice sounds in my head in response.

Real life. I clench my teeth. Which one, though? The one where you forever chase after things you don't even want just to impress people you don't actually care about? Sounds like hell to me. The nine circles of it.

"Honey," Mom says, shifting her gaze to Dad, exhaustion pouring out of her voice. "Please, don't..."

"It was *our* dream," I answer quietly, while all I want is to scream. Scream from the top of my lungs. Scream at them for forgetting they still have a daughter, for not believing in me, for not believing in us. For letting Alex die. And to scream at Alex for dying. But I can't do any of that out loud. All that is left for me is to scream on the inside and put my anger and frustration into my songs. *Our* songs. Because Alex could sing so much better than me. I was the songwriter of our duo, the one who would transform our ideas and emotions into beautiful lyrics and melodies. Alex was the one to bring them to life. Which is ironic, considering that he's the one who is dead. Will I even be able to do this without him? Do I want to do this without him? What if I'm not good enough?

"You could go back to studying education," Mom tries. "You always enjoyed teaching music."

"*You* wanted me to study education. We—*I* have always wanted to study music. There's a difference, Mom. You used to love our songs," I remind her. A sad, painful expression crosses her face as my dad shakes his head in disgust. Or maybe disappointment. Who knows?

"If you leave, you're on your own," he says, the warning in his voice loud and clear.

I glance back at Mom, but she remains silent, looking down at her feet. I guess some things don't change.

At last, I nod. "If that's what you guys want."

"I'm sorry, Sabrina," Mom says with a trembling voice.

"Me too, Mom. Me too," I answer, and it's true. I'm sorry. Sorry that I have to leave. Sorry that I, too, have dreams. And most of all, I'm sorry that my parents have just lost yet another child.

# One

Being late on the very first day of classes? Check. I could blame the annoying jet lag that I still haven't been able to entirely shake off and also the fact that I've spent the past two days unpacking and trying to understand the layout of our university campus, but I'm pretty sure the professor is going to blame *me*. It might not be helpful to my cause that I enter the classroom with a Starbucks cup in hand. As I do, all the heads in the room immediately turn in my direction. Fortunately, this week is a welcome week, so the real lessons haven't started yet. The point of the orientation class is to get to know each other and talk about our goals for the next four years. In my case, only three because I was able to test out of multiple subjects thanks to the first year of university studies I completed in Prague. The studies I believed would be a total waste of time. Well, that's something, at least. My thoughts wander back home, and I have to make a conscious effort to gather them.

"Miss…?" The professor's irritated voice helps draw me back to earth.

"Sabrina Fialová," I introduce myself quietly. "Sorry I'm late, I—"

"Will you sit down, or should we wait until you finish your coffee?"

Yep, I deserve that. Leave it to me to make the worst first impression possible. "Sorry," I mutter again, scanning the classroom for an empty spot to disappear into.

"Hey! Here!" A blonde girl with a friendly smile waves at me, gesturing to the seat next to her. A sense of relief washes over me. Fuck. This isn't how I envisioned the first day at my dream college.

"Thanks," I whisper as I slide into the seat.

She chuckles. "No problem. He's usually quite nice."

"Yeah." I shrug. Even if the guy were a jerk, he's a highly recognized musician, same as all the faculty here. A jazz musician, in this case, which is not something I'm particularly interested in, but still, being here, surrounded by such amazing people, is a dream come true. Our dream.

*It says they can offer a scholarship to only one of us.* Alex's words from the day we received our acceptance letter from BMC force their way into my head, and I try desperately to push them away. Now is not the time to think about that. I'm here, and that's what my brother would have wanted.

"I'm Isabela, but call me Bela." Alex's voice blends with that of my new friend, and I know, unfortunately, only one of them is real.

"Sorry. Sabrina. Nice to meet you." I reach out my hand, and she responds with a wide smile.

"Coffee after class?" she offers, despite my cup of coffee sitting right in front of her.

"Much-needed."

We laugh and then focus our attention on the professor, just in time to catch his question for this upcoming semester: "So, do you believe you have what it takes to be here?"

*

Bela's drowning a large, sprinkled donut in her latte, looking at me with sincere curiosity. "So you got a full scholarship?" she asks, but there isn't a note of envy in her voice. "God, you must be good." Taking another huge bite of her donut, she nods to herself. The tables around us are buzzing with energy. Blue Cats, the university coffee bar, is a beautiful, cozy place filled with light colors and signed photos of virtually every famous musician on the planet.

"Yeah, I don't know about that." I shrug.

"What's your major?" she asks.

"Songwriting. What about you?"

"Performance. I'm a singer. Isn't it obvious?" I chuckle as she points to herself. Bela looks like a singer. There's something about her that inevitably, but still very much effortlessly, screams, 'I'm here. Look at me.' Maybe it's her long blonde hair, elegantly cascading over her shoulders, combined with her green eyes, or her lips painted red into an almost perfect heart shape, or it might be her stamped floral minidress and high heels. Whatever it is, I instantly like her even though she's my opposite. Not that I don't put effort into my looks, but I'm more of a jeans and Converse girl. Plus, although I've always wished for blue or green eyes, mine are dark brown, very much the same as my hair. Still, I can't complain. I'm just not much of an attention seeker. Quite the contrary, actually.

"Songwriting is something I should definitely work on," Bela continues, and I instantly pick up on her slight but beautiful Spanish accent.

"Yeah, and singing is something *I* should work on." I laugh, but the reminder of the fact that I can't sing my own songs as well as Alex could only makes me anxious.

She grins at me. "Looks like we'll be sharing most of our courses. Awesome! I can introduce you to some people because I've been here since the summer."

I noticed earlier this week that most of my classmates already knew each other. The student visa offered the option of coming to Boston a month ahead of time to get familiar with the city and prepare for the upcoming semester without the stress of last-minute preparations, so it only made sense Bela had already made herself at home. Unfortunately, I didn't have the luxury of spending money just to make friends. Damn, I really need to work on that, though. But when? All the craziness hasn't even started yet, and here I am, already feeling overwhelmed.

"That would be nice, thanks. I'm just not sure how much time I'll have to socialize," I admit reluctantly, sipping from my third coffee of the day.

"Why? That's exactly why we're here."

Right. Everyone knows that one of the biggest benefits of getting into BMC is the networking—the contacts you can make here, the infinite amount of incredibly talented people you get to meet. "I start working at the university bookstore next week. And if I want to survive here, I should also find myself a job where they actually pay me. Everything is so damn expensive." I groan.

"You need an on-campus job?" Bela frowns, and I can see the wheels turning in her head. "Ooh, I see. Wait, because now that I'm thinking of it…" She jumps to her feet and rushes toward the counter. Once I made sure none of her coffee ended up on my shirt, my eyes curiously follow her. She leans against the counter, dangerously close to the barista, and starts animatedly throwing her arms and gesturing toward me. Umm, what?

"Sabrina! Come on! Get your ass over here!" she shouts, turning dozens of heads in the process. Perfect. That's just what I need after this morning.

I get up hesitantly, dragging my feet, and make my way across the café.

"This is Rodrigo. He is Spanish like me."

"Actually, I'm from Argentina," he objects, but Bela dismisses him.

"Yes, yes, right, you know what I mean, mi amor. Now, let's get to what's important here. Sabrina needs a job, and you could use the help." My friend smilingly gestures to the line of people starting to form behind us, even though she's clearly the one causing the backup.

Rodrigo, who must be at least a few years older than me, looks at me reluctantly. "Are you any good at making coffee?" he asks, with the obvious intention of getting rid of both Bela and me as quickly as possible.

"I—I guess…?"

Bela nudges me with her elbow, sending me a pointed look.

"Sure," I correct myself, not sounding sure at all. I've

exactly zero experience making coffee. Hell, I've only started drinking it recently.

"Good." He nods. "You start tomorrow at 3 p.m. Now stop blocking the counter, please."

What? That was easier than I thought.

"Amazing! Thank you so much, mi amor. I knew you were the best." Bela seals the deal before I can even react to the unexpected news of my employment.

"Thank you." I flash my best smile at Rodrigo, but he's already retreated to the coffee machine, forgetting all about us.

Bela loops her arm through mine as we head back to the table. "Well, guess that one's solved. Anything else?"

*

Living in a dorm was never my dream, but it's hard to object to free housing. I take off my jacket, and I'm hanging it up in the closet next to my bed, or what I established as my bed since I was the first one to arrive—leaving two more beds to be claimed—when the door opens.

"No, no, wait a minute! Why should you be the one next to the window?" A girl, potentially my new roommate, throws her hands up in the air without even bothering to say hi.

"Because I got here first?" I offer.

"So what?"

"So I get to choose?"

"That's bullshit," she replies, and if it wasn't for the fact that I have to actually live with her, I would probably laugh. She's obviously younger than me, likely eighteen or nineteen, and judging from the drumsticks she's pointing at my bed with, I would guess she's a drummer. It's also not surprising that her whole appearance is a little scary. Beautiful, but still scary. Her long black hair is completely braided, accompanied by thick lashes that are almost certainly fake, and her nails and lips are painted dark purple. This entire look is combined with jean shorts, a Metallica T-shirt, and leather cowboy boots.

"I'm Sabrina," I try again.

"Hmm." Annoyed, she throws me a look and leaves her luggage at the door before jumping on one of the available beds. I'm not at all surprised she chooses the one that's farthest away from me.

"Nyra," she finally says. "So you are a guitar player?" Her eyes wander to my old guitar case standing in the corner next to my bed.

"Songwriter."

She rolls her eyes. "Of course you are."

"What's that supposed to mean?"

"Nothing, just, you know…" She gestures toward me.

I frown. "Not sure I do."

"Doesn't matter." She waves her hand. "How old are you, anyway? Twenty?"

"Twenty-one," I say.

"Twenty-one? Why?"

"Why what?"

"I mean, you took a few years off after high school or something?"

"Or something." I have no intention of elaborating. Besides, it's not like I'm the oldest one here. Most international students in their first year at BMC are older than eighteen or nineteen, and sometimes it's even their second career. This college is the best in the world, but it's damn expensive, and so is Boston. Coming here involves sacrifices. A recognizable sting of pain shoots through my chest.

*Do you think yours was worth it, Alex?*

Silence.

I shake my head. *So now you only answer when it suits you?*

Before Nyra can come up with more questions, Bela's blonde head appears in the doorway.

"Bela? What are you doing here?" My surprise ratchets up at the sight of the luggage she's dragging behind her. "Wait, are you staying with us?" The joy in my voice doesn't go unnoticed.

"Are you?" Nyra frowns, eyeing my friend doubtfully.

Ignoring her, Bela's mouth stretches into a grin. "You wouldn't believe it, mi amor! My roommate suddenly decided she wanted to move off campus, and the office told me there was a free spot in your room. I specifically asked for you, and it wasn't easy, trust me, because I didn't know your last name. So I just kind of said, 'She's a songwriter, long dark brown hair, amazing body, chocolate eyes, very pretty, from the Czech Republic, has got a full scholarship...' and some of that information must have clicked. So, voilà! Here I am!"

By the time Bela finishes, I can barely control my laughter. Nyra appears far from thrilled, instead looking like she's plotting ten ways to kill us in our sleep. Still grinning, Bela looks around, her eyes landing on the available bed next to me. "So I guess this one is mine?"

Nyra snorts. "Yes, because Miss 'I got here first' already got the best one."

It's not until then that Bela actually looks at her. "And you are?"

"Nyra," she says, arms folded across her chest.

I bite back a laugh. If I thought Bela and I were different, these two are complete opposites.

"Nyra. That's a cool name. Well, I'm sure we can be friends."

Knowing Bela's enthusiasm is about to be crushed, I almost feel sorry for her.

"I doubt that, Barbie." Nyra gets up from her bed, confirming my guess. "Anyway. Since you two have obviously a lot to say to each other, I'm gonna go practice."

Bela shoots me a confused look as soon as the door closes after her. "What the hell is her problem?"

I shrug, still smiling. Bela being here is a gift from heaven. "She's from the Big Apple. It's the New York attitude. I'm sure she will warm up to us."

✳

I spend the rest of the morning writing and composing. Or at least I try. I've always found it difficult to focus on creative work with other people in the room. Except for Alex. Making music with my brother felt as natural as breathing.

*You better not be giving up already.*

*Really? Now you decide to talk to me?*

I throw the pen I've been chewing for the past two hours against the opposite wall.

Bela, who is comfortably lying down on her bed with her eyes closed, takes off her headphones. "Everything all right, mi amor?"

"Yep." I nod without looking at her. "I think I'm going to grab a bite. My new job starts in an hour. You know, the one you got me? Don't want to make you look bad." I force a smile.

She chuckles, lazily stretching her body. "Good. I'll drop by later for a cup of coffee. Rodrigo is working today, right?"

"Yeah. Why?"

A mischievous smile appears on her lips. "I like him."

Leave it to Bela not to dance around things. My skepticism peeks through, and I'm unable to hide it. "Do you even know anything about him?" I ask with a slight frown on my face.

"He plays the guitar and makes excellent coffee." She shrugs. "Oh, and don't get me started on his accent."

I snort, grabbing my jacket and checking its pockets for my student card. Got it. "Right. Sounds like a good start."

"Wait!" She stops me with my hand already on the knob. "What time do you get off?"

"Around seven. Why?"

"I'm headed to a concert on campus tonight. You want to come?"

Damn it. Going out is the last thing I should be doing. I need to register for a harmony class early in the morning, and I haven't had a full night's sleep in weeks. Time to get used to this rhythm, I guess.

"Who is playing?"

"River." Bela's face lights up.

"Who?" I frown, scanning my memory for any famous musician with that name.

"River Evans. Though he only goes by River. You don't know him?" she asks, making it sound like I've personally offended her. "How can you not know him?"

"Umm, I don't know. Is that his real name? River?" Sounds unusual. I'm pretty sure I would remember it.

"Yes, that's his real name." With a shake of her head, she lets out a sigh. "Mi amor, I'm sorry, but you can't call yourself a songwriter and not know this guy. He is one of the best. Quite big in the States right now."

"And he is a singer?" I ask, trying to catch up while making a mental note to google River Evans before tonight's concert. I don't want to look like a complete idiot. Again.

"He is *everything*," she says dreamily. "He plays the piano and sings. Writes his own songs, too. You'll love him."

Right. Not so sure about that. Wouldn't I have already heard of the guy if he really was that amazing?

Bela arches her eyebrows at me. "Mark my words."

"All right, count me in."

# Two

By the time I spot Bela at the café, my feet are absolutely killing me, and Rodrigo is about to kill *me*.

"You said you were an experienced barista!" he yells at me as soon as the long line of people—caused by my not-so-incredible cappuccino- and latte-making skills and speed—is finally gone.

I grit my teeth, trying to remind myself how much I need this job. "I didn't exactly say that I was experienced. I said I could make coffee, and I can. But you are asking me to draw freaking milk hearts and flowers on every single stupid cappuccino. This is a university café, for God's sake! I didn't know I needed a master's degree in coffee art!" Just one glance at Rodrigo, and it's clear that I'm not doing a great job at staying calm. Chances are I'm about to get fired on my first day.

He pinches the bridge of his nose with his left hand and directs his annoyed gaze at me. "Look, Sabrina, if people wanted to go to Starbucks, they would. In fact, there's one right across the street." He points toward Starbucks, where

I've been getting my morning coffee since I arrived. I'd never admit it aloud, but after trying the Blue Cat's coffee, I don't ever plan on going back. The cappuccino is not only better and cheaper here, but it also comes with adorable hearts and flowers. Or at least when Rodrigo makes them. Mine look more like abstract art.

"Look, I'm sorry, I will try harder, okay? I can learn. I really need this job."

"Yeah, yeah." He shakes his head. "You better be an excellent musician, girl, because you are sure as hell not making a living as a barista." I guess I should be offended, but as I look at Rodrigo, I see the corners of his mouth twitching, so I shake my head and burst into laughter.

"You're right. And since we've established that you are so much better at it, would you mind making me one of those super fancy cappuccinos?" I smile sheepishly, dodging the wet towel he throws at me.

"Well, well, seems like you're already becoming friends, mis amores!" Bela leans on the counter, flashing us one of her perfect smiles. Her lipstick is pink this time, accompanied by flawless smoky-eye makeup and wavy hair. She is wearing a fake leather miniskirt, knee-high boots, and a white long-sleeved T-shirt.

"I wouldn't go so far as to call us 'friends,'" Rodrigo says, rolling his eyes but handing me my cappuccino.

Bela chuckles before glancing at the shiny watch on her wrist. "You'll be off in fifteen minutes, right? Shit, you won't have time to get changed before the concert." Her eyes take in my outfit, the tiny crease on her forehead becoming more visible.

I make a face, looking down at my ripped jeans and

simple blue crop top. "Umm, I wasn't really thinking about changing. What's wrong with this outfit?"

Somewhere behind me, Rodrigo chuckles, shaking his head at both of us.

"Nothing's wrong with it. You look great, but I do remind you that there is a possibility, even if it's a small one, that we'll run into River tonight."

"Right. Like he'll care about us." I snort when I imagine a situation in which we actually get to meet the guy, and he not only talks to us but also takes the time to notice our outfits. Hmm, yep, still don't see it.

"So I take it you're going to River's concert tonight?" Rodrigo looks between us. "I may swing by after I close here."

Bela shoots me one of her 'You see? What did I tell you?' looks, causing me to scowl. Am I really the only one who doesn't know this mysterious singer-songwriter?

"Awesome! You like him?" she asks.

"Yep, I've seen him perform twice already, and he's fucking good. I tried to get someone to cover for me tonight, but it looks like everybody's going. I think I can still make it, though."

"Oh," I say, seeing the opportunity to redeem myself. "If you need to get out earlier, I can stay and close up for you," I offer, noticing their skeptical expressions right away.

"Yeah, that's not happening, but thanks for offering." Rodrigo shakes his head while Bela winks at him.

Seriously? My brows crease into a frown. I'm pretty sure I'm not *that* bad.

I turn to Bela, silently pleading for her support, only to

be betrayed by her wide grin. "That probably wouldn't be the best idea, mi amor. We really like this café, and I heard it has been standing for over a decade now. Let's keep it that way."

My confusion must be clearly written on my face because they both burst into laughter. "Fuck you, guys." I stick out my tongue and then laugh along with them.

✻

To say that the university concert hall is packed would be an understatement. Of course, I had no time to get changed or even google more information about tonight's concert, but at least I'm here, which feels like a big enough accomplishment after this week. As I look around, I notice a lot of familiar faces from our orientation week, not only singers and songwriters, but all kinds of musicians, from bass players, guitarists, and drummers to cellists, and I'm pretty sure I saw the guy from our dorm who plays some kind of weird ethnic instrument I don't even recognize. Honestly, I have no idea what to expect.

The lights begin to fade, eager applause and loud whistles replacing the noise in the concert hall. River's name is called several times, but it looks as though he likes to keep the crowd waiting. Bela enthusiastically claps her hands and then leans over to me. "Did you know he'll be staying on campus this semester?" she whispers.

"Who?"

"Who do you think? River! I heard he'll be giving a couple of master classes, helping some students. I don't know exactly, but the point is, he'll be around—" Her words get lost in another wave of applause, this time much louder, and I'm glad we got the best possible seats, right in the second row. I have to tilt my head just a little, but I finally see him approaching the grand piano at the center of the stage.

River Evans is tall, that much I can tell from my seat. He's wearing casual black pants and a simple white shirt that stretches across his broad shoulders and causes my eyes to linger on his muscled arms. His hair is thick and dark, and his eyes, at least in the spotlight, look like a combination of light green and gray. Fuck. River Evans may officially be the most attractive man I've ever seen. Why has no one told me that?

He slightly nods his head toward the crowd as he takes his place at the piano. The hall falls silent, punctuated only by the sound of people breathing. The first notes echo around the room, hitting my eardrums. His hands move on the keyboard effortlessly, his long fingers stroking the keys, creating the most beautiful melodies. The first piece he plays is a piano solo composition, and when I think this must have been one of the most beautiful tunes I've ever heard, he starts his second piece, and the sound of his deep, low voice fills the air. The atmosphere instantly transforms into a more intimate one. By the third song, it feels like the crowd has been enchanted. They sway slowly to the rhythm of River's songs, singing along. Bela isn't an exception, and even Rodrigo, who has just arrived and sat in the spot we've managed to save for him, is lip-syncing with the rest of the crowd. I wish I could join them, but I don't know the lyrics, so I take out my phone instead and press the record button. Most people are recording everything on video, but I just want to enjoy it, so I keep the phone on my leg and settle for the audio, so I can listen to it again later. I'd rather experience the performance firsthand than through a camera lens. Still, I can't resist snatching a few pictures toward the end of the concert.

"Thank you all for joining me tonight." River's voice resonates in the hall, earning him immediate applause. He quietly waits until it fades, then smiles and starts talking again. "It's always a pleasure to be playing in my hometown, especially here at BMC, where I studied and enjoyed some of the best years of my life." The crowd starts clapping again, and River laughs softly. "Now it's up to you guys to have some fun! And I'm really looking forward to sharing the stage with you in the future." Excited shouts erupt in the audience as River turns back to his piano, securing the microphone in its stand. "This is the last song I'll play for you. This one isn't mine, but it's one of my favorites. Thank you again for coming tonight, and I guess I'll be seeing you guys around."

The first notes of Elliott Smith's song 'Between the Bars' fill the air, and it suddenly becomes hard to breathe. My stomach knots up, the familiar anxiety hitting me all at once. *Please, not now. Not this damn song.* But I can't move. So I stay and listen, my nails digging into my palms, searching for relief but only finding more pain.

*You used to love this song, sis.* I can almost see Alex's big brown eyes looking at me.

*I used to love you singing it*, I respond, wishing for my brother's voice to be more than just a figment of my imagination. *I miss your voice so damn much it hurts. Can you forgive me? I'm so sorry, Alex. I'm so sorry I failed you.*

But the only answers I get this time are the anguished lyrics that continue to fill up the air. And even though it's not my brother's voice singing them, the tightness in my stomach remains, as if they were tearing me apart from within.

When the song finishes, people stand, clapping and whistling again while I struggle to my feet, focused on making my way out as fast as I can.

"Sabrina! Hey! Where are you going? Let's have some drinks. Rodrigo is buying," Bela shouts after me.

"Just text me. I'll catch up with you guys!" I shout, pushing through the crowd without glancing back. Unfortunately, the concert is over, causing hundreds of people to head for the main exit simultaneously. Damn it! What now? I've been through enough panic attacks to know it will pass, but right now, it feels like my lungs are closing in on me, and I'm on the verge of throwing up. My head buzzes as the main light of the hall flickers back on. Suddenly, everything around me feels too bright, too loud. The cacophony of voices and sounds engulfs me, making it hard to focus. Briefly losing my balance, I unintentionally grab onto someone's elbow before swiftly regaining my footing again. Air. I need air.

As I anxiously scan the crowded hall, I spot the emergency exit signs leading somewhere behind the stage. My legs instinctively follow, and a wave of relief flashes over me when a door comes into view. I push it, hoping not to trigger an alarm. Luckily enough, it opens easily, and I find myself in an empty back alley right behind the concert hall. A wave of momentary relief washes over me. This is good. I'm good. I take a few deep breaths, slowly sinking to the ground, leaning the back of my head against the wall, and hugging my knees close to my chest. The stupid song still rings in my ears, and I finally let out the tears I've been holding back.

*Breathe, breathe, breathe*, I repeat to myself.

The door swings open, making me jump in surprise. "Hey, what are you doing there? Are you all right?"

I recognize that beautiful, deep voice. This has to be a joke, right? Out of everyone who could have found me here, it's River Evans staring at me with a blend of confusion and concern on his face, and I must admit, he looks even more attractive up close.

"Are you okay?" he repeats and then surprises me by sliding down and sitting next to me when I don't answer. His eyes scan me from head to toe, and it doesn't take him long to figure out what's happening. He slowly touches my arm. His fingers are warm, but it still makes my bare skin erupt in goosebumps. "Look at me," he says, and I do. His eyes are, in fact, mint green with light shades of gray. "Everything is fine. You are fine. Just breathe in and out, very slowly," he says, his voice calm and sounding just as low and deep as when echoing through the concert hall.

I try to compose myself, but the shaking resumes. "I'm good, you can go. It will pass." I must look like a mess, and I'd rather be alone. I've worked through this before. I can stop it. Except I can't right now. Damn, this is ridiculous and embarrassing. Really embarrassing. Why is he still here?

"The hell I'm leaving you alone." With a frown, he moves closer and reaches for my hand. My eyes widen.

"Close your eyes," he orders.

Sitting in a back alley with a stranger holding my hand is definitely not a situation in which I'd ever consider closing my eyes. Though, there's something about River's calm expression, and the softness in his voice, that makes me trust him. It's either that or having a complete meltdown right in front of a stranger. So I take a deep breath and do as he says.

"Good girl," he whispers, his words sending involuntary shivers through my body. He lifts my hand and puts it on his chest. What the hell? There is something too intimate about this moment. I'm about to withdraw from him when he stops me, covering my hand with his own. "Breathe with me," he says.

I feel his heartbeat through the thin material of his shirt, his muscles moving underneath. Taking a deep breath, my lungs fill with his scent, making me lose my focus for a moment. He smells like ginger and something a little spicier. Fuck. I close my eyes tighter, trying to block out everything else and focus only on his beating heart. He is calm and warm, and I feel my breathing gradually syncing to his, becoming normal again. This feels good. It feels… safe.

"That's it. Keep breathing. You're doing good," he murmurs.

With each deep breath, the painful memory that had overwhelmed me earlier starts to fade. It doesn't fully disappear, but it becomes a little less excruciating. I notice the soft breeze caressing my skin and the faint sound of the city in the distance. As I slowly open my eyes, I realize my hand is still pressed against his chest. I take it back with what must be an embarrassed expression on my face.

"I'm sorry," I manage to say.

"You have nothing to be sorry for." He shrugs as he releases my hand. We stay still for a while, silently sitting next to each other, his arm and leg brushing against mine.

"I really liked your concert." I break the silence.

His eyebrows rise, a look of amusement appearing on his face as his mouth turns into a boyish grin. "Thanks. I can tell you enjoyed it."

I make a choking sound. "That had nothing to do with your show. Or not directly, at least…"

"Now I really want to know." His grin widens, revealing his flawless teeth. It looks like he hasn't shaved in a couple of days, but it suits him. River Evans is stunningly beautiful, and he's more than aware of it.

"I'm sure you've better things to do than sit in a back alley with a random girl after your show." I gesture toward the overflowing garbage bins in front of us to make my point. "What are you doing here, anyway? Don't tell me you escape through the emergency exit after all your concerts."

Quiet laughter bubbles from his throat. "Sometimes I do, actually."

"Well, there is no better way to make a glorious exit than by leaving through a dumpster-filled alley."

He shakes his head and chuckles again. There's another moment of silence.

"So, are you gonna tell me what happened tonight?"

"Nothing happened, really. It's just that"—I swallow the lump in my throat—"the last song you played reminded me of someone."

"Must be someone important." His eyes are fixed on

an unknown spot in front of us, making it much easier for me to answer.

"He was." I don't trust myself to say more. This isn't a story I can share.

Instead of pushing, River simply acknowledges my answer with a nod. Feeling slightly better, I become more aware of his presence. I'm sure I look terrible. My mascara must be smudged all over my face, and, as Bela tried to tell me this afternoon, I haven't exactly picked my best outfit for tonight. Not that it matters. I'm hoping he'll forget about this encounter as soon as possible. Of course he will. I glance at him, meeting his gaze.

"I should probably introduce myself." I lift the edges of my mouth into a half grin. "I'm Sabrina."

There's a small sparkle in his eyes as he accepts my hand, and I can't take my eyes off his long fingers, enjoying the tickling sensation of his touch. Shit. Even his hands are perfect. He doesn't bother introducing himself. "So, are you also a musician, Sabrina?"

I suppose it's more of a polite question since his concert took place on campus and was only open to BMC students, who are *all* musicians, but of course, I could also be a business major. It still takes me a moment to answer, not feeling quite confident in the presence of someone as accomplished as him.

"I'm a songwriter." My cheeks flush while River's face lights up with interest.

"Songwriter." He hums, studying me as if seeing me for the first time. "So, where can I listen to something of yours?"

"You can't." The sharp answer slips out of my mouth without me thinking.

He chuckles. "Why not?"

"I don't… I don't really have anything ready," I lie, internally kicking myself. I have one of the top singer-songwriters right in front of me, asking about my music, and I just completely killed my elevator pitch.

*Way to go.* I hear my brother's voice, and I can almost imagine him rolling his eyes at me.

*Shut up.*

A soft groan of frustration escapes me as I stand up, dusting off my ripped jeans. "Anyway, it was really nice meeting you, River. Thank you again for the amazing concert and… your help."

He follows my lead, getting to his feet, a tiny smile tugging on his lips.

"Wait," he calls after me when I start walking away. "You haven't told me your last name."

"What do you need it for?" A tiny frown forms between my brows as I remember what Bela told me. He'll be teaching at BMC this semester. What if he wants to report my meltdown? Could they take away my scholarship if they don't think I'm prepared to be here?

He must see the panic on my face. "So when your songs are ready, I can listen to them." He winks at me, and I can hear the challenge in his voice. There is no way in hell that River Evans would actually spend time listening to any of my songs, but I still can't stop myself from smiling.

"Right. Well, I don't think you're going to remember it, but anyway… Fialová."

His confusion at the mention of my last name is almost comical.

"I'm from the Czech Republic," I explain. "It means

'violet,' like the color. This way, if you forget it, you can just google the word," I offer. I'm obviously joking, but River's face breaks into a genuine smile.

"I'll make sure I remember that. See you around, Violet," he says as he turns and heads in the opposite direction, toward what I now realize must be his car.

"Bye, River," I whisper, but I don't think he hears me.

# Three

Autumn. I can never get enough of it. The first month of classes flew by. Between studying, practicing, and working at Blue Cats and the campus bookstore, which at least turned out to be an easy and fun job, I barely have time for anything else. Like sleeping, for example. Bela and Rodrigo have been trying to lure me into all kinds of student parties, but so far, they haven't been successful.

It's the end of September, and even though the weather is colder now, the city has never looked more beautiful—full of colorful leaves, with the characteristic smell of pumpkin spice in the air. As I walk through the streets, the rich hues of red, orange, and yellow leaves crunch under my feet. And no matter how hard I try to avoid thinking about my hometown, this season, with its unique colors, always reminds me of it. I also try not to think about the fact that I haven't called my parents since I left. Yes, I sent a few texts just to let them know I was all right. They replied but never asked about my lessons or music. Our conversation would always stick to safe topics like the weather, the new dog they got—probably to replace me—and my on-campus job. While they haven't gone ahead with their threats to completely cut me out of their lives, they haven't shown any intention to help me either. I guess they hoped this tactic would eventually lead me back home, but they hugely underestimated my motivation to be here.

"I swear I'm gonna scream if one more person asks for a pumpkin latte today," Rodrigo groans as he rounds the counter, grabbing another tray of our autumn special. Laughing at my colleague's frustration, I get ready to prepare a new one. True pumpkin latte lovers will never have enough.

"It's nice to see you laugh for a change."

His voice catches me off guard, nearly causing me to drop the cup, potentially spilling its contents on my white shirt. God, I'm sure Rodrigo would love my pumpkin smell. I spin around, blood rushing to my cheeks, and sure enough, River Evans is standing right in front of me. There's a twinkle in his eyes, and his lips are drawn into a broad smile.

It shouldn't really be much of a surprise, given that he's been working on campus, but I haven't seen him once since our back-alley encounter. It would be a lie if I said I haven't tried to gather more information on him… or that I haven't listened to all his albums over and over, even learned to play some of his songs. And despite Bela and Rodrigo complaining about waiting outside the concert hall to meet him, I still couldn't bring myself to tell them I actually had the pleasure. Forgetting about my embarrassing moment of weakness seemed like a better option. Hence why I also haven't gone to his master class, open to all students upon registration a few weeks ago, even though I would have killed for that lesson. He was visiting certain courses, as I heard, but since BMC works on the principle of the highest ratings—the higher your rating, the better professors you can choose and the more access you get to all kinds of campus activities and events—I wasn't worried he would visit any of *my* classes.

I'm still technically a freshman, even though I was able to get almost an entire year of credits thanks to my previous studies. For better or worse, whatever status I reached or not reached as a musician during my life in Prague doesn't apply here. BMC and the city of Boston are like a battlefield. A battlefield full of musicians fighting for their place in the sun. And even though I love being surrounded by so many inspiring, like-minded people, I'm still not sure I'm cut out for the battle part.

"Would you believe me if I told you I don't hide crying in back alleys most days?" I grin at him.

The corners of his mouth tug, and the sound of his laugh makes my heart stupidly jump. The café is nearly packed, and every gaze is fixed on us, or rather, on River. His outfit is much more casual today—blue jeans and a green hoodie with the university logo. One could almost mistake him for one of us if it weren't for the superstar aura surrounding him. But no, River Evans is most definitely not one of us—and I had better remember that.

"I would." He smirks. "Your laugh is way too nice to hide it."

My eyes flicker to his, his words catching me off guard for a moment. "Is there anything I can get you?"

"Please, don't say pumpkin latte," Rodrigo murmurs warningly, appearing right behind him.

River laughs again. "Nope, no pumpkins for me. I'll have an espresso and a bottle of water. Thank you," he says, keeping his gaze on me.

"On it. Feel free to sit, and I'll bring it to you. Unless you want it to go?"

"No. I'll be sitting back there. I'm… meeting someone." He points toward a table with a beautiful blonde sitting alone with her notebook and a cappuccino. Right. Of course. I try to hide the absurd feeling of disappointment that washes over me.

"Thanks, Violet," I hear him say before he heads to his table.

My lips twitch at his use of that name, but I don't turn around.

"What. The. Fuck?" Rodrigo is looking right at me.

"What?" I ask, trying not to sound irritated.

"You didn't tell me you know the guy! And what's up with the nickname? Or is that your new artistic name?" He raises his eyebrows, and seeing his amused expression makes me want to throw something at him. Instead, I groan.

"I don't know him. Not really. It's kind of a long story, but let's say our paths crossed very briefly. He helped me with something when I needed it and was really nice about it."

"Are we talking about sex?" Rodrigo's eyes are wide open.

"What?" I raise my voice, noticing several curious heads turning toward us. "Why would you… Uhhh.

Are you even listening to me?" I'm not doing a great job explaining myself, but I don't feel like telling Rodrigo about my panic attack after the show. Coming to Boston was supposed to be my chance to show myself that I can do this.

"Oh, yeah, I'm listening to you." He chuckles. "No sex, got it. And while I think you deserve to have some fun because we only ever see you working or studying, I've got to tell you that River Evans may not be the right guy for it. And you know I love him." He winks at me.

"What do you mean?" I don't know why I'm even asking. That thought itself is obviously ridiculous. But still, there's something about River Evans that draws me to him every time our paths cross. And for some reason, they keep crossing.

Rodrigo puts down the tray he's holding and looks at me. "Look, we're talking about a musician who's not only great at what he does but also has the looks to go with it. And he knows how to use all of that to his advantage. Who can blame the guy, right?" He lets out a laugh but stops short when he sees my face. "What I'm trying to say is, River Evans can have anyone he wants, and he *is having* anyone he wants, if you know what I mean. So my brief advice as your friend is… if you don't want to get your heart broken, stay the fuck away from him."

Rodrigo's words hit me like a cold shower, and I try not to show any reaction, hiding my face in the dishwasher instead. He's right, of course. "No need to tell me that. As I said, there is nothing going on. I barely know him, and I'm not interested." In him, or anyone else, I should add, because that's true. I know why I'm here, and that's the only thing I want to be focusing on. Besides, River Evans may be a little out of my league, and he's most definitely not interested in me. There you go. Nothing to worry about.

"Okay, great." Rodrigo nods and hands me the tray. "Go give him his coffee, then."

I head to the table, trying to convince myself of what I just told Rodrigo. Music is why I'm here. I need to focus on my dream. On showing Alex I can do this. Showing myself. Right now, there's no room for anything or anyone else in my life. So why is my heart racing so damn fast?

Approaching the table, I hear them laughing at something, and I see the blonde—likely a cellist, judging by the blue cello case next to her—briefly touch River's hand in an intimate we-know-each-other way. She withdraws it only when I awkwardly stop in front of them. His eyes find mine, and I swallow hard, keeping myself busy placing their order on the table. I do it as quickly as I can, ignoring his gaze, and get back to the counter, almost running.

"You were saying?" Rodrigo raises his eyebrows skeptically at me as I return to safety.

"Shut up."

His laugh rings in my ears long after.

*

"Aaaall right, folks, let's do this again!" Professor Jameson's voice echoes loudly through the room. He's a large man, a renowned saxophone player and a producer who's worked with some of the best musicians in the industry, or so it says in his bio. I was lucky enough to be able to choose most of my courses for the first semester, and they all have to do with music one way or another, so I can't complain. My schedule includes piano and guitar lessons, music production, songwriting, and even yoga for musicians, whatever the point of that one is, but the course I'm in right now I did not choose. None of us did. It's a requirement for all freshmen, and I'm convinced it's been created with the sole purpose of making us suffer.

There are more coffee cups on the classroom desks than anyone could ever count, and that's probably because it's only eight thirty in the morning and chilly. Professor Jameson steps away from the board, pointing his finger at Nyra, who I'm sure is not only thrilled to be sharing the dorm room with us but also this unusual course, suitably called What and Why.

"Tell me *why* you're here," he demands.

"On this planet? Fuck, I wish I knew," Bela whispers, and I bite my tongue not to laugh. While the first month of the course was dedicated mostly to getting to know each other, it seems like now the fun is finally over.

Nyra glances around the classroom as if seeking our help before returning her gaze to the board. "Because I… I'm a musician?" she tries.

"Is that a question?" His voice grows even louder, making me wish I'd brought my earplugs.

Nyra shakes her head. "I'm here because I'm a musician, and I love to play," she says, much more convincingly now, and I send her an encouraging smile. Not that she cares.

Professor Jameson stares at our roommate like she's grown a second head. I stifle a laugh, not wanting to draw attention to myself. It's not like I have the right answer, either.

"And what makes you think anybody would care about that?" he asks, and a few gasps and "oohs" immediately travel through the classroom. Professor Jameson raises both his hands in the air. "Calm down, folks! All I'm saying is that the only person who cares about *your* dream of being a musician is *you*." He lets his words sink in and turns back to Nyra. "What you said is not an answer to my question." He surveys the room, his eyes settling on me for a moment, but I pretend I'm too busy studying the wooden desk in front of me. "Anybody else want to give it a try and give me an *actual* answer?"

The room becomes completely silent once more. The kind of silence where you could hear a pin or a guitar pick drop. No one is dropping anything, though, quite the opposite. We try to move and breathe as little as possible.

"Nobody? Really, folks?" Professor Jameson's voice sounds disappointed, and I almost feel sorry for him.

A red-haired guy, with his long legs stretched dangerously across the aisle, raises his hand.

Professor Jameson looks at his waving arm with notable relief. "Go on…?"

"Jeffrey."

"Go on, Jeffrey. What's your answer?"

Jeffrey takes a deep breath, flashing his confident smile. "I'm here because this is what I'm good at."

Our heads instinctively turn back to Professor Jameson as we wait for his reaction.

He shakes his head and pinches the bridge of his nose, which is probably not the best sign. "You realize that's practically the same answer Nyra gave us, don't you?"

"Is it?" Jeffrey's look is anything but confident now.

Professor Jameson looks at his watch and sighs. "Let's leave it here today. This question will be *the* question of this course, so think about it. I'm expecting much better answers in our next class. Now go!" He raises his voice again, and this time, we happily follow his command.

＊

On Saturday morning, I head to the bookstore for my weekend shift. I haven't had breakfast, and my stomach is loudly protesting.

"I can hear your growling stomach from here!" my colleague, Connor, shouts at me from one of the bookshelves. "Just go grab something from the café. You're making me nervous."

Connor is a piano player in his last year of studies. He's originally from New York, but fortunately, he doesn't show any of the famous New York attitude our dear roommate proudly exhibits every day. Quite the contrary. He's actually nice, and in addition, he's good-looking, with thick, dark blond hair, green eyes, and the physique of someone who's definitely using the amazing on-campus gym I haven't had the pleasure to visit yet, let alone use.

"Thanks, but I'm working at the café later. I'll just grab something then," I say. What I leave out is that I had to skip the breakfast that's included in my scholarship, and I'm not planning on spending money on food I can have for free later. My budget is stretched thin this week because of all the books and class materials I had to buy.

"You're working double shifts now? Girl, what are you? Wonder Woman?" He laughs.

"Yeah, something like that." I wink at him while cutting open the box of promotional material that arrived this morning. I pull out a keychain shaped like a small grand piano with our university's logo and wave it in front of him. "Look, that's cute. You should get one."

He laughs. "No way. These things are fucking overpriced."

My stomach growls again, and I start disassembling the now empty box in order to disguise the noise. Organizing myself a little better food- and time-wise would be a good idea, and I promise myself I will as soon as I've got a better handle on everything.

"Hey, can you take care of the cash register if someone comes in? I gotta run some errands," Connor shouts from somewhere behind me.

"Sure, no problem."

He grabs his jacket and leaves, and I take a slow look around, scanning the store. Everything looks in order with all the new merchandise, from keychains and pencils to T-shirts stored on shelves. I have two hours left at the bookstore and three more at the café, but what I'm worried about is not having time to study for my Monday songwriting class. A wave of anxiety causes my stomach to tighten. We're supposed to play one of our original songs. My gaze wanders to the upright piano standing in the corner near a small reading area. The bookstore is empty at the moment. Would it be such a bad idea? I glance around once more, then hesitantly take a seat at the piano, opening it and gently running my fingers over the keys. There's a song I've been working on, but it's not finished, and I don't know if it will ever be. Not without Alex. I miss the way he could bring our songs to life. He had a knack for knowing exactly what was missing. How to make a song sound so much better. And his voice. His voice was incomparable.

With closed eyes, I let my fingers glide across the keys, allowing the lyrics to flow from my lips. In my head, though, it's not my voice singing them. It's my brother's.

Why wouldn't you just listen?
Keep going, there is nothing we can't do
And I believed you, always so damn sure
Was it me who didn't see the storm coming?
Was it you?

You left me alone
Surrounded by those I don't even know
You asked me to keep smiling
But my heart doesn't hold

Not hearing the door open, it takes me a moment to realize I'm not alone.

"Don't stop, it's beautiful. Your voice is beautiful." His voice comes out soft and slow, but his presence startles me enough that I stop playing. And even though I haven't looked at him yet, I know River Evans is standing right behind me. I'd recognize his voice anywhere, same as his smell, that rich combination of ginger, orange, and spice that has all my sensory cells on high alert.

"I… I was just… I thought I was alone."

He stares at me with such intensity it makes me want to check that my lipstick isn't smudged. "How long have you been listening?"

"Long enough."

I swallow nervously. I'd have never played if I knew anyone was here. If I knew *he* was here.

"Can I help you with anything?" I ask, getting up from the piano while trying to remember the basics of my job.

"You work here?" He frowns, his voice laced with confusion.

"I do."

"And at the café?"

"Right. That too." I offer him a brief smile.

Curiosity flickers in his eyes as he turns around, grabbing a bright red T-shirt with a BMC logo from a shelf behind him. Without uttering a word, he hands it to me.

"Umm, these are for girls, actually." I frown at the small shirt in my hand. "I can help you find your size if you need," I offer, checking him out quickly. He's dressed simply, in gray joggers, a white shirt, and a casually open black jacket, and looking as jaw-dropping as always. His lips curve into a lazy smile, and I realize he's caught me staring.

"I know. It's not for me."

"Of course—" I start while mentally cursing myself. How do I manage to make myself look and sound like a complete idiot every damn time I meet this guy? Just as I spin around, heading to the cash register, he gently grabs my arm. It looks like he's about to say something, but then the door opens, and I spot Connor's blond head. He hasn't seen us yet, but as soon as River notices him, he lets go of my arm. What was that about?

"Hey, I know you!" Connor states as soon as he spots River. I use the opportunity to slip behind the register.

River looks unimpressed, but he acknowledges Connor with a slight nod, a stark contrast to the friendly and easy-going vibe he was showing just five minutes ago. Connor doesn't seem to get the message, though.

"You're River Evans, right? Man, my ex was in love with you. That was annoying. I swear she wouldn't stop talking about you," he says, only half joking, and I stifle a laugh when I see River's frown. Opting to spare him from Connor's trip down the failed relationship memory lane, I hand over his purchase. "It's going to be twenty-eight dollars."

He hands me his credit card, and his fingers briefly brush against mine. I'm pretty sure it wasn't intentional, but when I look up, his eyes are locked on me. I quickly swipe his card and hand it back to him.

"Thanks," he murmurs. He's almost to the door when he stops. "Violet?" he calls, and I can see the confusion in Connor's eyes.

"Yeah?" I try not to smile at the nickname he keeps using.

"I still wanna hear that song," he says simply, heading out and not giving me the time to answer. Not that I could.

When I remember how to breathe again, I reach for a stack of books that need to be put back on the shelves. Anything to distract myself.

"What song was he talking about?" Connor's expression is still puzzled. I guess there's no way around this.

"My song. I used the piano to practice for a couple of minutes. Sorry about that." I cringe. Even though Connor is a student, just like me, he has been working here since the first year of his studies and is the one in charge of the store. I need this job to maintain my scholarship, and to do that, I can't have Connor thinking that I'm slacking.

"Wait a moment. He asked you to play your song for him? Are you kidding?"

"I think it was more like he accidentally heard a part of it and then asked me to play it again," I explain reluctantly.

"And you did?" Connor insists.

"No, I didn't."

"What?" He frowns. "Why not?"

"Umm, where do these books go again?" I try. Unfortunately, Connor is not that easily distracted.

"Sabrina, do you even know who that guy is?"

"Sure, I went to his last concert," I say, hoping to end this conversation.

"Okay, well, I haven't, for obvious reasons. I've been listening to my ex talking about him for two years nonstop, and there were even posters hanging in our bedroom—" I snort out a laugh, and Connor offers me a defeated smile. "But I know the guy, and he's fucking good, not to mention extremely well connected. No one in their right mind would say no to him. Hell, I wouldn't say no, and I can't stand the guy!"

I burst out laughing. "Then maybe you should do it," I suggest.

He shoots me an annoyed look. "You still don't get it. I haven't tried, but I know people who have, and he never replies to anyone."

I shrug. No wonder he doesn't answer. He probably has to deal with constant requests for favors and attention.

The door opens, and our conversation is interrupted by

a group of students talking and laughing loudly. They ask about piano book recommendations, and Connor seems more than happy to help them out. We don't talk for the rest of my shift, but I still can't stop thinking about his words. *He never replies to anyone.* Was he serious when he said he wanted to hear my song? *Don't stop, it's beautiful. Your voice is beautiful.* Is there a chance he actually liked it?

∗

When I finish my shifts at the bookstore and the café, the only thing I want to do is catch up on some much-needed sleep, but instead, I head for the practice rooms. I know I won't be able to get anything done at the dorms. Fortunately, the practice rooms are open until 2 a.m., and I manage to get a small room all to myself.

Taking out my phone, I scroll down through my last recordings. There's one I saved from River's concert, and even though I've listened to his albums on iTunes, I haven't had the chance to go back and listen to the actual live audio. Pressing play, I hear his low, deep voice instantly fill the small room. Choosing a song that's now my favorite, I replay it twice. The first time I heard it, I was immediately drawn to its beautiful melody. It took me a couple of hours to learn to play it, but since then, it has been stuck in my head on loop. I close my eyes, and as my fingers start moving, I'm surprised to realize that I don't even have to look at the lyrics. I remember them perfectly. The song is beautiful, simple yet so complex, and I wish I could ask him about it. How did he come up with it? Does he enjoy performing it? Does it remind him of someone?

Feeling a little more determined, I take out a piece of paper and a pen from my bag and put both in front of me.

Performing one of my old songs in our songwriting class doesn't seem right. Not without Alex. My best chance right now is to finish the song I've been working on. Right. As if it is that easy.

*Would you stop looking for excuses?* Alex's voice is a soft caress on my skin, and it draws a smile to my lips because I'm sure it's precisely what he would say if he were here.

*That's not what this is.*

*It's not?* His chuckle resonates in my ears, bringing tears to my eyes, but I swiftly push them back. *Correct me if I'm wrong, but we both got in, didn't we?* he asks.

I grit my teeth. *Just because we auditioned together.*

There is no response from my brother. Funny how even in my head, I know exactly when he would disagree with me.

Shaking my head, I grab my guitar again and spend at least ten minutes going back and forth, scratching out every idea I write down. Frustrated, I tear out the messy page, crumpling it into a ball and throwing it angrily at the door. It strikes the small glass window placed in the center, and for a moment, I'm almost certain I glimpsed some movement behind it. Is someone waiting for the room? Because I'm pretty sure I booked it for the rest of the night. Still, I get up and head toward the door, realizing I must have left it slightly ajar. I peek out just in case, but there is no one. The only sounds that can be heard are random notes and voices coming out of other practice rooms. Perfect. I'm officially losing it.

I spend the rest of my practice time going over and

over the same song, but it remains incomplete, and I don't feel confident enough to sing it. What I do feel is too tired to keep going, so I pack my things and head to the dorms.

Bela isn't there when I open the door, and I suddenly remember that she mentioned some kind of late-night jam session, trying to get me to join her, as always. I silently promise myself to try harder next week. There must be a way to study, work, and socialize at the same time, and if not, I better find it. It's late, and the room is dark. I tiptoe silently toward my bed to avoid waking Nyra, not wanting to turn on the light. That's when I hear something that resembles muffled sobs. I stop in the middle of the room and listen. The silent sobbing starts again. "Nyra?" I whisper, still not seeing anything. The sobbing stops, but there's no answer. "Are you okay?" I try again, finally reaching my bed.

"I'm fine. Go to sleep!" Her voice is angry, and as my eyes adjust to the darkness of the room, I notice her silhouette sitting on the bed and wrestling with something that looks like a piece of white gauze.

"Are you hurt?" I ask, bracing myself for another wave of her anger.

"Why don't you mind your own fucking business?" There you go.

"Did something happen to your wrist?" I grimace as I watch her struggle to wrap and secure her right hand.

"Oh my God, you're a genius. My wrist fucking hurts, okay? Happy? Now, can you shut the fuck up and sleep already?" she snaps at me, but her voice trembles. To avoid alarming her further, I get up slowly and walk over.

"What are you doing? Didn't you hear me?" she asks as soon as she sees me moving closer.

I sit beside her, switch on the small bedside lamp, and reach for her hand. "Just let me help. You can save your bitchy attitude for later. Maybe when you feel better?" I suggest, and surprisingly enough, it works.

She tenses her jaw but lets me take her hand and put it into my lap. I seize the gauze from her and use my teeth to tear a long enough piece to secure her wrist.

"You know there is an on-campus doctor, right?" I ask as I wrap it around, making sure the gauze stays in place.

"Yes, I fucking know," she says, her voice lacking anger now and sounding almost defeated. "I can't go there." She bites her lip as she glances at me. "There's a recording tomorrow I can't miss."

"Okay." I nod carefully. Telling her to go to the doctor and skip the recording would be the right thing to do, not that she would listen, but it somehow still feels wrong. We all battle with similar issues, whether it's back or neck pain, carpal tunnel syndrome, or vocal strain from singing too loud or for too long. Each instrument has its own challenges. When it comes down to it, musicians are no different from dancers or athletes. The outside world only perceives our smiles and performances, unaware of the hidden world of pain, blood, and tears that lies beneath.

"Try not to move it until tomorrow, and don't sleep on it. I'm sure it will be fine, but maybe you can have it checked after your recording. Have you taken some ibuprofen?" I ask.

She nods, her tiny braids moving around her head in a Medusa-like way. "It was really hard to get this recording, you know?" she whispers. "I'm the only freshman who was asked to participate." It doesn't sound like she's bragging, more like she's putting a lot of pressure on herself without even realizing it.

"Well, I'm sure you'll have fun tomorrow," I say, getting up and heading to my bed. I'm so tired, every step feels like ten.

"Thank you, Sabrina." She turns off the light on her nightstand. "Good night," she adds reluctantly, and I smile into the darkness. Every small victory counts.

# Four

"What did you think the name 'Yoga for Musicians' meant when you registered for this course? Because I'm pretty sure I got it wrong." Even after a month of classes, I still struggle to follow the impossibly flexible movements Jennifer, our yoga teacher, is showing us. "We should have just joined the hip-hop course. I'm seriously convinced there is less sweating involved," I complain to Bela while trying to catch my breath.

Next to me, Bela is panting and shaking her head. "I'm just thinking about the ways of implementing this into my shows."

"I don't think you are meant to do that," I snort out as I try to imitate the perfect downward dog pose. "Are you sure you don't want to join the hip-hop course?"

Bela bursts into laughter, and Jennifer's head turns in our direction. "Girls, you wanna show us how it's done?"

"Do you?" I whisper to Bela.

"Nope, we're fine. Thank you!" she shouts loudly, and I chuckle.

This is our first class of the day, which doesn't leave enough time to get back to the dorms for a nice, long shower before the start of our songwriting class. So instead, we take a quick gym shower, and both end up with damp hair, very little makeup, and an outfit consisting of yoga pants matched with a long white V-neck sweater in my case and a short pink crop sweater in Bela's case.

"I'm really looking forward to today's class," Bela says as we run across the campus to make it on time.

I swallow the lump in my throat. I wish I could feel the same, but my anxiety and nerves are getting the best of me. Part of it is because I'm still not sure I belong in this class. The other reason is that although I've managed to avoid performing any of my songs so far, it's not like I can keep flying under the radar the entire semester. I'm pretty sure the teacher would notice. And if I'm honest with myself, so would I. I came here to learn, not to hide, but… What if I make a fool out of myself? What if I can't sing? And even worse, what if nobody likes my music? What if this is not what I'm meant to do after all?

*Music is not our fucking hobby.* The words Alex used to say, especially when arguing with our parents, repeat in my head, reminding me why I'm here, and I clutch onto them tightly.

"Do you?" I hear Bela asking as she catches a breath, opening the heavy door of the main building.

"Fuck. I'm sorry. I spaced out. Do I what?"

"You do that a lot, mi amor," she says, throwing me a concerned sideways glance. "Is everything all right?"

"Yes, sorry, guess I'm just tired." That, at least, is not a complete lie.

"I was asking if you have anything you want to sing today," she repeats patiently, but fortunately, I don't get the chance to answer since we're already entering our classroom.

"Good morning, ladies! Take a seat, please. We're about to start." The professor points to a couple of chairs right in front of her. Bela and I exchange a grin. Hers is excited. Mine a little less. The first row it is. Perfect. More familiar faces come into view as Rodrigo waves at us from behind. He's actually the one who recommended this course. Apparently, he studied with the same professor last year and claimed it was the best course he's ever taken.

In her forties, Charlotte Williams is a stunning, tall woman with dark hair and a refined elegance. I had listened to her albums even before applying to BMC and fallen in love with her music, a flawless fusion of country and pop accompanied by her guitar and an incredibly sweet voice.

With an energetic clap, she scans the room to ensure she has our full attention. "Okay, guys, the first month of our course is over, and today, I'm looking forward to finally hearing some of your songs. But before we get to that part, I have some great news for you—"

A light knock on the door interrupts her words.

"Come on in!" she shouts, and our heads turn in unison to follow the sound of the door opening.

The class gasps in surprise as River Evans strolls into the room like he owns it, a confident smile on his lips. What the hell? What's he doing here?

"Now that is a nice surprise," Bela whispers, leaning in.

My mouth dries, and a knot the size of a cricket ball forms in my stomach as the class erupts in excited chatter. He slowly walks to the board, and his gaze locks with mine. His eyes widen a little, but if he's surprised to see me here, he doesn't let on.

"Guys, calm down!" Professor Williams waves her hand in the air until the room falls quiet again. "As I was saying, I have some great news for you. River Evans will be joining us during this course and—" The classroom fills with excited whispers and spontaneous applause. I reluctantly clap my hands—I can't be the only one not to show enthusiasm—but there is no way I'm excited about his presence. And if I was already freaked out about performing my songs in front of Professor Williams and the entire class, there is no way in hell I will be able to do it if River Evans is here. I don't know why exactly, but there is something unnerving about his presence. Something I feel every time I see him.

"Guys, please, can we show Mr. Evans that you not only know how to behave but you are also amazing musicians?" Professor Williams pleads while River swiftly grabs a chair from somewhere in the third row. He positions himself in front of the board but slightly to the side, as if to say he'll only be observing for now. Or at least I hope that's what it means. He's sitting practically in front of me, but I do my best not to look at him.

"The guy's fucking hot," Bela whispers to me, and I shoot her a warning glance, anxious he might hear. Damn it. He does look good in his faded jeans, black sweater, and Boston Red Sox baseball cap with a red letter B.

"It's a pleasure to be here. I don't want to interrupt

your class too much, and I won't be assisting every week since you already have a great teacher," he says with a smile, causing our professor to blush like a teenager asked to prom. Looks like no one is immune to River Evans's charm. "But I'll be present throughout the course to listen to your music, offer input, and share some of my experience," he says, his voice low but captivating. It's the first time I really notice his strong Boston accent and funny pronunciation of certain words, dropping the final 'r' and replacing it with 'ah,' making the word teacher sound more like 'teachah,' but what really annoys me is that this little detail somehow makes him even more attractive— not that I'm attracted to him.

"Guys, this is a great opportunity for you, so let's hear some of your music. Any volunteers?" Professor Williams asks, looking around the room, causing me to sink deeper into my seat.

"I can give it a try!" Bela's hand goes up, and I let out a sigh of relief. The professor nods in appreciation and gestures toward the baby grand piano in the left corner of the room.

River takes off his cap and leans back comfortably, slightly turning his body for a better view.

Seated at the piano, Bela readjusts the microphone closer to her mouth, and after taking a few deep breaths, she starts playing. I realize she has chosen a song she's already played for me a couple of times. I like it, but I think the lyrics still need some improvement, which is what I told her when she asked me. She laughed and said she knew she was a brilliant singer but a terrible songwriter. "I can't have it all, mi amor," she joked. Her voice, though, is beautiful—bright and powerful, filling every inch of the classroom. I peek at River, but his expression isn't giving anything away. Does he like it? Would he also ask her not to stop?

She gets to the last part of her song, elegantly dropping her voice to a lower tone, and I'm the first one to applaud when the last note fades away. Rodrigo and the rest of the class join me right away. Turning her head toward the board, Bela smiles and gazes first at Professor Williams, then at River.

Surprisingly, River is the one to speak first. "It was good," he says. "You have a great voice, but this song still needs a lot of improvement." Professor Williams nods in agreement. "Work more on the lyrics, make them stronger, feel them. You're focusing too much on the interpretation itself, but when you believe in your song, you don't have to do that. It'll speak for you."

There are four more volunteers, who also receive similar feedback, either asking them to improve their writing or to work on their interpretation. One of them, a guy from England whose name I can't recall, is actually pretty good, but not even he escapes their scrutiny.

There is no way in hell I'm playing one of my songs today. Professor Williams, almost as if reading my mind, looks around the room again.

"Anyone else?" she asks as I study my sneakers. "Sabrina?" She stops in front of me, making it impossible to ignore her.

River looks up, our eyes finally meeting, the corners of his lips lifting into a playful, almost daring smile.

Fuck. "Umm, I don't really have anything ready yet," I say and notice River raising his eyebrows.

"You can sing it even if it's not finished," he cuts in. Of course he would see right through me.

"I appreciate your help, umm… Mr. Evans, but I'd rather have more time to work on it," I say and feel Bela's leg quietly kicking me.

With a hint of curiosity, he fixes his gaze on me, slightly squinting, as if trying to figure out what's going on in my head. *Good luck with that.*

"Sure, then why don't you just pick a song you like and sing it?" he suggests.

"That would also work, Sabrina," Professor Williams chimes in, trying to save the situation. "In fact, I see there are no more original songs ready today. Why don't you all pick a singer-songwriter you admire and sing one of their songs?"

The idea doesn't seem that bad. I consider myself more of a songwriter than a singer, but I can get by singing the songs of other artists. Maybe I could go with one of Damien Rice's songs and ask Rodrigo to let me use his guitar. It's certainly not as frightening as singing my own songs.

"Actually," Professor Williams continues, "let's make it more interesting… Sabrina!" Her eyes land back on me.

"Yeah?" I answer, praying that her new idea won't be worse than the original one.

"You pick an artist for Rodrigo since he also hasn't played any of his originals and"—she looks around, her eyes stopping at one of the girls who's already performed—"Olivia, you pick a songwriter for Sabrina."

I frown. All right, that idea *is* worse than expected. I'm just hoping my classmate won't have me singing Taylor Swift, because I wouldn't know any of the lyrics and would probably embarrass myself. "Choose known musicians, though," Professor Williams adds, obviously pleased with her idea. "Go on."

I suggest Damien Rice for Rodrigo since I can't sing him myself, and Rodrigo winks approvingly at me before grabbing his guitar and letting out the first notes of 'Volcano.' I sit back, silently moving my lips in sync, and when the song is almost over, I notice River's gaze on me, even though I'm not the one currently performing. Rodrigo receives quite an applause, and we spend a while analyzing Damien Rice and his songwriting. There are only ten minutes left for class, and it almost looks like I won't get my turn today. Of course, I'm not that lucky.

"Olivia!" Professor Williams cuts short the heated conversation about which Damien Rice album is the best, clearly remembering that I've yet to perform. Damn it.

"It's your turn. Who is your favorite artist?" she asks my classmate, and I brace myself for her answer. She definitely looks like a Swiftie. Olivia looks around the class until her gaze rests on River. Is she seeking his approval of whichever artist she chooses?

She bats her long lashes at him and smiles. I'm starting to feel uneasy about this whole thing.

"My favorite artist is River Evans," she says sweetly, and several things happen at the same time: Bela chokes on the water she was gulping, the class starts laughing quietly and whispering, Professor Williams seems surprised, and, at the same time, slightly annoyed by Olivia's blunt flirtation, and River, of course, looks amused. I'm in shock. What the actual fuck?

Professor Williams is the first one to collect herself.

"Well, I guess we can't really argue with that, and I definitely agree with your choice." She nods, smiling.

"You are screwed, mi amor," Bela whispers, and I'm thinking the exact same thing. Fuck me. And fuck Olivia for her stupid little crush on River.

"Sabrina?" Professor Williams turns to me.

"Isn't that unfair?" The sound of Rodrigo's voice comes from behind me. "I mean, I'm not sure how I'd feel about Damien Rice listening to my interpretation," he says, and the class bursts into laughter.

River opens his mouth to say something, but Olivia is faster. "I can do it if Sabrina can't."

What? I have had enough of this girl. And I have also had enough of River's amused face.

Standing up, I make my way to the piano. River's jaw drops, and a range of expressions from surprise to intrigue to curiosity cross his face all at once. He leans forward and rests his elbows on his knees. The class falls into sudden silence, where the only sounds that can be heard are breathing and the noise of chairs scratching the floor as my classmates move in their seats in anticipation.

Closing my eyes and focusing on my own breathing, I let my fingers dance over the keys. The lyrics flow out of my lips automatically. I already know them by heart.

Look at me one more time
Just once more before you walk away
We all look for someone to stay when things get tough
You say we end up alone no matter what
And yes, I know, darlin'
You have already made up your mind

Stay or leave, I swear it will make no difference
Oh, there is no such thing as innocence
When I tell you to believe
Everything in life is just a fucking game
A sense of trepidation
Would you still decide to play?

We could just admit that we are scared
Looking for the easy way out
You say there is no point in believing in fairy tales
We have seen too much, and it's too late

No need to turn off the light on your way out, darlin'
But it's probably easier
So much for the long run
Oh, but you already knew

Stay or leave, I swear it will make no difference
Oh, there is no such thing as innocence
When I tell you to believe
Everything in life is just a fucking game
A sense of trepidation
Would you still decide to play?

Oh, there is no such thing as innocence
Believe me

When I press the last key and the final note dies out, I can hear the absolute silence in the room. Thankfully, it transforms into a burst of applause almost immediately. I glance at River, hoping that he didn't hate it and I didn't make a fool of myself, but his intense gaze catches me off guard. I'm just not sure what it means. He doesn't say anything. Instead, he gets up and leaves as soon as Professor Williams thanks me for my performance, not without reminding me that she wants to hear my own song soon, and announces the end of the class. Go figure. This guy is as confusing as it gets.

*

"I'm so happy we're doing this!" Bela is hovering over me, the eye pencil in her hand dangerously close to my left eye.

"Are you sure you know what you're doing?" I ask for the tenth time.

"Yes, of course, but only if you stay still and shut up," she warns, while I'm starting to rethink this whole Halloween idea.

I'm still not sure I should have let Bela convince me to join her for the Halloween jam happening outside of campus. It's been a challenging couple of weeks, and I know I should prioritize practicing and working on my song. The idea of having to go back to our songwriting class next week just to say for the thousandth time I'm still not ready is haunting me more than any Halloween ghost ever could. So is the fact that River Evans hasn't made another appearance in our class. Professor Williams said he's been busy recording his new album, and he hopes to join us again soon. I haven't run into him since my involuntary performance of his song, and it bothers me that he might think that not only am I incapable of singing my own songs, but I'm also ruining his. The irony of the name of his song 'Ruin You' is not lost on me. I think I may have just given it a whole new meaning. I'm telling myself that his opinion only matters to me because he's practically one of my teachers now, and I respect him as an artist, but that's not the only reason. There is also something about his music that really resonates with me, something I don't feel that easily with other musicians, not even the ones I've always admired.

"What is it again that you are going to be wearing tonight?" Bela snaps me out of my thoughts.

"Umm, this is pretty much it. This party was kind of short notice." I grin, gesturing at my simple outfit made up of dark blue jeans, a black asymmetrical shirt with no sleeves, black boots, and lots of leather accessories embellishing my neck and wrists, all paired with my fake leather jacket. My makeup is in the nineties style, and my long brown hair is loose and curlier than normal. I also have a red winter hat I'm planning on using to make sure people understand I'm going for Alanis Morissette's look.

"What about you? Who are you supposed to be?" I ask once I'm able to open both of my eyes again.

Bela puts down the eye pencil and spins around.

"Can't you tell?" she asks.

I furrow my eyebrows and look at her more thoroughly. She's dressed in a white minidress that reveals more than it covers. Extremely long and shiny earrings hang from her ears, and her hair is styled into a loose top bun. Her makeup is much stronger than mine, with dominant golden eye shadow and fake eyelashes.

I lean closer and reach toward her ears. "Have you stolen these from Nyra?"

She chuckles. "Yes, I did actually. I told her it was a crucial aspect of my J.Lo costume, and she threw them at me, literally."

"That's who you are supposed to be! Got it." I grin. "Whose idea was this, anyway? To have us dress as famous musicians? Couldn't we just do normal Halloween? I saw a really cute Minion outfit."

"Mi amor, you don't want to see drunk Minions or Harry Potters singing and playing in a jam session. This is much better. This is us in the future!"

"I don't know if I want to see any drunk singing at all," I assure her. "Do you think any teachers will be there tonight?"

Bela frowns at my question, slightly narrowing her eyes. "I certainly hope not. Are you looking for anyone in particular?"

"No, just asking." I shrug. I definitely wouldn't want Professor Williams seeing me partying, since I've been coming up with a new excuse every week as to why I haven't finished my song yet. But would I like to see *him*? It doesn't matter because the chances of River Evans appearing at a student Halloween party are slim to none.

"All right, let's do this," Bela says, and I follow her out, but not before grabbing my jacket and red winter cap. Hopefully, this will be enough to hide.

# Five

As expected, the club is packed. I soak in the sight of the impeccably equipped stage, all set for the performance to start.

As Bela drags me across the place, I spot Bob Marley, Michael Jackson, Shakira, Amy Winehouse, and I'm pretty sure I also saw Jimi Hendrix, Ringo Starr, and Billie Eilish. Dead and living musicians are getting mixed up, and most of the time, I can't tell who's behind the costume.

"Wait a minute!" I shout as I accidentally step on Marilyn Manson's foot on our way to the bar. "Was that the quiet guy from our harmony class?" I ask Bela, still in shock.

"Umm, I think so, hard to say, but whoever he was, he is the winner!" She laughs while I try to shake off the slightly creepy vibe of that costume.

We finally reach the bar just as someone takes hold of the microphone. "Good evening, ladies and gentlemen. Welcome to our annual Halloween Jam Session!" We all turn toward the stage. I stand on my tiptoes to get a better look at the young, blond, blue-eyed guy, who didn't have to try too hard to look like Kurt Cobain—before all the drugs, obviously—but if there was ever any doubt, he's also wearing a Nirvana T-shirt and hugging a guitar. The only thing that is a little off is his accent, which points to somewhere in Northern Europe, probably Norway or Sweden. But who am I to judge? I highly doubt I sound like a native Canadian.

"Sooo… this is how it's gonna work tonight," he continues, waving his guitar. "This stage is open to everyone and anyone who wants to play. We wanna hear you!" He raises his voice once again, and people start whistling and cheering. "Anything's allowed, as long as it's good." He laughs at his own joke as he places the microphone back into the holder. "And since you can already guess what my favorite band is, I don't mind starting the party."

We join the crowd and clap enthusiastically as more musicians step on the stage, and the first notes of 'Heart-Shaped Box' fill our ears.

"I think I'm in love," Bela says dreamily, sipping from her cocktail.

"I thought you were in love with Rodrigo." I chuckle and accept the glass of wine she is handing me.

"Yeah, but that's not going to work, so I have to expand my horizons."

"Why not?"

"He's playing for a different league. I told him I didn't care, but apparently, that's not how it works." She grins.

"Wait a minute. I don't know which information I should try to process first… but I'll go with the fact that you told Rodrigo that he could switch his sexual preferences in your favor." I burst out laughing, trying not to ruin my makeup.

"Mi amor, have you met me?" She grins, pointing at her sexy outfit, and I can't argue with that. Instead, I let her drag me to the dance floor, where we both surrender to the rhythm of our classmates' performances. It's only when a girl in a Spice Girls costume takes over the stage that I leave the dance floor and head back to the bar. Bela stays slow-dancing with the Nirvana guy, and Rodrigo's enjoying the company of a charming dancing partner of his own.

I lean on the bar and ask for another glass of wine and a bottle of water, which I gulp almost immediately. While the night is still young, I'm noticing too many drunk music stars. The jam session hasn't stopped for a minute, but some interpretations are so terrible that I pray those students are from MIT or some other college.

"I was hoping to hear you sing tonight." The voice coming from behind me causes a tickling sensation as warm breath caresses my neck.

I slowly turn to face him. His voice is unmistakable. It's the Elvis Presley costume that confuses me for a moment. River Evans is the last person I'd have expected to see here tonight. He is, in fact, almost unrecognizable, which makes me want to know how long he's been here. He's fully clad in fake leather, with black pants that hug him in all the right places and a jacket that almost matches mine. Except that he isn't wearing a shirt, and the jacket is left half open, revealing his muscular chest, where a small piece of a tattoo is peeking out, which I'm pretty sure is his own and not Elvis's. His dark, thick hair is brushed back.

He's wearing big golden sunglasses, shielding his eyes, but I feel his gaze burning into me as he, too, studies my costume.

I take a few sips of wine to buy myself a little extra time before answering.

"Really? Is that why you ran away the last time you heard me sing?" I don't know what got into me, but my own surprise mirrors River's as he opens his mouth, then closes it just as quickly. The idea that he might know how much his reaction affected me bothers me, but the words are already out.

"Wait, what?" He frowns. "That's not what happened."

"Sure looked like it to me." I shrug.

He steps closer, taking off his glasses. His green eyes burn into mine, and in his heated stare, I notice their color shift to a beautiful mix of gray and almost blue.

"I'm sorry if that's what you thought," he says, his voice softening a little.

The Spice Girl finishes her cover, and a different student takes over, playing an original.

"It took me by surprise, that's all. Your voice, singing my song, is my new favorite sound."

"Right." I shake my head, unsure if he's making fun of me. Standing so close, our significant height difference means I have to tilt my head back to meet his eyes. "Anything else while you're at it?" I ask, not trying to hide the hostility in my voice.

Confusion flickers across his face, but then he grins at me. "Actually, yes. I can't figure out who you're supposed to be."

"Seriously?"

"Sorry." He lets out a deep laugh that I try not to enjoy too much. "Wait, let me guess." He scans me from head to toe.

I lift an eyebrow, waiting for his answer.

"Avril Lavigne?"

"Nope, wrong Canadian. Besides, do I look like a punk-rock girl to you?"

He chuckles. "I honestly never know with you. You're full of surprises. That's the only thing I've learned so far. Come on, Violet, give me a clue. Sing for me?" he asks softly.

I shake my head again. This guy is unbelievable. Since this is my second glass of wine and the background music makes everything seem less real, I stand on my tiptoes and lean toward him, steadying myself with a light grasp on his shoulder. He puts his arm on my back, helping me reach him as his hand lands on my shirt underneath my short jacket, his touch burning into my skin. When I start whisper-singing into his ear, he tenses, and I can feel him holding his breath. I sing the first verse of no other song than 'Ironic,' but River remains quiet, pressing his hand to my back as though he needs to hear more. I'm pretty sure he must have recognized it. It's a well-known song and all, but I keep humming into his ear until after the chorus.

"Alanis Morissette," he finally says, his voice coming out raspy.

I retreat slightly, and he reluctantly removes his hand from my back.

"Were you even alive when that song came out?" The sexy smirk on his face makes a reappearance.

"Almost."

"Hmm, almost, right. How old are you? Twenty?" He looks at me with an amused expression, narrowing his eyes as if challenging me to answer.

"Twenty-one, actually. Almost twenty-two."

His eyes flicker with surprise, but he doesn't ask more questions, and I don't ask about his age either. Wikipedia already informed me he is twenty-eight.

"You want me to tell you something, Violet?" he asks when the music stops again.

I look up at him, and he surprises me by grabbing my arm gently yet firmly. Then he leans down and whispers in my ear, and my body shudders.

"I understand that 'Ironic' is your favorite Alanis song, but do you know her 'Thank You' music video?" I try to think about that particular music video, but my mind is blank right now. "That outfit might have been more interesting…"

Someone bumps into me from behind, and a small group of people surrounds the bar. River puts his glasses back on. I suppose he isn't interested in anyone else recognizing him tonight. It takes me a moment to realize what he has just said, and when I do, he's already gone.

By the time I get back to the dance floor, Bela is nowhere to be seen, nor is the Kurt guy. Good for her, I guess. Rodrigo is still around but not paying much attention to anyone but his dancing partner.

"Hey!" Someone puts a hand on my shoulder. I turn around and spot Connor. "I wasn't sure it was you!" He yells to be heard over the music. I have no idea who he's supposed to be, but he looks great, as always.

"Hey, my favorite bookstore colleague." I smile at him.

"I believe, technically, I'm your boss." He laughs.

"Semantics." I wave my hand in the air.

Connor starts dancing, and I join him, glad to have someone to dance with since, apparently, I've been left on my own. At this point, I've taken off my winter cap and tied my jacket around my waist. The heat is unbearable, and I'm starting to think River was right and I should have just come naked. Might have been fun.

Connor doesn't seem to mind the temperature. He's getting a little too close for my comfort. The song certainly doesn't call for it. This is exactly why I don't go to college parties. I put my hand between us, gently pushing him away, but he responds by placing his hand on my back and pulling me closer again.

"Umm, Connor, are you drunk?" I joke and try again to push him a little harder without causing a scene or hurting his feelings. He's always been great to me, and I know he means no harm. He probably just had a bit too much to drink.

"That's enough, buddy." The voice comes from behind me, and my heart skips a beat. He sounds different, though. The coldness in his tone is almost enough to give me chills. How does he keep sneaking up on me?

Connor appears equally surprised, but it's clear he has no clue who's behind the Elvis costume. "Just dancing," he says, his words somewhat slurred, before taking a few steps back as if just realizing how close he was.

River doesn't take off his glasses, but his jaw is twitching, and I can tell he's upset. "Come on, Violet," he says, grabbing my hand and leading me across the dance floor.

I'm so confused that I don't resist. But then my frustration takes over. What's he thinking, barging in here like that? I don't need his help. And why does he even care? As my annoyance builds, I halt my steps and tug at his hand. "I was handling it," I say, gritting my teeth. My anger is obviously misplaced. I'm really just mad at myself for wasting my time at this stupid party instead of working on my music. But does he have to always be around at the worst moments possible?

He stops walking but doesn't let go of my hand. People continue to dance around us, absorbed in their own worlds. An unhappy expression plays across River's face, but he seems calmer now. Forcing a slow breath out, he finally looks at me. "I know you were. *He* wasn't. I just thought you could use some fresh air." He runs an anxious hand through his hair, messing up his perfect Elvis look. The sunglasses he's wearing obscure his eyes in the dim light, but I can hear the softness in his voice. That's the voice I'm used to hearing. The one he uses with *me*. He nods toward the emergency exit, and I follow him without a word. We end up in a back alley similar to the last one. Bins overflowing with garbage, parked cars, and smoke coming from the nearby bars and restaurants. Lovely.

River leans against the wall, finally taking off his glasses. I put my jacket back on, leaving the hat in my pocket, and adopt the same position.

I break the silence. "This kind of seems to be our thing."

"I guess it does." He chuckles.

"What are you doing here, anyway?"

"What do you mean?"

"Come on." I raise my eyebrows, sneaking a sideways glance at him. "Does the great River Evans usually frequent student Halloween parties impersonating Elvis Presley?"

He lets out a laugh. "Not usually, no. I'm accompanying someone."

I try not to show any reaction, but it's kind of hard because this guy always manages to throw me off. I haven't seen him here with anyone, but if that's the case, why would he come running to my rescue? Could it be the cello student I saw him with at the café? I look away, trying to stop my brain from running through all kinds of different scenarios. I have no reason to care. And I don't. Yet I can't keep from asking, "So isn't she wondering where you are right now?" Rodrigo's words sound in my head, warning me to stay away from River Evans: *He can have anyone he wants, and he is having anyone he wants.*

"I haven't said it's *she*," he says.

"What?" I ask but realize my mistake immediately.

He chuckles. "I'm here with my sister. And I'm sure she's more than happy to escape my supervision for a moment."

I cast a surprised look in his direction. Didn't see that one coming. "I didn't know you had a sister. Is she a student here?"

"No." He hesitates. "Mayra is graduating from high school this year. She wants to come to BMC, so I've been showing her around."

"Buying her T-shirts?" I ask, remembering our encounter at the bookstore.

He laughs. "Yeah, that too."

"She must look up to you," I say, but he shrugs as if that thought didn't even occur to him.

"Why don't we talk about you?" he suggests.

I let out a nervous laugh. "Me? Why? What do you want to know?"

His eyes sharpen on me, his bent leg brushing against mine, just a few inches away, like last time, and the touch feels familiar. It's not the cold that causes shivers to run through me.

"I want to know why you didn't sing your song in class."

What? Okay. This isn't where I saw our conversation going. "Umm… it just… it wasn't ready."

"It wasn't ready, or *you* weren't ready?" he presses.

"I… Both?" I frown at him. "All right, that's enough about me. Let's talk about something else—"

"I heard you," he says.

"What do you mean?" There's a momentary pause in my heartbeat.

He sighs, but his gaze doesn't leave mine. "I heard you in the practice room the other day," he clarifies, and my surprise increases. "Sounded ready to me. Actually, it sounded quite good, if you ask me."

So there *was* someone behind that door, after all. I should have known. Why didn't he say something, though? And for how long had he been standing there? Blood rushes to my cheeks. Did he also hear me singing *his* song? Right now, I wish for the ground to open up and swallow me.

"Why do you keep saying that?" I groan.

"Saying what?"

"That you like my singing." I'm trying not to sound irritated, but probably failing. Is this a joke to him?

"Because I do."

"Right." I press my lips together.

He frowns in confusion, and, for some reason, it seems sincere.

"Did you write it yourself?" he asks.

"Of course I fucking wrote it myself! I just can't sing it," I snap and see the look of surprise on his face.

"I'm sorry." I shake my head, biting my lip.

He turns toward me, and I mirror his movement until we are facing each other.

"What is it that you are scared of, Violet?" he asks softly. By now, I know that this tone of voice is reserved for me. And I wonder if also for someone else.

A sigh of frustration escapes me. "I don't know how to do this," I admit, trying to keep my voice steady. "I'm not used to writing songs for myself."

"I don't understand," he says. "Were you in a duo with someone?"

I nod but look away. "My brother."

"And you don't play together anymore?" he asks carefully.

I take a deep breath, shaking my head. I have no intention of crying or breaking down again in front of River, but then again, that's usually not something I can control. Digging my nails into my palms, I try to focus on the physical pain. That almost always works.

"We don't. Alex died a few years ago." I think it's the first time I actually say it aloud, and it still doesn't sound right. Will it ever? "It feels like I'm letting him down," I whisper. Damn it. Why am I even telling him this?

"Why?" His head tilts to the side, his eyes studying me with interest.

Because he never gave up on our dreams, I did. Because he was the one who kept pushing. Except he pushed too hard and in the wrong direction. Still, he deserved this chance so much more than I do, and he would have known how to seize it. I have no fucking idea, and I miss him too fucking much.

"Doesn't matter." I shrug. River Evans already knows more than he should, and nothing good can come out of that. Would he think differently of me if he knew the entire story? That thought bothers me much more than I care to admit.

Silence settles between us, neither of us moving for a while. All I can hear is the loud beat coming from the club.

"Violet?" he asks quietly.

"Yeah?"

"Your voice is still my favorite sound. You should use it."

# Six

The bookstore is almost empty today. It has been raining nonstop for three days, and the atmosphere inside the store reflects the gloomy weather outside, as only a few scattered customers browse the shelves. With strong winds expected, most activities and classes have been canceled. Including our songwriting class. I feel relieved and disappointed at the same time. Relieved that I don't have to sing my song in front of everyone, and stupidly disappointed that I won't have the chance to see River. I don't want to think about the 'why' of this feeling. I try not to think of him at all, but the universe apparently doesn't share my plan.

The Music Awards from a couple of days ago are being broadcast on the massive TV screen in front of our cash register. I couldn't watch them because I was working at the café all afternoon, but Rodrigo caught me checking my phone right when the results were posted online.

River Evans won Male Artist of the Year. No surprise there. And he looked more handsome than ever in his black suit. As I try to push those currently unwelcome thoughts out of my head, an interview with River, right after receiving his award, pops up on the screen.

Connor, who stands behind me, turns the volume up, and I'm torn between feigning disinterest and asking him to increase the volume even further.

The interviewer congratulates River on his latest success, the new album, and his upcoming tour, and River thanks him, the smile never quite reaching his eyes. He sounds so different. Much more serious. Almost unapproachable. Not at all the River I know. I finally abandon the pile of shirts I was folding, directing all my attention to the screen. Despite River's calm tone, his discomfort becomes more palpable as the questions grow more personal.

"Is your family here tonight? Anyone cheering for you?" the interviewer asks, and before I can catch River's answer, I see Connor shaking his head. "That guy is a fucking idiot. Don't they do any research before interviewing people? How do these people even get a job as journalists?"

"Why?" I ask. His question seemed pretty normal to me. Even nice. Something to break the ice.

Connor looks at me. "Everyone knows River Evans grew up in a foster home. He has no family."

"What?" My heart skips a few beats. Is that true? Why didn't he say anything? But then, why would he? We are practically strangers, after all. Yet he mentioned his sister. Perhaps she is not his real sister. I suddenly have a strong urge to learn more about him.

"Was he ever adopted?" I ask.

"I don't think so. He never talks about this stuff."

Huh. I turn back to the screen just in time to catch the interviewer's last question. "So, who's the beautiful woman with you tonight?" My chest tightens at seeing a photo of River with his arm around a beautiful tall blonde as the interviewer waits for his answer. I don't even realize I'm holding my breath until I hear his voice. "That would be Riley Clark," he simply says and politely nods to thank the interviewer, letting him know their conversation is over. The interviewer thanks him again, and once River is out of his sight, he goes on to inform the audience about Riley Clark, a model and actress. Of course she is. A pang of something that can't be jealousy, but it's awfully similar, tugs at me.

"He is kind of a jerk," Connor says while turning the volume back down.

"The interviewer?" I ask absentmindedly, the name of Riley Clark sounding in my head. Is she his girlfriend? Because if she is, she's exactly the kind of girlfriend I imagine him being with. Stunning and successful. And again, why do I care?

"No, River Evans," he says, snapping me out of my thoughts.

"Why?"

"I don't know. I like his music, but I don't especially like him. He keeps to himself. Most of the time, anyway. And I heard he's tough in class."

"You think he's unfair, though?" I ask, thinking about River's comments in class. Sure, they could be harsh, but not at all in a putting-another-artist-down way. Everything he said was true and useful, but I know perfectly well how easy it is to bruise a musician's ego. Sharing our music is an act of vulnerability. It exposes our deepest fears and secrets. Something not everyone is willing to do.

"Probably not." Connor shrugs. "But he's still weird. He came here yesterday, you know? To pick up some books."

"What's weird about that?"

He frowns. "He was rude and didn't even say hi."

I try not to laugh. He still hasn't realized River was behind the Elvis mask. I'm not sure how much Connor remembers from Halloween night, although he repeatedly said he was sorry if he acted inappropriately. He even brought me lunch. And coffee. And then chocolate. After which he handed me a pack of guitar strings, claiming they arrived extra in the last order. I doubt that, but who am I to say no to free guitar strings?

The Music Awards continue for a little while, but I go back to organizing shelves and folding T-shirts. The rain outside is getting stronger, and so is the wind, judging from the sea of colored umbrellas swaying from one side to the other.

When I'm done and there is nothing else left to do, I decide to take out my harmony book and use the time to study.

Connor's talking to someone on the phone, and since there are no students coming in, I'm sure he won't mind.

"Sabrina?" he calls out from somewhere in the storage room when he finishes his call.

"Yeah?"

"You can go home. No one's coming in this weather anyway, and we'll be closing early."

"Ooh. Are you sure?" I ask. Having the rest of the

afternoon to myself sounds great, but I can't afford to cut my hours since I rely on my scholarship.

"Yes, please, go. And I won't tell anyone." He grins.

"Appreciate that." I smile at him.

"No problem."

Not needing more convincing, I grab my jacket and head for the practice rooms. They're as empty as the bookstore, with the exception of a bored receptionist, a girl I believe is Nyra's friend since I almost always see them together. She's chewing gum and air-drumming an imaginary set of drums. I smile to myself. Yep, definitely Nyra's friend.

Of course, I'm completely soaked because my five-dollar umbrella didn't do a thing to keep me dry in this stupid weather. It would probably make much more sense to go home, take a hot shower, and try to get things done from there. Not that I'm considering it.

"Hey, is there a guitar available?" I ask the receptionist. Usually, I would bring mine, but I'm certainly glad I didn't bring it today.

"Umm, yeah, I think so." She stops air-drumming for a moment, looking at the computer screen in front of her as she blows a gigantic bubble. "There's one in room number two, right next to yours. The room is taken, but I don't think the guitar is being used. Maybe just knock and ask?" she suggests.

"Great, will do. Thanks." I nod and head straight to the restroom. Entering a practice room with any kind of liquid is strictly prohibited, and even though I'm not sure this would classify as such, there's water dripping from my hair and clothes. I squeeze the excess water out of my hair and then rub it with a paper towel, but there's not much I can do about my wet clothes. Taking off my sweater and tying it around my waist, I check myself in the mirror. Even my shirt is half soaked, and my jeans are uncomfortably glued to my legs, but this will have to do. At least I was clever enough to wear rain boots this morning.

I press my ear to the door of practice room two, but there is only silence. Considering that all rooms are soundproofed, it's a waste of time. So is knocking, though, and there's no door window to see who's in there. I don't mean to interrupt, but I really need that guitar. I quietly press down the handle and step inside. The room is much bigger than the one I was in last time. The lights are low, but I can distinguish the silhouette of a guy sitting at a grand piano in the center of the room. His back is turned to me, and he is playing, completely unaware of my presence. Not wanting to interrupt, I stay still by the door, listening and waiting for him to finish his song. I personally hate being interrupted when I'm playing or, even worse, when I'm composing. The melody that fills the room is beautiful and delicate, and I catch myself wishing for it not to end. And then a low, deep voice joins the notes, slowly dancing over them, and my breath catches in my throat, and my pulse quickens. It's *his* voice. What's he doing here, using the students' practice rooms? I'm pretty sure he has his own studio with more than just a piano and a couple of guitars.

Suddenly, I feel like I shouldn't be here. It's not only because he hasn't noticed me yet, but also because the way he's playing and singing just feels so… intimate. And even though I'm pretty sure most people would gladly pay for this private show, it doesn't feel right to intrude. Peeling my eyes off him, I quietly tiptoe back to the door, pressing down on the handle once more, when the music stops abruptly. "Hey, this room is booked for tonight. You can't be here."

Shit. Biting my lip, I turn slowly to face him. "I'm really sorry, I didn't mean to interrupt. I just wanted to ask if I could grab a guitar."

"Violet?" Confusion appears on his face, but the harsh tone is gone.

"Hi." I nod but remain at the door. "Sorry," I say again. "I didn't know you were here. I don't want to disturb you." My hand goes back to the handle as I forget about the guitar I actually came for.

"Wait." His voice stops me once again. "You said you need a guitar?" he asks, nodding to the guitar resting on the stand next to him.

"Umm, yeah." I hesitate. "If you're not using it?"

He chuckles. "I wish, but I'm a piano player."

"I figured." I can't hold back my grin when our eyes finally meet.

He stands up and holds the guitar out to me. Our fingers briefly brush as I take it from him, the tickling sensation causing me to pull back quickly. A slight flicker appears in his eyes, but his expression remains guarded.

"I thought you played the piano?" There's a note of curiosity in his voice.

"I do, but not very well." I pause. "Definitely not like you. My main instrument has always been the guitar. Anyway"—I swallow—"I'm sorry again for interrupting."

He shakes his head. "That's okay. I don't usually rehearse here, but with afternoon classes canceled, I thought I'd stick around for a while, see if the rain stops." His eyes wander over my wet hair and soaked T-shirt, and I suppress the urge to cross my arms over my chest. Exactly how revealing is this stupid shirt?

"Yep, still raining," I confirm, noticing a smile tugging at his lips. With my hand on the door, I hesitate a moment longer. He's sitting back at the piano, but his eyes are still on me. "By the way, umm... Congratulations on your award."

I catch a flash of surprise in his eyes, even though he's probably heard it a thousand times before.

"Thank you." He nods, not giving anything else away as I quietly close the door behind me and head to my own practice room.

This one's much smaller, and the only piece of furniture is an upright piano with a bench occupying one wall.

To make more space, I move the bench under the piano and settle on the floor with my guitar, then take out a notebook. Throughout the years, Alex and I have composed more songs than would fit on an album. The system we had back then was flawless. I'd come up with ideas, and Alex would make them work. Simple as that.

Since Alex died, I've worked on many new songs but never finished any of them. Partially because I am lost without his guidance, but also because... is there even a point in doing this without him? Even though we both had an equal passion for music, Alex was the more talented one of our duo and also the one who constantly motivated us to move forward. It was his idea to start playing small gigs in Prague, to forget about covers and focus on writing our own music. He was also the one who suggested we should apply for BMC. And when we got in and were offered only one scholarship, and our parents refused to help us, he never lost hope, determined to find a way for both of us to go.

A twinge of pain spirals through me.

"You should have gone alone, Alex. That's what you should have done, because if you had, you would still be alive," I whisper, but of course, he doesn't answer. He never does when he disagrees.

Playing my new song on repeat, I scribble down ideas just to cross them out in frustration moments later. The sound of the door opening catches my attention, and I see River standing in the doorway, balancing two cups of coffee. "Need a break?" he asks, a hint of hesitation in his voice. My surprise is hard to mask. Did he come looking for me? *Don't be ridiculous,* I scold myself. He was probably just bored. We must be the only ones here tonight.

I clear my throat. "Why not? I'm pretty sure coffee isn't allowed here, though."

"Then it's a good thing there's no one around." He chuckles, throwing me a mischievous wink. I'm not sure why my heart skips a few beats, but it does. It could be because of how good he looks in his tight, gray pants and blue sweater, emphasizing his strong chest and arms, with his messy, dark hair falling into his eyes. The room is so small that it fills instantly with his captivating scent of orange and ginger. He hands me one of the paper cups, and I expect him to leave or maybe stay in the doorway and chat for a while, but instead, he surprises me by sliding to the ground next to me.

"Keep playing," he says, making himself comfortable and successfully ignoring my puzzled look.

"What?" The right side of his body is brushing against me, given the limited space, and I know that if I couldn't focus before, there is no way I'm focusing now. And there's no way I'm playing for him.

"Remember the panic attack you had the night after my concert?" he asks out of the blue.

Blood rushes into my cheeks. Why is he bringing that up now? "Yes, what about it?"

"I used to have those before performing," he says.

My brows knit together in doubt. "I'm not sure whether to believe that."

"Believe it or not, it's true." He shrugs.

I sneak a glance at him, gently running my fingers over the polished wood of my guitar. "And how did you get past it? Wait, let me guess. Were you picturing the audience naked?"

His laughter echoes through the room. "I haven't tried that one, but now that you say it, I'm almost tempted to. But no, it took a lot of time and practice before I could stand before an audience and actually enjoy it."

"Well, then I guess there is still hope for me," I murmur, still not sure why he is telling me all of this.

He takes a few sips of his coffee before leaning in and taking my unfinished cup out of my hand. "Play," he says again, his beautiful voice low and commanding.

I frown, letting out a frustrated sigh. "I can't play with you looking at me." This is probably not helping my professional image, but I don't care.

He gives me a skeptical look, raising his eyebrows, but then he leans his head against the wall and closes his eyes. Umm, seriously? This guy is incredible. Incredibly annoying, that is. I don't know if I should be angry at him for crashing my practice time or feel flattered that River Evans wants to hear my music. I glance at him again. His eyes are shut, and I can hear him breathing and swallowing quietly. All right, this is weird. Keeping my eyes on him, I start playing, fully prepared to stop if I see so much as a tiny movement behind his eyelids. He remains completely still, except for the unconscious gesture of wetting his lips, while his breathing quickens slightly. That and the heat of his body so close to mine is a continuous distraction I can't ignore. Following River's example, I shut my eyes to give the song the attention it deserves.

Why wouldn't you just listen?
Keep going, there is nothing we can't do
And I believed you, always so damn sure
Was it me who didn't see the storm coming?
Was it you?

You left me alone
Surrounded by those I don't even know
You asked me to keep smiling
But my heart doesn't hold

They say if you don't decide who you are
The world will tell you
But do they know?
Did you?
Why wouldn't you listen?
Keep going, there is nothing we can't do

And I believed you, always so damn sure
Was it me who didn't see the storm coming?
Was it you?

When I finish and slowly open my eyes, River's intense gaze is focused on me, but he stays quiet.

"It's not finished," I say, interrupting the silence, suddenly feeling really nervous again. Did he not like it? What am I even thinking, singing in front of him? The situation repeats itself. It feels like the last time I sang his song and he ran out on me. Except that he's still here. Isn't he? Damn it. I wish I didn't care so much about his opinion.

He doesn't respond. Instead, his eyes once more vanish under his thick lashes. "Play it again."

What? "I don't thi—"

"Sabrina, please," he says softly, and I'm so surprised he used my actual name that I stop objecting and start playing again. He makes me repeat the same unfinished song four times, and on the last attempt, I catch a glimpse of his beautiful lashes moving and his eyes opening cautiously. Strangely enough, I don't even mind at this point. I feel his gaze on me as I keep going, noticing a slight change in the air around us.

This time, when I finish, his face lights up, and he flashes me a broad smile, revealing his perfect teeth.

My nerves kick in. "You are freaking me out. Say something, please."

He chuckles and then shakes his head. "I will tell you one thing."

I turn to him, trying not to show how much his opinion means to me. Not only because of the amazing musician he is but also because he has somehow been there for me every time I needed it since I arrived in Boston.

"Finish it," he says simply.

"Yeah, I know, but—"

He puts his hand on my leg. It's a gentle touch, but it burns through the thin fabric of my jeans. "There are no 'buts' in this industry, Sabrina. There are a lot of talented people, but there's also a lot of work and a lot of sacrifice. Some days you feel like singing, some days you don't, but as long as you know your reason for doing it, it's all worth it," he says.

My reason for doing it... I suddenly remember Professor Jameson and his question '*Tell me why you are here*' that most of us still haven't been able to answer correctly.

"What's your reason?" I ask quietly.

He smiles, taking his hand off my leg but still looking into my eyes. "Music saved my life," he says simply, but there is so much power in his words. Maybe because I know exactly what he means. Even though I haven't been able to compose since Alex died, music was the only thing that kept me going. The only solace amid the darkness I fell into in the months after my brother's death. And it was the letter I received from BMC that finally pulled me out of that darkness. The letter that said this was my last chance to come before losing my spot and, with it, the offered scholarship.

River suddenly clears his throat and gets up. "It's late. I should probably get going, see if the rain stopped. Do you... umm... do you need a ride?" he asks a bit awkwardly.

"No, I'm good, thanks. I think I'll stay a little longer. Plus, I'm living in the dorms, so…"

"Right," he says, frowning slightly. He turns to the door, but then he stops with his hand on the handle, looking back at me.

"I meant what I said, Violet. You have everything you need, and trust me, you are doing just fine. Finish the song," he says, leaving me speechless as he closes the door behind him.

Did I hear him right?

✳

"It just feels a little excessive. That's all I'm saying." With a shake of my head, I hang two massive Christmas branches wrapped in lights over the bar counter. Somewhere behind me, Rodrigo chuckles while digging up more Christmas decorations from a paper box he brought this morning. It's Saturday, not that it makes much difference to me. I work at the café in the morning and at the bookstore in the afternoon. All that while my classmates are having fun, playing jams, and currently relishing their coffee after what appears to be one hell of a hangover from Friday night. That part, at least, I don't envy.

"There's nothing better than a bit of Christmas spirit!" He hands me a box filled with small snowflakes and star-shaped lights, his mood suspiciously cheerful.

"Yeah, but there's still over a month and a half until Christmas. The only motive behind creating Christmas spirit ahead of time is to boost sales," I point out, mimicking his cheery tone.

He shakes his head, laughing. "Come on, Sabrina! Don't be such a Scrooge! Are you going home for Christmas? Or are your parents planning on coming here?"

Leaning on a chair for balance, I carefully lower myself to the floor, handing him the empty container. "Neither." I shrug. There's no point in explaining that I don't have the money to go back to Prague and my parents won't come here, even though they have more than enough. "What are your plans?" I ask instead. "Are you going home?"

"No," he says. "It's ridiculously expensive during Christmas. My plan is to travel around a little. Maybe take the bus to New York. I also have a friend in Rhode Island, so I might drop by for a visit."

I conceal my smile, well aware of who his friend from Rhode Island is. "Are we talking about a certain tall, handsome guy from the Halloween party that I might or might not have seen you kissing?" I wink at him. As it turns out, it's not at all unusual for Rhode Island students to come to Boston on weekends and crash our parties.

"Oh, shut up." Rodrigo hands me an incredibly tangled-up set of Christmas lights. "Like I didn't see you leaving with that Elvis guy," he says.

"What Elvis guy?" Bela's high-pitched question comes from behind the bar. Of course she overheard that. That woman has a talent for appearing at the most inconvenient moments. I give her a quick hug as Rodrigo starts preparing her latte.

"Forget about it," I say.

"Are you kidding? Oh, I'm *so* not going to forget about it, mi amor." She laughs, her long earrings tinkling as she shakes her head. Yep, I've brought this on myself, mentioning that night.

"You went home with someone?" she continues.

"You mean I brought someone to our dorm?" I let out a laugh. "I'm not that desperate. Nope."

"She prefers a quickie in the back alley," Rodrigo chimes in innocently, putting a tempting-looking latte in front of our friend.

"Ugh, for God's sake. Stop it, both of you!" I roll my eyes. "I was with River, and we were talking. That's it," I clarify, with the solemn intention of saving myself from their interrogation, but instead, I somehow manage to trigger an absolute avalanche of new questions and comments of all kinds.

"What River? Wait a minute. Are we talking about River Evans?" Bela stares at me, her eyes wide.

"What was River Evans doing at our Halloween party?" Rodrigo asks.

"Wait, I heard he was fucking that cello player. You think it's true?"

"Probably," Rodrigo answers. "It's a new one every week. He was with Riley Clark at the Music Awards."

"Oh my God, I'd absolutely fuck that guy." Bela grins.

"Who wouldn't?" Rodrigo agrees, and both of them burst into laughter.

I finally manage to untangle the damn Christmas lights, sacrificing one of my nails in the process, and victoriously toss them at Rodrigo. "I'm taking five," I blurt out, earning their surprised looks. At least they pause the ridiculous conversation. Not waiting for Rodrigo's permission, I grab my jacket and hurry out to get some fresh air. As much as I would like to think that my sudden frustration has nothing to do with their comments, that would be a lie. Then again, they aren't really saying anything new. Are they? I let out a sigh when my phone starts buzzing. My parents. Just what I need right now. I wait a few seconds before deciding there's not much sense in delaying the inevitable.

"Hi, Mom."

"Sabrina?" Hearing her voice instantly makes me miss her, even though I don't want to. "How are you? We haven't heard from you in a while."

I sit on the stairs outside, switching my phone from hand to hand, giving myself some extra time to come up with an answer. "You haven't called either," I say after a moment. Probably not the best response.

"Your dad thought you may come back," she whispers. "Are you doing all right, darling?"

All of a sudden, I feel bad. And exhausted. So fucking exhausted. What's all this fighting for? It's not like it's going to bring Alex back. "I'm fine, Mom," I say. "I'm learning a lot. I was even able to—"

"Will you come home for Christmas?" she interrupts me. Of course this is what it's all about.

"No," I say quietly. "But you can come here if you want. I could show you around," I try, knowing well that it's useless.

Silence is the only answer I get. Not that I expected anything else. Disappointment isn't something I allow myself to feel anymore.

"How are you doing with money?" she asks after a while.

"Fine." The lie comes out easily. Even though most of my school expenses are covered, the money I'm making at the café is nowhere near enough to live comfortably in this city. The main difficulty lies in books and meals. Books because they cost a ridiculous amount of money, but fortunately, I can photocopy most of them at the bookstore, to which Connor generously turns a blind eye, and meals because the campus diner's hours don't always match my hectic schedule.

"You know you could have everything here," Mom says, probably sensing that I'm lying to her, the subtle reproach in her voice more than obvious.

I sigh. It really is a never-ending story. "Doing what, Mom?"

"Anything you want!" she says. "Well… something that will allow you to make a living. Teaching, for example. We talked about it—"

"Yeah, we did," I agree. "I have to go, Mom."

"This dream of yours, Sabrina, it's foolish and you know it. It's what took Alex from us and it will—"

*I'm so fucking tired of being what they want me to be. Aren't you?* Memories of my brother's angry voice come rushing back to me.

*So am I. So damn tired of never being enough and never having their support.*

I can't bear to listen to her anymore. I hang up, slowly breathing in and out, just like I learned through my two years of therapy, before heading back inside.

# Seven

"You seem like you're about to doze off," Bela whispers to me in our yoga class while we're hanging upside down in a dog pose.

"I'm fine," I say. My exhaustion from the weekend somehow spilled into the beginning of the week. It's not helping either that the weather is getting colder each day.

"Just didn't get much sleep." *Or breakfast. Or dinner.* In addition to practicing until late last night so I would be ready for our songwriting class today. My song still isn't finished, but I'm hoping I'll at least be able to perform what I have so far.

When we get to the classroom, our hair wet and wearing the usual post-yoga outfits, Professor Williams is already there, and so is River. He's talking to one of our classmates, the same girl who made me sing his song, and I can see she still hasn't stopped trying. Leaning toward him, she points to something on her tablet, all the while offering a perfect view of her cleavage. I suppress the urge to roll my eyes. *Being a little too obvious, Olivia?* Yet his gaze finds me as soon as I sit down, making my heart pound a little faster against my rib cage. I give him a slight nod and focus my attention on Professor Williams instead.

I'm mad at myself, not only for being so easily distracted but also for not being able to get River out of my head. Unfortunately, his presence fills the room, making it hard for me to focus on anything else. It's been a week since we last spoke, but our encounter in the rehearsal room has been replaying in my mind repeatedly. How his body was so close to mine that I could feel his every breath. How incredibly beautiful his eyes looked when he opened them after hearing me play, a smile forming on his lips. Damn it. I try to push those thoughts aside. Thinking about River is the last thing I should be doing. Especially thinking about him *like that*.

"Sabrina, are you ready today? Would you like to start?" Professor Williams asks, and despite my knowledge of what was coming and the week-long preparation, my anxiety immediately kicks in. Using my leggings to wipe my sweaty hands, I reach for my guitar. As I brush the strings with my fingertips, my eyes nervously wander around the classroom. Were there this many people last time? And do they all need to be looking at me?

River's gaze meets mine from across the room. His look is intense but, at the same time, soft and reassuring. I try to imagine that his eyes are the only ones in the room staring at me but fail miserably. My heartbeat quickens, and I suck in a deep breath to calm myself. *Come on, you have rehearsed for this at least a hundred times. What's the worst that could happen?* Alex's voice echoes in my head, and I know he would have laughed if he could see me right now.

*Easy for you to say.*

Amid my mental conversation with my brother, River clears his throat, causing all heads to turn to him. "Actually, if you don't mind, I'd like to try something different today," he says, looking at Professor Williams, who simply nods for him to continue. "Why don't you all close your eyes while you listen to Sabrina so you can really focus on her song?" he suggests, his voice as deep and mesmerizing as ever, with his charming Boston accent slightly marking each word. "Let's try it for all of you playing today," he adds, leaving no space for objections, making it sound like a random experiment that has just occurred to him. I frown in confusion. Does he really want me to play with everyone's eyes closed? But he isn't looking at me. Instead, he leans comfortably into his chair, stretching his legs out in front of him and closing his eyes. What on earth? Professor Williams follows his example, and so does the rest of the class.

I shake my head in disbelief, but his gesture is not at all lost on me. *He is doing this for me.* Another person I shouldn't let down. Damn it. When did he become *that kind* of person to me? Taking a deep breath, I push aside all my thoughts and start playing.

As my voice joins the first notes traveling across the room, River's eyes gradually open. He silently mouths, "Keep going," while his lips lift into an encouraging smile. And so I do. I focus on him and continue. Somewhere in the middle of the song, I completely forget where I am. My eyes stay on River, and his stay on me, making it seem like it's just the two of us. Surprisingly, none of my classmates open their eyes, nor does Professor Williams. I don't know if they're actually listening, or, more likely, taking a nap, but I don't care. For a moment, it feels just like it used to when I played with Alex. It feels right.

As the final notes fade away, River's green eyes quickly close again. He opens them along with the rest of the class, a few seconds later than everybody else, silently joining their applause. Our eyes briefly meet again only when everybody's attention shifts back to Professor Williams.

"Good job, Sabrina. It's a powerful song. Keep working on it. I'm looking forward to hearing it when it's finished," she says simply, and I nod, both grateful and infinitely relieved.

Another student takes my place, and I can't tell if it's the aftermath of my performance or all the exhaustion suddenly crashing down on me, but my head starts spinning, and my vision becomes blurry. Trying not to interrupt my classmate's performance, I lean over to Bela, giving her arm a gentle shake. "I'm not feeling good. I need to get out," I whisper as quietly as possible, yet River's eyes immediately snap to me with a questioning look.

"Why? What's going on? Do you want me to come with you?" she whispers back, already grabbing her bag from the floor.

I shake my head. "No, no, stay. I'm fine. Just need to get some air."

A tiny frown between her eyebrows tells me she doesn't like the idea, but she nods. "Let me know if you need me."

Quietly but as fast as I can, I sneak out of the room, hoping that Professor Williams won't hold it against me. Our classroom is on the second floor and the elevators are always crowded, so I opt for the stairs, praying not to trip before reaching the exit. A broken leg definitely wouldn't help. I'm used to panic attacks, but this feels different. My legs are shaky and the stairs in front of me appear out of focus. Fuck. How many are there, anyway? Taking a hesitant step, I grasp the handrail for support.

"Violet!" I hear behind me, but it sounds like it's coming from much farther away. Hands wrap around my arm, and I look up to see worry plastered over River's face. "What's up with you?"

"I'm fine. Just need to get some air," I say, at this point highly doubting it will actually solve anything.

"Come here." He grabs my waist and guides me to a bench by the stairs. I feel his touch, light but firm at the same time. Being so near to him, inhaling his scent, and feeling his hands on me makes me even dizzier, although for completely different reasons. I let him help me sit down, but then, changing my mind, not wanting to show any more weakness, try to get up almost as quickly. My mistake becomes apparent when my legs give out, and my mind goes blank, causing everything to vanish momentarily.

"Is she going to be all right? I don't understand what happened." River's voice sounds in my ears as I try to open my eyes. Blinking a couple of times, I take in my surroundings. What the hell? Why am I in the infirmary? And most importantly, how did I get here?

"Honey, when was the last time you ate?"

I narrow my eyes at the older woman leaning down in front of me. Her hair is gray, elegantly styled into a bun, and her eyes share a similar color with little hints of blue. She hands me a glass of water that I gladly take, finishing it in one gulp.

"I… umm… yesterday?" I say tentatively, ignoring the surprised look in River's eyes and shifting uncomfortably on the infirmary bed. Why is he still here?

"Yesterday, what time? Dinner?" she insists.

"Lunch, probably," I mutter, trying not to look at either of them, suddenly feeling ashamed.

"I see," she says, nodding. Still, her voice is sweet, no sign of reproach. "You need to eat, honey. I know you guys have so many things going on, but we can't have you fainting here, can we? Go get something to eat. Come on!" she orders, and I start getting up, happy to oblige as long as it gets me out of here.

River's at my side before I know it, his hands finding their way to my waist once more. "I'll make sure she eats," he promises.

"You do that, boy." The woman smiles, and I'm surprised to see her giving him a small kiss on his cheek. Seeing my confused look, she winks at me, nodding toward River. "I remember this one, way before he became such a superstar." She laughs. "He has always been a good one," she adds, and River chuckles in my ear, so close to me that I can feel the vibration of his laughter traveling through my body.

We leave the infirmary, and even though the glass of cold water helped, my legs don't feel completely steady. Clearing my throat, I glance at River, who's keeping a firm hold on me.

"Sorry about that," I start. "I can manage from here. You can go back to class. I'll get some snacks from the vending machine and be right back, too."

His mint-green eyes pierce through me like an arrow,

his eyebrows furrowed together. If I had to guess, I'd say he's angry. What at or who at, I'm not sure.

"We are *not* going back to class." He growls. "And you aren't getting a fucking snack from the vending machine."

I frown at him. He may have saved me again, but there's no reason for him to be biting my head off. It's not like I starved myself on purpose. I mentally remind myself to buy protein bars to throw into my purse, a handy snack for emergencies. Problem solved.

"Care to explain what has gotten into you?" I ask.

"Stay here," he orders, not acknowledging my question as he guides me to sit on a couch in the reception area. "I'm gonna get your guitar." Leaving me no time to react, he darts up the stairs toward our classroom. Next thing I know, he's leading me to his car.

"Wait, I have more lessons today. I can't just leave!"

"What lessons?" He still sounds upset. What the hell is his problem?

"Piano." I look around the parking lot. Is he taking me to the dorms? I could easily walk from here. This is ridiculous.

"Who's your teacher?" he asks, opening the door of his SUV for me.

"Professor Brown. Why?" I inhale his scent as he leans in to secure my seat belt.

Again, he doesn't answer. Instead, he takes out his phone and starts typing. "Done. You'll do a makeup lesson tomorrow. Something else?" He raises his eyebrows at me, starting the car.

"Umm... did you just text my professor?"

"Yes."

His short answer leaves me even more puzzled. "Are you mad at me for some reason?" I scowl, letting my voice go up a little.

With his eyes fixed on the road, he takes a couple of breaths before answering. "Yes, I'm fucking mad at you!" he snaps, and I can tell the breathing exercise did little to calm him down.

"What? Why?" I glance at him, fiddling with my hands. "Look, I get it. I'm being a pain in the ass, and I'm really sorry this all somehow keeps happening when you are around... But I told you I don't need your help. I'm fine."

"You're fine?" He looks at me, stopping at the traffic light, his voice cold and serious. "You fainted, Sabrina," he reminds me, as if I don't remember it myself. I've been so used to him calling me Violet, at least when we're alone, that I instantly frown at his use of my actual name.

"Okay, look. This is the first time it's happened, and it was an accident. I was busy, and I... forgot to eat," I try to explain, unsure if I'm making it any better.

"Forgot?" he asks doubtfully.

"Well, technically, I didn't forget, but let's just say that my work schedule doesn't always align with the business hours of the campus diner," I admit reluctantly.

His eyes shoot to me in surprise. "Okay, but why wouldn't you just buy something?"

I don't answer, turning my head to the window.

He sighs but doesn't keep insisting, which I'm grateful for.

"I still don't get why you're angry," I whisper after a moment of somewhat comfortable silence.

His eyes narrow at the road in front of us, and I notice his grip on the steering wheel tightening a little. "You scared me, that's all," he says, much to my surprise. "I'm sorry I snapped at you."

"You kind of saved me… again, so I think we're good," I say with a grin, watching him relax and shake his head in amusement.

"By the way"—I give him a small side glance—"how exactly did I get to the infirmary?"

"I carried you," he says calmly, his eyes not leaving the road.

"What?" My mouth drops open, heat rushing to my cheeks. "All the way?"

He chuckles, and I hate admitting how much I enjoy the sound of his laughter. "Violet, I promise you, I can carry you much longer than that if ever needed." His words are accompanied by a mischievous wink. Right. I don't doubt it. I've seen his muscles moving under his shirt. Most professional musicians work out religiously, as it is the only way to not end up in pain after so many hours of playing. Hence the campus gym I've yet to get acquainted with.

I shake my head and give him a slight shove, using it as a way to distract myself from overthinking his words. Even though I'm pretty sure he was joking, my stomach still does a few stupid somersaults.

The car suddenly stops, and I realize where we are. "Is this Cambridge?" I peek out of the window. I haven't had much time to explore Boston, but I've been to Cambridge a couple of times. There is something very bohemian about this part of the city. Perhaps it's because it's the only place where most of the famous food and coffee chains suddenly vanish, leaving the area with more original, cozy places to enjoy, along with charming art shops and bookstores.

"Yeah, it is." He nods as he gets out of the car, circling it to open my door. "Come on," he says.

"Where are we going?" I obediently hop out, my curiosity getting the best of me.

He gestures for us to cross the street. "We're going for lunch because that's what you need right now."

He canceled my lessons and left campus to bring me to lunch? "Why are you using that tone with me?" I scowl, noticing his voice has gone serious again.

"What tone?" He gives me a surprised look.

"The one you use when you talk to other people," I say before realizing how it may have sounded. Perfect.

"Umm, I haven't realized that," he says. "Does it mean I'm using a different tone when I'm talking to you?" he asks, amusement seeping through his voice.

I shrug. "Usually."

He smiles but stays silent, coming to a halt in front of what looks like a Mexican restaurant. Fueled by curiosity, I press my nose against the glass and peek inside. The space looks big, mostly furnished in wood, with walls covered in black paint and decorated with colorful skulls and flowers. My eyes nearly pop out of my head as I scan the menu prices by the entrance. Damn it. These prices should be criminal. How much can you charge for a burrito, anyway?

"Hope you like Mexican," River says as he ushers me inside, and even though I'm glad his voice has softened once more, my rising panic doesn't let me enjoy the moment.

The waiter shows up immediately. "Table for two?" he asks, and River simply nods, putting his hand on the small of my back. A feeling of uneasiness settles over me. How do I always end up in these situations around him? A growl leaves my throat before I even notice it.

"What's wrong?" He frowns, glancing down at me with a questioning look. God, this guy is tall.

To save myself from more embarrassment, I lean closer to him, making sure he's the only one who can hear me. His touch on my back tightens as he tilts his head to me. It's the simplest gesture, but it makes my heart skip a beat.

"Umm, maybe we could go somewhere… less fancy?" I try.

River throws me a look laced with confusion, and I can't say I blame him. "I'm not sure I'd call this 'fancy,' but the food here is good." He shrugs. "But, of course, if you don't like it, we can go somewhere else."

Ugh. Does he think I'm being ungrateful? Of course he does. I slowly shake my head. "No, it looks great. Let's stay here," I say, taking a seat at the table at the back of the restaurant we have been shown to. The waiter returns in less than five minutes, bringing two glasses of water and homemade lemonade. "Have you guys chosen anything yet?"

River gives me a nod to go first.

"I'll go with the salad." I motion toward one of the starters on the menu. The one I can actually pay for.

"Anything else?" he asks with a strong, I suppose Mexican, accent.

"That will be all, thank you." Giving him my best smile, I close the menu and hand it to him. I try not to look at

River in the process, but that doesn't mean I don't catch his disapproving look.

"And for you, sir?" It's clear from the admiration in the waiter's voice that he knows perfectly well who River is.

"I'll have the burrito," he says, pointing at a picture of a delicious-looking burrito. More delicious than my salad, that's for sure. "Actually, make it two," he corrects himself. "And some nachos, please."

"You got it." The waiter walks away, and I grin at River. "Look who is the hungry one!"

He leans forward, resting his elbows on the table. "Is there a reason you are not eating?" he asks.

"What?"

"You heard me, Violet," he says softly.

"No, of course not. I assure you I'm quite an eater, actually." My cheeks go red, but I give him a wide smile, hoping he believes me. That part is completely true. My stomach is growling just from the smell coming out of the kitchen.

"Hmm, I'll have to see that to believe it," he says, shaking his head but returning my smile. "You did well in class today," he adds, surprising me.

I glance at him, but the only thing I see in his eyes is sincerity. "Could have been better." I shrug. "But I appreciate you saying that, and I appreciate what you did back there."

River is the one shrugging now. "I have no idea what you're talking about."

"Liar." I throw back and notice him hiding his smile.

"Tell me more about your brother." He surprises me again by completely changing the topic.

"My brother? Why?" The familiar pain spirals through me. Talking to River is easy, but talking about Alex is a whole different matter. And just like that, that same thought that has occurred to me so many times returns, making my stomach churn. What would he think if he knew what happened to Alex? Would he judge him as everyone else did? As our parents did? Would he judge *me*? Would his opinion of me change?

*I found a job where I can make good money… enough money.* The words Alex spoke to me only a couple of months before his death—and that should have served as a warning if I'd only listened better—resurface in my head.

"Please," River adds.

"What do you want to know?" I ask quietly.

"When did you guys start playing together?" he asks, and I immediately smile at the memory. That's an easy one. Sucking in a breath, I allow my eyes to wander out the window. The square is buzzing with life at this hour, yet it feels like we're in our little Mexican oasis, hidden from the outside world.

"It was on our eighth birthday. Dad bought us guitars and got us into music lessons. We'd never been so excited about anything. It was love at first sight." I chuckle, but it doesn't come out quite right.

"I think I know what you mean." River's lips curve into a soft smile. "So you both got the same present for your birthday?"

"Yeah, well, we usually did. Alex… he was my twin, and I think we were the epitome of twins, to be honest." I wince, the memory of Alex bringing an entire cocktail of different feelings, both sad and happy. "We used to be inseparable and did everything together." Alex and I didn't have best friends, *we were* best friends. River nods, and judging from the warmth in his eyes, I would say he understands. I make a mental note to ask him for more details about his sister. It's clear that he doesn't like discussing his nonexistent family, so I may have to find a way to bring it up without him shutting me down, just like he does in all his interviews.

"That was some great gift your dad gave you. He must be proud of you." He smiles.

His words, though well-intentioned, leave me choking on air. Because… isn't that just the problem?

"Yeah, I wish that were the case." Here I am, complaining to someone who never even had a family. How is that fair?

"Violet?" he encourages softly, noticing I'm lost in my thoughts.

I sigh. "Our parents have always been obsessed with appearances. Dad especially. As kids, we didn't get to pick the activities we liked. We had to take the ones that were 'trendy.'" I grimace, slightly pausing at that word to make sure River is still following. He's quiet, but his eyes haven't left mine, and I know I have his complete attention. That alone makes the weight pressing on my chest feel a little lighter. Saying all of this out loud also feels strangely freeing. "So we were taking all kinds of classes besides music—from English and French to painting, tennis, swimming, math, karate… you name it," I say and see his eyebrows go up in amusement after the last one. "But music was the only one we really fell in love with, and also the only one we were actually good at."

"So you weren't any good at karate? That's a bummer." He chuckles, lightening the mood with what has become my favorite sound, right next to the steady beat of his heart.

"Oh, shut up! I still have some moves." I grin.

"I can't imagine your dad wouldn't be happy hearing you play," he says after a few seconds of silence.

"It's not that he wasn't happy to hear us play. At least at the beginning, anyway. The thing is, for him, music was just another way of showing off his kids in front of his friends and colleagues, but for us, it became… everything."

He seems to think about that for a moment, carefully swallowing as if deciding to keep his opinion to himself. "So when did you guys decide you wanted to become professional musicians?" he asks.

I look back out of the window. The square brims with college students, many of them wearing Harvard hoodies, walking fast, zipping up their jackets, some of them sipping on hot coffees, all of them headed somewhere, probably to work on their dreams.

Dreams, such a beautiful but dangerous thing to have.

My fingers clench into a fist under the table. "We played a lot, wrote our own songs. Once we got a little better, we started getting small gigs around the city, sometimes in clubs, sometimes we would just play on the street or in subway stations. Until, at one point, it stopped being enough. So we decided we would apply to BMC. Alex came up with the idea, and we knew it was the best university out there, so in our heads, there was never really any doubt that Boston was where we had to go. That day, we took a train to Vienna, where the audition was taking place"—I inhale deeply, this memory being one of the most beautiful and painful ones because of how much it meant to both of us—"and we made a deal. We would only go if we both got in. And if we did, and our parents refused to help us, we'd find a way to make it happen no matter what."

"And?" River asks quietly, most likely trying to understand the exact moment things went to hell. He doesn't ask, but I can see the question in his eyes.

"And we both got in," I say. "We auditioned separately in the theoretical part of the exam, and then we performed together for the practical one, playing a couple of our songs. One month later, we got the admission letter." I pause for a moment, letting the memory sink in. "It said we both got in, but they could only offer a full scholarship to one of us."

A flicker of understanding flashes across his face. "So you told your parents?" he asks.

"We did," I whisper. "And they said they wouldn't help. To them, music isn't a real career. God, I really wish they could meet you." A dry laugh leaves my throat as River shakes his head.

"You'll show them yourself, Violet. I don't doubt that," he says, his voice tender. How can he believe in me so much when I can't believe in myself? The question never leaves my lips, though. My stomach growls as the waiter puts our order on the table, placing a bowl of salad in front of me, the nachos in the middle of the table, and two huge burritos—which make my mouth water from how good they look and smell—in front of River. Doing my best not to stare at them, I gleefully pierce a few pieces of lettuce with my fork.

"Anything else, Mr. Evans?" Huh, of course he knows who River is, and so does the rest of the restaurant, judging by the open glances. What must it be like to have people following your every move? River doesn't seem to care. He's always so calm and composed, almost like he was born for this role.

"No, thank you." He gives him a polite half smile before returning his attention to me. "Do you like your salad?" he asks, raising his eyebrows as he takes a bite of his burrito.

"Ummm, it's delicious." I nod. It's not bad, but no one in their right mind would ever compare it to a burrito.

He shakes his head, a smile playing on his lips as he pushes the other burrito in front of me. "Eat, Violet."

What? "You don't want it?" I ask, a look of embarrassment on my face.

"I ordered it for you," he says simply.

We look at each other for a moment, but I have no idea what to say. So I don't say anything, and neither does River.

"Try some nachos," he murmurs a couple of minutes later, as if it isn't a big deal. And to him it probably isn't, but to me, it's another tiny piece of a puzzle helping me to understand the man in front of me. The media's depiction of him as cold and guarded couldn't be further from the truth.

"So," I start, after swallowing the most delicious taste of burrito I've ever had. "I feel like I told you a lot about myself, and I know nothing about *you*."

River looks up from his plate, and I could almost swear he suddenly looks nervous. "What would you like to know?" he asks, slowly chewing.

"How did you become a musician?" I try, hoping this

is a broad enough question for him to decide if he wants to tell me more about how he grew up.

"I loved playing the piano since I was little," he says, "and continued as a teenager, then started singing and composing my own songs. Got a full scholarship, just like you, recorded my first album when I was a student, and the rest kind of just happened."

"Really?" I look at him, but he doesn't return my gaze. Instead, he gives his full attention to his burrito.

"Huh, really," he mutters.

"Okay. Now that I have heard the Wikipedia version—thank you very much, by the way, but I have already read that one—will you tell me the real one?"

His eyes immediately snap to mine, and his gaze lingers on me for a split second until he finally cracks a smile. "You're much bossier when you aren't hungry, you know that? I'm not sure I should keep feeding you. Maybe I'm creating a monster."

I snort. "Told you I could eat. Now, come on, let me hear your story!" I give him my best begging look.

"Don't look at me like that. You know that's not a fair game—" he starts, an expression in his eyes I struggle to interpret, but he stops without finishing the thought. And for a moment, something changes between us, and I can feel my heart beat a little faster.

"Please," I finally say again, and he sighs.

"Only if you have a dessert with me," he says with all seriousness, and I laugh at his request, letting him pick the best one, along with two coffees. I wish I didn't have to leave for my afternoon shift at the bookstore. These couple of hours have passed so quickly that I'd give anything to hang on to them for a little longer. And it crosses my mind that maybe, just maybe, it's not the restaurant or the food, but the company that's actually responsible for this feeling. But of course, I already knew that.

*If you don't want to get your heart broken, stay the fuck away from River Evans.* Rodrigo's words pop into my head, but I quickly push them away.

When our dessert, something similar to a rice pudding, with the delicious smell of vanilla, is finally in front of us, River clears his throat and looks at me.

"So the real version," he says, only half smiling, "really isn't that interesting. You may be disappointed."

"Yeah, I highly doubt that. Try me." I wave my spoon in front of his eyes, and he shakes his head, chuckling and whispering something that sounds very much like "little monster."

"I grew up in a foster home, but I guess you already knew that," he says. "It wasn't all that bad, but I can't really compare it to anything else because it's the only thing I've ever known." My heart squeezes, but I stay silent, hoping he'll continue. "Some days it felt like home, and others it felt like anything but that," he admits, his eyes darkening just a little but enough to make me understand that these aren't all happy memories.

"I'm sorry," I say. "You don't... we don't have to talk about it if you don't want to," I whisper, knowing very well that he never willingly shares any information about his past.

He shakes his head. "It doesn't matter, I guess. It's in the past now. And as I said, it wasn't all that bad. I met some great kids there."

"Your sister?" I ask softly.

His smile is immediate, his eyes lighting up. "Yes, Mayra got there when she was five. She was just a little kid, and I was a teenager already, but she was so different from the other children—so much fun to be around. She was never afraid of anything and was always smiling and laughing. It was refreshing. She was like this completely unexpected rainbow in the middle of a fucking never-ending storm. Something to remind you that the sun's always there, even on the darkest days. We became friends right away."

Clenching his glass of water, he hesitates for a moment. "We used to take care of each other. Mayra was under my protection, which meant that none of the older kids could pick on her or bother her in any way, but she was as protective of me as I was of her. We'd get punished when we didn't behave well. You know—didn't clean our room, forgot to do the laundry or the kitchen work assigned to us every week, or just talked after our bedtime, those kinds of things. So when any of that happened, they'd leave us without a meal—lunch or dinner, sometimes both."

My jaw tightens, and I struggle to maintain a neutral expression. A surge of conflicting emotions washes over me, but I push them aside, not wanting River to see how much his story pains me. He says it with his usual calmness and distance, as if none of it could have hurt him, but I don't believe that for a minute. There is no chance things like that don't leave scars. He just learned to hide his all too well.

"I'd get punished all the time, so Mayra used to hide food in her pockets and sneak it to me at night once everyone fell asleep," he continues, actually smiling at that particular memory, the muscles in his shoulders relaxing.

I try to smile back, but it probably turns out to be more of a grimace. And then it hits me. Is this why he was upset earlier about me not eating? Seeing how much he insisted on feeding me, it must have triggered something in him. Fuck. Was that my fault?

"I didn't mean to upset you," he says softly, noticing the wrinkle forming on my forehead. "Why don't we change the topic?"

I shake my head. "No, please don't. I want to hear it. It's just that this punishment… it seems messed up." Who the hell does that to kids who have already been punished enough by life itself?

River shrugs. "There were too many of us, so the rules were strict. Every foster home I've ever been to has been the same in that regard. Only the punishments might have been different. It's just something you get used to. But to get to the good part—" His lips curl up in a smile, and I can't help but admire his calm and the way he carries himself through life. I wish I knew how to deal with my past in the same way. I wish I knew how to use that pain in the same way he did. "Growing up, I moved around a lot, lived in different foster homes every couple of years or so. None of them felt special until the last one where I met Mayra. It had this beautiful, old upright piano, and every once in a while we would have music teachers come in, all of them volunteers who worked with kids in similar situations. That's how I met my piano teacher. The guy was in his sixties, already retired, his wife recently died—they never had kids—and we just… clicked. I guess you could say we had a special connection."

River lifts the corners of his mouth into the warmest

smile I've ever seen on him. "He started teaching me. At the beginning, he would come once or twice a month, but then he started coming every week. He taught me everything he knew and helped me apply for BMC." He grows silent and looks at me with such sadness in his eyes that I'm almost afraid to ask. But I do.

"Do you still keep in touch with him?"

River shakes his head. "He died a few weeks before my audition, a week before my eighteenth birthday. I got in and was lucky enough to get a full scholarship. Right after that, I moved out."

"And Mayra?" I ask.

"Mayra wasn't there anymore at that time. She got adopted when she was seven. It rarely happens with older kids, but she was really lucky and found a great family. They would occasionally bring her to see me on weekends because they knew we missed each other, and sometimes they would even take me out for a day."

I try to picture it, and my heart aches for the young boy who never had a family to call his own, being borrowed for the weekend, just to be returned as if he was nothing more than a thing you can move around.

"And you were never adopted?" The question slips out without me realizing it. Shit. Did I actually say that out loud? But from what I understand, River was in the system since he was a baby, so how is it possible that no one was ever interested in him? And how did that make him feel?

"I'm sorry," I blurt out as soon as I realize my mistake. "I'm overstepping here, and that really came out wrong." I hide my face in my hands.

River softly chuckles and reaches for me. "Don't worry.

Forget about it," he says, his brief touch sending a tingling sensation through my fingers. "Let's get out of here."

My shoulders drop slightly, realizing our time is up. "Right, I should get going." I nod. "I have a shift at the bookstore."

"Oh no, you don't." He shakes his head.

I narrow my gaze at him. "What do you mean I don't?"

"The check, please." He waves at our waiter.

"River!"

"Your shift got canceled." He flashes me an innocent smile.

What? "I'm sorry, how did it get canceled exactly?"

"Because you were sick," he says like it's obvious, while taking out his credit card.

"Let's split." I reach for my wallet.

"No, I invited you," he dismisses me, handing his card over.

"You still haven't answered my question, and you're not paying for the entire meal," I say, trying to give him my part in cash once the waiter is gone.

He frowns at me. "It was an invitation, Violet, get over it. And you have a free afternoon because you were sick, and I may or may not have informed the school about it," he says sheepishly.

"You have not!"

He flashes me a broad smile.

"Connor is going to kill me." I shake my head. Not that I'm not secretly happy about having the afternoon to myself after what feels like a lifetime.

A disapproving growl leaves River's throat at the mention of Connor's name.

I glance at him. "What's that for?"

"Nothing, I just don't like the guy." He shrugs, putting his jacket on.

"What? Why don't you like him? You don't even know him," I point out. Funny that Connor said the exact thing about him, not that I'd ever tell him that.

"Saw enough," he murmurs.

I bite back my smile. Honestly, I still can't wrap my head around River's protectiveness, but after today, it feels like some of those puzzle pieces finally start to fit. The only question I still ask myself is... why is he actually doing all of this? He's more than busy right now, recording a new album and preparing for an upcoming tour. So why would he choose to spend time with a student, an aspiring musician, someone not particularly interesting, at least for a guy like him? One who could have anyone he wants, or as Rodrigo likes to remind me, *is having* anyone he wants. I do wonder if that's true. And could he ever be interested in *me*? These thoughts are both unrealistic and distracting, and I don't like that, but they are also getting more difficult to ignore.

# Eight

As we leave the restaurant, I'm once more reminded of who River is as people from nearby tables approach us, hoping to get a picture with their favorite musician. And while he tries to include me in every single one, I volunteer to take them.

"Thank you for the lunch," I say as soon as we manage to get out.

River doesn't answer. He seems to have disappeared in his thoughts. Suddenly, he stops in his tracks and turns to me, causing me to nearly collide with him.

"I have an idea," he says, and there's a glimmer of devilry in his eyes.

"Hmm, okay?"

"Are you tired? Are you feeling better?" He studies me with a slight crease between his brows.

"What? No. I'm as good as new." A full stomach can work miracles. That and the cup of coffee I had. "You're making me nervous. Care to share your idea with me?"

A mischievous look crosses his face. "You will see," he

says, surprising me by intertwining our fingers and leading me to his car. I'm torn between focusing on the warmth of his hand or him briskly pulling me along. We get to the car, but to my surprise, he doesn't open the driver's door. Instead, he opens his trunk, pulling out my guitar, a couple of microphones, and a small amplifier, handing me the first and taking the rest.

"Umm… What are we going to do with all of this stuff, and why do you carry an amplifier and microphones in your trunk?" I ask, my voice rising. It's not like he's carrying duct tape and a shovel, but still.

"I don't," he says, grinning. "It's actually not even mine. A friend left it in my car the other day, but we'll borrow it. I'm sure he won't mind." Locking the car once more, he propels me toward the square.

"But what are we going to do with it?" I ask, still confused as to why we aren't headed back to the campus.

"We are busking!" he says.

"Busking?" I mentally search for the word in my vocabulary but come up short. "I have no idea what that means. Sorry."

He chuckles but doesn't answer. It's become clear that we're heading toward the subway station.

"Are we taking the train somewhere?" I try again.

"Nope," he says as he takes the stairs down to the tracks. If this were anyone else, I would suspect he's trying to lead me somewhere and… kill me? Which, I suppose, wouldn't make much sense either, in broad daylight amid one of the busiest subway stations.

"River! Talk to me!" I shout after him but continue to follow him down the stairs, holding my guitar and trying not to trip. He struggles to pull a black Boston Red Sox cap with the red letter B onto his head. If that is meant as a disguise, I don't know, but the truth is that dressed in slightly ripped blue jeans and one of his favorite sweatshirts with our university logo, he looks like any of the hundreds of university students around us. Just more handsome. Or I should say *much more* handsome. Fortunately, I have no time to dwell on that thought because River heads to an empty spot next to one of the station benches and puts down the amplifier, scanning the area. We're standing right in front of the tracks yet are somehow shielded from the crowds getting on and off the train.

"Perfect spot," he says, looking around, his devilish mint-green eyes happily assessing the place.

"Perfect spot for what?" My voice is going into panic mode because I may be starting to get the idea of his plan. It's a terrible plan. A plan I have absolutely no intention of following.

"Come on, Violet. Take out your guitar," he says.

"Absolutely fucking not." I realize this isn't a mature adult answer, probably also not an answer one would expect from the professional musician I'm aiming to become, but I don't care. "You can't ask me to play here!"

His expression is one of amusement. Of course, he's finding this situation funny. "We'll play together," he says, his voice calm, the kind of calmness that's getting on my nerves right now.

"That's even worse." I growl. "I'm definitely not playing with *you*!"

"Why not?" He frowns, and for a moment, I almost feel bad.

"Because you are… you."

He lets out a laugh and, shaking his head, takes my guitar from me. Then he opens the case, his eyes briefly lingering on the picture of me and Alex. "You said this is what you guys used to do." He looks at me, his voice so low it contrasts with all the noise surrounding us—people walking fast, talking on phones, laughing with friends, and getting on and off the train.

"We did," I whisper.

"Okay, so let's do it." He hands me back my guitar and sets up the microphones. "Let's just have some fun today. There are musicians busking all around Boston. It's not like people will be paying special attention." He grins, showing his beautiful teeth, a look of anticipation mixed with excitement in his eyes. I'm not sure if that's what ultimately makes me give in.

"Ugh, okay! I think I hate you right now. What do you want to play? Your songs?" I ask, adjusting the strap of my guitar around my neck.

"I was thinking more about *your* songs. We can't play my stuff, people could recognize me." A sexy, innocent smirk crosses his face, but I'm not falling for it.

"You don't know my songs," I argue, holding on to the last glimmer of hope that I may be able to get out of this.

"I don't need to. I will just go along." He shrugs. "You know, I actually have a bit of experience—"

"All right, just shut up, please," I say, rolling my eyes but also resisting the urge to laugh. How I've found myself on a subway platform in Cambridge, thousands and thousands of miles from home, with River Evans, a musician whose usual venues are theaters and crowded stadiums, definitely not subway stations, I really don't know.

"Let's start with some Damien Rice," I suggest, playing the first notes of 'Delicate' and catching a glimpse of River's smile from the corner of my eye. He waits for me to sing the first verse, then joins in at the chorus. The sound of his voice dancing with mine gives me a thrill I hadn't realized I needed, sending a buzzing sensation through every inch of my body. I know River feels the same from the way his eyes lock with mine and his gaze stays on me while his lips move along.

The station is crowded because it's rush hour and trains run every five minutes. People standing nearby gradually start to notice us, some of them coming closer, others looking up from their books or taking off their headphones. Their attention doesn't make me nervous, though. My focus is on River. The only person able to make me feel like everything around us suddenly disappears.

His voice is beautiful, low and deep, almost haunting, definitely giving Damien Rice a run for his money, and I know I could get drunk on that sound. Hell, I could probably come just from listening to his voice. I immediately scold myself for even putting sex and River in the same damn thought, but I believe it's too late—and I also blame the song.

We continue with two more Damien Rice songs, and when another train leaves the station, and only those who weren't fast enough to catch it are left standing at the tracks, I close my eyes and play the first chords of one of my songs. A song that Alex and I wrote right after we got accepted to BMC, still full of hopes and dreams, believing the world lay at our feet. *How wrong were we?*

River joins me in the chorus as soon as he hears it repeated for the second time, and I continue with my guitar solo, playing the interlude. When my eyes open again, I notice a small crowd of people surrounding us. A surge of panic floods over me, but as I see him mouthing the words "keep going," I draw a deep breath, hoping that my heart will follow the lead and calm down. His smile widens as his voice rejoins me, his gaze never leaving mine.

It's only toward the end of the song that I'm slightly distracted by a strange clinking sound I can't quite place, and it's not until the end of it I realize its source. Not until I see my guitar case, I hadn't even realized I left open, covered by small, shiny coins. River sees the surprise in my eyes and quietly laughs, urging me to continue. I shake my head in wonder but follow his lead. Some songs feel easier to get through, and some make me cry no matter how hard I try to keep my tears locked. If River notices, he doesn't let on. I resist the temptation to shut my eyes, locking them instead with the man who once more managed to remind me of the joy music used to bring me. It's only then that I hear another voice joining us. And I wish that strong, raspy voice I've been crazily missing every single day didn't exist only in my head.

I'm not sure how long we play, but when we finally switch off the amplifier and start packing up, my guitar case is overflowing with both coins and small bills. Money that could cover quite a few shifts at the café.

"So this was quite... unexpected," I say, suddenly even more self-conscious. Why does being in River's presence feel like such a roller coaster?

He simply smiles.

"What do we do with this?" I point to today's earnings, bending down to collect them so I can put my guitar back in the case. He leans in, his breath delicately tickling my neck.

"Buy some food when the diner is closed?" he suggests, half amused, half serious.

I chuckle. "Fine. But you'll have to come with me because half of it is yours."

Not hearing any answer, I close the case and stand, unaware of how close River is to me. His face is mere inches from mine, and the piercing look in his eyes confuses me. I stumble and move backward a few steps. His hand instantly finds the small of my back, helping me to regain balance, but also, maybe unintentionally, causing me to lose it all over again.

"I'll tell you what," he finally says, his eyes lingering on my lips. "You keep it, but I may take you up on that offer." His hand doesn't let go of my back as he gently pulls me closer. The station is almost empty right now. One train has just left, and most passengers waiting for the next ride are lost in their cell phones, indifferent to their surroundings.

We both stay completely still, my sudden nervousness causing my heart to beat so fast it almost hurts.

"Your voice, Violet," he whispers in my ear, his lips nearly touching my skin and sending shivers through my body, "is still my favorite sound."

I open my mouth, then close it just as quickly, sensing that something has shifted between us. His touch on my back tightens, and his gaze drops to my lips again. "Fuck it," he says. "I thought I could do this." The next thing I know, his mouth is crashing down on mine. First, with a slight air of hesitation, as if testing me, but at the same time with confidence, not asking for permission, almost as if this is the most normal thing to do, as if he is only claiming what is already his. And it leaves me wondering if he's right. When I put my arms around his neck, and my mouth opens, welcoming his tongue, he pushes back with hunger. His free hand caresses my cheeks, slipping to my neck and holding me in place. He tastes like coffee and vanilla and something comforting but hazardous at the same time. It's only when our lips are completely swollen and we are almost out of breath that we reluctantly break our kiss, the announcement of the next train arriving at the station reminding us of where we are but also *who* we are.

"Should we be doing this?" I whisper, our lips still brushing.

"Fuck. I don't know, but it feels too good," he whispers, his voice husky, but his arms, in contradiction to his own words, finally let me go.

Taking a step back, I start collecting my things. What the hell just happened? *You wanted it to happen*, my inner voice reminds me unnecessarily. My heart is racing, but I try my best not to look at him, the heat of our kiss still too obvious on my cheeks.

River stands there for a while, breathing unevenly, not uttering a word, then he bends down to gather the rest of our gear. Neither of us talks on our way to the car, which is quite awkward after what just happened, but also after the entire afternoon spent together without a minute of silence. And I wonder if we've made a mistake. Most likely, but I can still feel him on my lips and know without a doubt there is no going back. There is no world in which I can forget how it feels to have that extra bit of River Evans.

We drive back to campus, still mostly in silence, interrupted only by a couple of failed attempts at conversation about classes and music in general. I don't think either of us really cares about the topics we try to come up with to avoid the giant elephant in the room. And, of course, it's not working.

When he finally parks near my dorm and turns off the engine, the air is laden with tension, and I wish I could just go back and undo that stupid kiss. Because if this results in losing his friendship, it wasn't worth it. I'm not sure how it happened, but in this short time, I got so used to somehow having him in my corner, and I want to continue having that privilege. The privilege of knowing him better than most people do and sharing our music together. Right, that should be enough. I try to ignore the annoying little voice in my head, making me question that very idea. What if it's not enough?

Unbuckling my seat belt, I slowly turn to face him. "Can we, please, just forget about what happened?"

A look of surprise flashes across his face. It lasts only a few seconds. His jaw tenses and his fingers tighten slightly around the steering wheel, but then he smiles, flashing me one of his perfect camera smiles that doesn't quite reach his eyes, and he nods. "Sure. I'm sorry," he says. "My mistake. I got carried away. It won't happen again."

*Mistake?* Huh, okay. I'd definitely prefer for him not to add that last part, but I guess this will have to do. So I smile back, and it takes everything in me not to make it look like I'm about to throw up.

"Thank you again for the lunch and for… playing with me," I say, reaching for the door handle, the double meaning unfortunately not lost on me, and judging by the quick flicker in River's eyes, nor is it lost on him.

He shakes his head, finally meeting my gaze, but his usually so vivid eyes are spent. Nowhere near what they look like when filled with excitement and desire.

"Thank *you*," he says. "I will see you in class."

"Right. See you in class." Getting out of the car as quickly as possible, I grab my guitar, and just as I'm about to close the passenger door, his voice echoes in my ears again. "Violet?" he calls. My heart stops for a moment, stupid enough to hope…

"Promise me you'll take care of yourself," he says, his tone soft but leaving no room for argument, something he apparently does so well.

"Promise," I murmur, and only then do I see an actual smile tug at his lips.

# Nine

"Earth calling Sabrina!" Connor's touch on my arm makes me jump in surprise.

"What?" I ask, meeting his amused expression.

"What's going on with you?"

"What do you mean?" A frown tugs at my lips as I get back to folding the new hoodies that came in this morning, trying not to think about how good one of these would look on River. Especially the green one. It would match his eyes.

"You're being weird this week," he says.

"Sorry. I've had a lot on my mind lately." It's not exactly a lie, but I'm also hoping he'll leave it alone. God, I'm using this excuse way too often.

"Yeah, I guess it's getting crazier with midterms and Christmas coming." He nods. I sense his gaze on me, seeing from the corner of my eye as he nervously rubs the back of his neck, shifting his weight from one foot to the other.

I stop folding and shoot him a curious glance. His green

eyes are, in fact, fixed on me. They're not at all the same green as River's. Connor's eyes are much darker, closer to deep forest green. Ugh, why on earth am I comparing them? And why can't I get River out of my head?

"I was wondering…" Connor bites at his lip. There's something different about him today, although I can't quite put my finger on it. It could be the black long-sleeved shirt he's wearing instead of his usual T-shirt, or maybe it's the nice citrus smell of his cologne. Does he usually wear cologne?

"Would you go out with me?" he blurts.

"What?" I ask for the second time in probably less than ten minutes, but this time, slightly more shocked. Where is this coming from?

"Connor," I begin, thinking of the best way of saying no without offending him. I'm sure he has plenty of girls who would jump at his offer of taking them out for a date. He's handsome with his messy blond hair, green eyes, and seemingly flawless body. With the exception of one drunken night, he's also attentive, sweet, and funny, but he is not… him.

"You are my—"

"Boss?" he suggests, grinning at me.

"No, I was going to say friend." I laugh, giving him a gentle poke in the side.

"Okay, I see. Don't worry about it," he says, not quite able to hide his disappointment but forcing a smile for me nonetheless.

Our conversation gets interrupted by a couple of students asking about the best ear-training books, and Connor seizes the opportunity to hide from me. The rest of the afternoon goes by quickly, and I only realize my shift is over when I receive a text from Bela asking me to meet her at Blue Cats. I'm looking forward to enjoying a cup of coffee for once, not having to worry about the misshaped foam hearts on my cappuccinos.

It's been four days since our performance at the subway station. And to say I was surprised when I got home and counted all the money that magically appeared in my guitar case would be an understatement. I was in shock. Four hundred dollars in less than an hour. I feel slightly bad, though, because theoretically, half of that money is not mine. Not that River needs it, and he did say I could keep it all, but still. He also said he would take me up on my offer to have lunch together, but then he suggested our kiss was a mistake and decided to ghost me instead. So… there is that.

Connor only appears back at the cash register when I'm putting on my jacket, ready to head out. As I try to zip it up, my long hair gets in the way. He quietly leans toward me, gently flipping my hair over onto my back. "If you ever change your mind, Sabrina, just let me know," he says, leaving me with my mouth open, since I'd assumed our earlier conversation was over.

"Uh, sure. Thanks, Connor," I stammer, not quite sure how to respond. I'm almost about to add the 'you really are a great friend' part, but fortunately stop myself in time. I can't imagine he would appreciate any more praise for our friendship right now.

The café is as busy as usual, with the scent of fresh coffee and the sound of chatter filling the air. Quickly scanning the place, I spot Bela's blonde head at a corner table, absorbed in her laptop like most students around her. Rodrigo is nowhere to be seen, which means we are both off today. Although he's probably much smarter than me, enjoying his day off far away from his place of work. Behind the counter, there are two girls struggling with the coffee machine, trying to fill it with fresh coffee beans but repeatedly lifting the wrong lid. I've only seen them a couple of times, and I'm sure they'll figure it out eventually, so I order my coffee, leaving them to their destiny. It's safe to assume there will be no foam drawing involved today.

"Hey!" I wave my hand in front of Bela's eyes. Taking off her headphones, she stops tapping her foot along with the music and looks at me.

"Mi amor! Sit down, you have to see this." She turns her laptop to me, her earrings, this time large hoops decorated with tiny golden charms, loudly clinking with each movement. I'm almost tempted to sample that sound. It reminds me of the wind chimes that used to hang in my window back home.

"You will come, right?"

"Where?" I try to mask my momentary confusion, refocusing my attention on Bela and her laptop screen. "What is this place?"

"I just told you! It's a jazz club. I'm going tomorrow, and you are coming with me," she says, her tone, as usual, leaving no room for debate.

"A jazz club? Why? You don't even listen to jazz." Bela is definitely more of a pop diva, no question about that.

"That's not true. I may not have been to a jazz concert yet, but I will have you know that I fully intend to take jazz lessons next semester."

"Okay, but what does that have to do with this concert?" I ask, mentally preparing myself for losing this battle. Because there's no doubt in my mind that I *will* lose it.

"Well, that's the thing. The professor I want to study with happens to be the singer in this band. She's like the new Diana Krall. We have to see her. Plus, I need her signature so I can register for the class."

"Right. And you think assaulting her at her own concert is the best way to get it? There's this thing called office hours," I suggest, grinning at the cappuccino that's finally handed to me. No foam drawings, of course, and looking much more like a giant cup of soup. Rodrigo would have a heart attack. With that in mind, I snap a picture and send it to him, letting him know I've been officially promoted and am no longer the worst employee of Blue Cats.

"Of course I know that." Bela shakes her head. "But the spots in her class are already taken, so this may be my only chance at convincing her. After all, you know I'm irresistibly charming in person."

"That you are." I smile and take a sip of my coffee.

With a winning grin on her face, she loudly closes her laptop. "So, that's settled. By the way, the ticket is thirty-five dollars. And you better bring someone because Anders is coming too."

Oh, no way I'm doing that. "So why do you need *me* to go? And who is Anders? The Kurt guy?"

"Kurt guy?" She shoots me a confused look.

"The Norwegian guy from the Halloween party," I clarify.

"Aah, that's right." She giggles. "But he's Swedish. And you have to come because he asked me out, and I don't want to go alone."

Sensing an inevitable headache, I massage the back of my neck. "Isn't that kind of the whole point of going out with someone?"

"Yeah, maybe… But you will come, won't you? Please?" She claps her hands, giving me sad puppy eyes.

"I will come," I confirm, inwardly saying goodbye to thirty-five dollars and wondering if it's a terrible idea to accept Connor's offer after all. And I'm pretty sure it is.

*

"No way." I shake my head. "I'm not wearing a dress. It's way too cold for that."

Bela scowls at me, hands on her hips. "Come on, that's what winter dresses are for. I'll let you borrow one of mine. Look at this one." She hands me a hanger with a long, black sleeveless cashmere dress with a mock neck and high slits on both sides, probably quite revealing, but truth be told, also elegant and sexy. I wouldn't expect any less of Bela and her wardrobe.

"Nyra, what do you think? Isn't this going to look amazing on her?" Bela, optimistic as usual, turns to our roommate, waving the dress in question in front of her eyes.

"I couldn't fucking care less." Nyra, who is sitting on her bed and reading, rolls her eyes in annoyance, slightly shaking her head, her braids moving around her like tiny, angry snakes.

I chuckle. "Thank you, girl."

Bela arches one of her perfectly plucked eyebrows at me. "You know who *is* going to care?"

"You?" I try.

"Connor!"

"Oh, come on. Don't start with that again. I told you we are going as friends," I say, seriously starting to regret this whole mess I got myself into. Asking Connor to come with me to the jazz concert was obviously a bad idea because even though I repeated the word 'friends' about ten times, he kept smiling like I just told him he won the freaking lottery.

"Connor? Connor from the bookstore?" Nyra snaps to attention, suddenly sounding much more interested in our conversation. "He's going out with *you*?" she asks, making her words sound like something between an insult and an accusation.

I narrow my eyes at her. "You like him!" Trying to hide my surprise, I struggle to picture those two together. Yes, they are both from New York, and they are both very good-looking, but the similarities pretty much end there. Connor would get eaten alive by Nyra before the end of their first date.

"I do not!" She frowns and directs her attention back to her book, but her quick denial tells me all I need to know.

I bite my lip to suppress a laugh. She may be a great drummer, but she's a terrible actress. "Well, in case you *do* like him, we are going as friends, and that's it," I say, loud enough to make sure both of them hear me. Nyra shrugs, faking disinterest, and Bela chuckles.

I take the damn dress from her hand. Another lost battle. This better be worth it.

✳

"Are you guys sure this is the right place?" I ask for the third time, slowly taking in the spacious hotel lobby with its leather sofas, dark furniture, a breathtaking chandelier made of thousands of tiny crystal raindrops— much like Bela's earrings tonight, complementing her blue minidress—a beautiful fireplace, and, of course, a massive illuminated Christmas tree. That one, though, only reminds me of the upcoming festivities I'm not at all looking forward to.

It's safe to say I'm glad Bela made me forget about wearing jeans tonight. What I'm not as happy about are the high heels she also insisted on, because they are currently killing my feet, making me feel like I'm walking on sharp razor blades.

Connor, on the other hand, looks more than happy, dressed in black pants, a blue woolen sweater, and smiling from ear to ear. I don't know how to feel about that because this does seem like a date, no matter how many times I throw around the word 'friends.' And that's probably my fault. I should tell him that I'm not interested in boys right now, that there's no time for distractions, but would that be true? Maybe I'm not interested in boys because I'm interested in a certain *man*, definitely not a boy anymore… One I *shouldn't* be interested in. Ugh, I hate that my thoughts keep wandering to our subway kiss, and what I hate even more is that I can still feel

128

the warmth of his lips on mine. Because that kiss was…
*everything.*

"Yep, I'm pretty sure this is the place," Anders says, running his hand through his shoulder-length blond hair. He still looks like Kurt Cobain, whether it's because of his hair or because he's the only one of us wearing jeans combined with a black sweater and a casually open leather jacket. It suits him, and I like the contrast between his rugged looks and my friend's sweet, goddess-like appearance.

"The jazz club is supposed to be on the top floor," Bela says, leading us to the elevator.

"Isn't it weird—a jazz club inside a luxury hotel?" I ask no one in particular as I press the button with number fifteen on, noticing that number thirteen is missing. Wow, Americans really take superstitions to another level.

"Not really." Connor shrugs. "It's pretty common for jazz clubs to be located in hotels. It's the same in New York. I could take you sometime," he says softly, and I know that last part was meant for my ears only. Luckily, I'm literally saved by the bell. With a slight thump, the elevator comes to a stop, and the door opens. The lighting on this floor is much softer, and the plush red carpet extending from the elevator to the club entrance allows my heels to sink in comfortably. We hand our phones to the young hostess at the reception desk. She scans our tickets and shows us inside. "You can choose your table," she says, offering a smile.

All right, this may actually be worth my thirty-five dollars. My eyes survey the room. There are about twenty small tables, most of them meant for couples, and some of them offering a third or a fourth chair, the small candles flickering on each one of them adding to the intimate vibe of the club.

We quickly choose our table, noticing that the place is filling up fast. We don't get to sit right in front of the stage that is already being set up for tonight's performance, but the view from the second row seems equally good. I happily sink into my chair, my aching feet immediately singing in victory.

"I wasn't aware that you could book your table." Bela's expression changes to a frown as she notices that the first-row tables are decorated with little *reserved* signs.

"They're probably VIP," I offer. Although it's a logical assumption, my friend still doesn't seem happy, casting an annoyed look at those she spots heading toward one of her chosen tables. I bite back a laugh, turning my attention to Connor and Anders, who seem to be in the middle of a passionate debate. I learn that Anders not only listens to rock but actually likes a whole variety of styles, from rock, pop, and hip-hop to country and jazz, and so does Connor, but the most surprising discovery is that Connor actually *is* a jazz musician. Huh, I guess I've never really asked him about his music. They're both apparently quite familiar with the band we've come to see, so I'm the only one in the dark about what to expect tonight.

As the waiter arrives to take our order, I realize that Connor and I are the only ones who can legally order alcohol. Bela is still twenty, old enough to drink in Spain but not in the US, and Anders said he'd be celebrating his twenty-first birthday in January. Connor asks for a beer, and I order tonic water in solidarity with the rest of our group.

When my lips finally touch the bitter-tasting drink, Bela nudges me with her elbow. "Hey, isn't that River Evans?" she asks, nodding toward the left side of the room. What? My heart leaps into my throat. I refuse to turn my head, tightening the hold on the glass in my hand. How would he act if we met here? I have no idea, but I know I'm not ready to see him.

"Yes, that's him," Connor confirms. "And that's the girl he brought to the Music Awards, right? Riley? Man, she's hot," he says and then likely realizes I'm sitting right beside him. His face turns red when both Bela and Anders direct their questioning gazes at him. "I mean, she's a model and actress. She looks good, obviously, but I didn't mean..."

I'm not listening to Connor's blabbering, and I also couldn't care less. Still, my tonic water goes up the wrong way, causing the inside of my nose to feel like it's fucking burning. I try hard not to cough, my eyes tearing up from the superhuman effort. Luckily, River hasn't noticed us. He's facing away, and neither he nor Riley have taken their seats at the VIP table yet. Instead, they do a small round, greeting people.

I recognize some other faculty members in the group, but none of them are our professors, at least not this year. River's palm is resting on Riley's back as they make their way to the table in front of us. I try to sink deeper into my chair, moving slightly away from the table and making myself as invisible as possible, pleased to discover that Connor's broad back serves as a great hiding wall.

That's until Bela opens her mouth. "Mr. Evans! Hi!" she shouts across the room, making the blood in my veins freeze. Fuck. So much for hiding. Why is she calling him?

In those split seconds, I pray to the universe he didn't hear her. But he did, and I can see the surprise on his face when he spots us, spots me. Our eyes meet, and a muscle flexes in his jaw, but his expression remains neutral. As neutral as the tone of his voice when he approaches us, his hand still on Riley's back, just as it was on mine only last week, gently guiding her to our table. Rodrigo's words ring in my ears, causing me to take a deep breath and blink a few times, just to ground myself. *River Evans can have anyone he wants, and he is having anyone he wants.*

"Guys, it's nice seeing you here," he says, his stupid Boston accent not quite so charming tonight. "Come to enjoy the concert?"

"Yes. We came to see Eloy," Bela offers. "I'm hoping I can study with her next semester." She prattles on, completely oblivious to my internal struggle.

River's piercing gaze returns to me and then finds Connor, and I can clearly see the slight furrow between his eyebrows. Two can play this game... I put on my best 'don't care' face just as River seems to remember his manners and shifts his attention to his girlfriend. "Riley," he says, finally taking his hand off her back and waving toward us. "These are my *students*."

His words land on me like a cold shower.

"Hi, Riley." My friends nod politely, not at all bothered by his introduction. Because honestly, why would they be? Technically, that's what we are. His students. And I know it would be incredibly naïve to think he could ever see me as anything more than that. I do the same, forcing a half smile. She looks absolutely stunning, dressed in a long golden dress, not a cashmere, winter one like me but a cocktail one, hugging her perfect curves, unconcerned about freezing to death in Boston's cold. I also bet she didn't take the subway to get here. Her heels are much higher than mine, and she wears them with such ease, as if they were a pair of the most comfortable sneakers. I hate her, and I don't even know why. Or I do. The reason is standing right next to her, looking equally beautiful in his black dress pants and beige turtleneck pullover. I hate him, too.

"Hi, guys, it's always nice to meet River's students," she says, a smile lighting up her perfect face. And, of course, she must also be nice.

Gritting my teeth, I avert my gaze to the stage, barely registering Connor's arm on my chair.

"Welcome, everyone! Thank you for coming." A sweet but unexpectedly deep feminine voice comes from the stage, saving us from any more awkward conversation. River takes it as his cue to leave, leading Riley back to their table, but not before he looks directly at me.

"Enjoy the concert," he says, his eyes lingering on Connor's arm, which is almost touching me but not quite. I haven't paid much attention to it until now, and in other circumstances, I'd have him remove it in an instant, but in this case, I choose not to.

The jazz trio is led by Eloy Mendoza, who can't be much older than River. She's dressed in black bellbottoms and a spaghetti-strap red top, her raven hair falling over her shoulders. I wish I could focus on the music, but all I can focus on is the first-row table on our left and the couple sitting there, the candle in front of them casting small shadows on their faces, especially when they lean close, whispering in each other's ear.

"You like it, mi amor?" Bela asks.

"Yeah, they are great," I say, hoping she doesn't notice the knot in my throat. If this isn't the sign I was looking for, I don't know what is. I need to get a grip. I wonder what Alex would think of River. My brother was very protective of me. There's no way he'd approve of him. At least this version of him. But is there any other, or is it just me wanting to see him for someone he's not?

When the notes of yet another beautiful, original tune fade away, Eloy speaks again. "I'd like to invite one of my dearest friends to join me on stage. It's an honor to have him here tonight, knowing how busy he is." A burst of laughter comes from the first-row tables, clearly aware of who she's referring to. I suppose it must be one of her colleagues, and I'm curious to see another BMC teacher performing, so I lean forward in my chair, finally clearing my mind a little.

"It has been a long time since we've played together, but those were always my favorite moments. Ladies and gentlemen, I believe this man doesn't need an introduction… River, are you coming up?"

Seriously? This must be some kind of joke the universe is playing on me. River isn't a jazz singer, but he's probably Eloy's former classmate, which would explain his presence tonight.

"Fuck yeah! Love that guy," Anders says, his fingers laced through Bela's. Not helpful. At least Connor doesn't seem particularly thrilled.

River steps on the stage, walking with his usual confident stride. "It's always a pleasure to play with you, El. Thank you for having me tonight," he says while switching

134

places with Eloy's pianist, who happily hops off the stage and sits at River's table, immediately being served a cold beer. A technician approaches and sets up a microphone stand for River next to the piano. "This one's mine." River clears his throat, his eyes traveling to me. "I thought it'd be a good one for tonight. Hope you enjoy it." His beautiful, low, deep voice hits my eardrums, and it's only then that I realize he chose the tune I sang in class. *Your voice, singing my song, is my new favorite sound.* Isn't that what he told me afterward? Why would he choose this particular song? It's not even one of the newest ones. The haunting melody and anguished lyrics enter every possible pore of my skin, traveling through my body and making me shiver.

> We could just admit that we are scared
> Looking for the easy way out
> You say there is no point in believing in fairy tales
> We have seen too much, and it's too late
>
> No need to turn off the light on your way out, darlin'
> But it's probably easier
> So much for the long run
> Oh, but you already knew

Eloy's voice joins River's after the first verse, but in my head, there is no one else on the stage. Not Eloy, not the bass player, and not the drummer, only River with his alluring voice and long fingers stroking the keys. The same fingers that not so long ago touched my face and held me in place while kissing me like I was all the air he needed. Turns out it wasn't true.

The song ends, and River gives Eloy a friendly hug before making his way back to his table, accompanied by a cheerful wave of applause.

"I think I need a drink after all," I say. I'm pretty sure there is no drink that could make me feel better right now, but it's worth a try, and I need to breathe for a moment without Connor's arm around me and without my eyes on *him*.

"I'll go with you," Connor offers, getting up to his feet.

"No, that's okay." I stop him. "I'll be quick. I also need to use the bathroom."

"Sure, no problem." He shrugs, turning his head back to the stage. Hurting Connor is the last thing I want to do, but I don't believe for a moment that he actually has feelings for me. He likes me, I know that, and he's probably curious where this could lead, trying to get the full college experience and all that, but I also know I'm easily replaceable in that experience.

"Do you want me to bring you anything, guys?" I check, making my escape a little less suspicious.

"Nope, thanks, mi amor, we're fine." Bela raises her bottle of Diet Coke, grinning at me.

I head for the bathroom first, checking my makeup and washing and drying my hands in slow motion, hoping the band will finish soon so we can get out of here. Something I've never wished for while attending a concert, not even concerts I didn't particularly like, but this has nothing to do with the music and everything to do with a certain infuriating musician.

The bar is strategically situated on the opposite side of the stage, close to the entrance, so that people can enjoy a drink and conversation without disrupting the performance yet still hear the music coming from the numerous speakers hanging on the walls. I hop on one of the barstools, crossing my legs, making sure that the high slits on both sides of my dress aren't revealing too much, and wave at the bartender. "Could I have a glass of white wine, please?" His eyes scan me, moving from my face to my body and back. Seriously? I refrain from rolling my eyes, only slightly arching my eyebrows at him.

"Do you have an ID?"

"Umm, right, an ID… I think I have a copy of my passport on my phone. Would that be enough?" I should have thought of that, of course, but I'm not used to having to show my ID in order to buy myself a glass of wine.

"She's with me." I hear the familiar voice from behind me, and my heart races.

"Mr. Evans, of course. I apologize." The bartender does a complete 180 right in front of my eyes and rushes to get my drink.

I shake my head. Oh, no, no. No fucking way.

"I'm not here with you," I say, slowly turning to him. "Someone else is, in case you forgot."

A look of surprise flashes across River's beautiful face, my words landing harder than expected. I shouldn't let him see it bothers me. Why do I care anyway? One small kiss in the heat of the moment doesn't mean anything. And it obviously didn't mean anything to him.

"Right." He stares back at me, no trace of a smile. "So why isn't Connor getting your drink?" His voice is chilly, and his eyes seem almost gray, stormy and unreadable.

"Here's your wine, miss." The bartender hands me a

glass of wine, and I swipe my credit card, this time not caring about rolling my eyes at him.

"I can get my own drink. If that's all, Mr. Evans, I will see you in class," I say as calmly as possible, trying to soothe the raging storm inside me. As I hop off my stool, his hand wraps around my wrist.

"Don't," he says, his tone suddenly much softer.

"Don't what?" I whisper back, hating how weak I sound around him.

"Don't act like we don't know each other." An unhappy expression appears on his face, his thumb brushing over my wrist, still holding me.

"I'm not sure we do. Maybe you should get back to your girlfriend," I suggest, holding his gaze and trying to ignore the feeling of his touch. It's light enough that I could shake him off if I wanted to, but I don't.

"Are you jealous, Violet?" he asks with an arrogant smirk, his voice coming out slow and whispery.

I take a deep breath, resisting the urge to slap him. "Why would I be? I don't care about the love life of my teachers."

His gaze hardens, and his thumb softly caresses my wrist again. "Is that so?"

"It is," I answer, this time yanking my hand out of his grip. What the hell does he think he's doing, playing this stupid game? I leave him standing there in silence, even though it takes every ounce of me to move my legs and find my way back to the table. Same as it takes every ounce of me not to look at him for the rest of the night. Because now I know I was wrong. There is no being friends with River Evans.

# Ten

"I'm not going today." I groan, covering myself again with the duvet Bela is desperately trying to tear off me. "I'm sick."

"Hmmm, you don't look sick to me." She hovers above my bed, the signature sound of her long earrings chiming in my ears.

"You know, Miss Full Scholarship, some of us actually pay a lot of money for those classes," Nyra throws in, fortunately already on her way out. Yep, she definitely still hates me for going out with Connor. Doesn't like him, my ass. She'd be pleased if she knew our non-date ended on a very awkward note when Connor tried to kiss me, and I cowardly backed away, his kiss landing somewhere between my cheek and my left ear. It vividly reminded me of my first kiss, which was, in fact, equally awkward. Luckily, we both laughed it off, and Connor finally gave up. I don't think he'll be crying over me for long. Or at all.

"What are you hiding from?" Bela raises her eyebrows

and crosses her arms. "Is it because of Connor? Are you working at the bookstore today?"

"Connor and I are fine."

"Then what?" she insists.

"Nothing. I just don't want to go to class. That's all." I'm not the best liar, and I'm sure Bela can see through me easily.

"Is it the yoga class you're trying to avoid, or are you suddenly afraid of Professor Williams? Because if it's the latter, don't worry. I'm pretty sure I'll be the one to take today's heat. I have my song ready, but I'm not happy with it, so I totally expect her to tear it apart. And if not her, then Mr. Evans, for sure. Girl, I'm telling you, the guy is sexy as hell, but he can be really mean sometimes. Wait—" She pulls my duvet straight off me and pins me with her gaze. "Does this have anything to do with Mr. Evans?"

"What? No!" Denial seems like the best option, but unfortunately for me, Bela is not that easily fooled.

"Are you sure? Because you acted weird the other day."

Sitting on my bed, she scratches her neck and tilts her head slightly. I'm not sure I want to know what she means. Has she noticed that while at the beginning of the evening I couldn't look away from River, toward the end I couldn't get out of the club fast enough? So much so that I waited outside, of course, hidden from the main entrance, to avoid running into him, or even worse, them again. All while Bela went on her mission to get Eloy to sign her application and admit her into her class next semester. That at least went well, apparently.

I decide that getting out of bed and dressed is, after all, the best way of dodging Bela's questions. As I do, I put on my black yoga pants paired with a white sweater hanging off one shoulder, revealing my pink sports bra, and I tie my hair into a bun, not bothering with makeup. I can always borrow some of Bela's after our yoga class.

"I wasn't acting weird. And please, stop calling him Mr. Evans." I frown.

"Why?" Bela looks amused.

"Because he isn't our teacher." I grab my gym bag and throw it over my shoulder.

"Hmm, I'm sorry to break it to you, mi amor, but he is. At least for this semester." She chuckles, closing the door of our room as she trails after me. "It doesn't make a difference, though. I mean, unless you want to fuck—"

I stop in my tracks and turn so quickly that Bela bumps into me. "Don't even finish that sentence," I warn her. She shakes her head and chuckles again.

"I'm convinced I'm missing something here, but no worries, you can fill me in anytime." She's still talking when we enter our yoga class. I believe we may be late, which is definitely my fault this morning, but I also believe we may be in the wrong class, so…

"What is this? Wait, did we get the room wrong?" Bela seems equally confused.

"Nope, doesn't look like it. Unless all our classmates collectively changed their course."

"Girls! You are late!"

I focus on the beautiful, dark-skinned woman dressed in bright purple baggy pants and an oversized black crop top impatiently waving at us.

"That's an unusual yoga outfit," Bela whispers, a tiny wrinkle appearing on her forehead.

"Come on! Take your place! You won't need your yoga mats today. Leave them at the entrance. We need space."

"Space for what?" I whisper.

"All right. Let's go again, guys, now that you are all here. As I was saying, your teacher is sick today, but no need to worry, because we're gonna have a lot of fun. Are you ready?

"You think she's still talking about yoga?" Bela asks as we obediently leave our mats at the door and take off our sweaters.

"I don't think so. I believe we may get to try our hip-hop class after all."

*

"That was brutal." I step out of the shower, drying my hair with a towel.

"Don't even tell me about it. There isn't a muscle in my body that doesn't hurt right now." Bela laughs, putting on her pants.

"I don't think I've ever sweated this much in my entire life." I cringe, but strangely enough, apart from all my muscles hurting, I feel much better and somewhat more relaxed. Like I may even be able to survive our next class.

"I'm going to get us some coffee," Bela says. "See you in ten?"

"Sure. Could you get me a protein bar or something?" I ask, handing her some money. All right, so I haven't had my breakfast again, thinking I could survive until lunch. Turns out I didn't count on burning a thousand calories this morning. I'll just have to make sure I don't pass out this time. At least not in front of him.

Bela nods and rushes off to grab our coffees while I finish getting ready. It's only when I put my pants on that I realize I forgot to pack another bra I could change into. Fuck. Normally this wouldn't be an issue as I never sweat that much in our yoga class to not be able to use my sports bra for another couple of hours. However, that's definitely not the case today. No bra it is then, perfect.

While I run across campus, I'm silently cursing whoever is in charge of our class scheduling, along with the architect of this stupid complex, because showering after a class and then racing to the building that's literally on the opposite side of the campus is a mission impossible. But somehow, Bela challenges that theory. When I open the classroom door, she's happily sitting in her chair with both of our coffees in hand. So is the rest of the class, no coffees in their case, and so is Professor Williams and, of course, River. Damn it.

"Sabrina, take your seat, please," Professor Williams says.

"Umm, right. Sorry I'm late." I head to my chair, keeping my eyes on the floor like there is nothing more interesting than my classmates' footwear.

"Is there a reason for your late arrival, Ms. Fialová, or have you just decided to keep us waiting?"

It's the absolute chill in his voice and his use of my last name that make my heart stop. Whispers fill the air as my classmates shift their attention to us. River usually sticks to music-related comments. One could argue that he is not the professor of this class, but I'm sure raising that point wouldn't help my cause right now.

"I… I was—" I struggle to explain myself, his behavior

143

leaving me too stunned to speak. Although River Evans is known for being harsh, his harshness has never been directed toward me, at least not in class. And I can't say it doesn't bother me.

"The gym showers were very busy this morning, Mr. Evans." Bela comes to my rescue, Rodrigo chuckling behind us.

I shrug, taking a seat and kicking Rodrigo's leg in the process.

"It's okay, Sabrina. We were just getting started," Professor Williams says, probably equally confused by River's unfriendly behavior. "Let's do this!" She claps her hands. We spent the next half hour analyzing lyrics of some of the best songs in history, and if I wasn't angry at River, I'd have to admit that his insight is not only helpful but also quite fascinating and inspiring. There are moments I can feel his eyes on me, but I make it my personal mission not to look at him. The second half of the class is dedicated to performances, and Bela is the first one to volunteer, just as she promised. Her song is not torn apart as she feared, but close enough. River says she's on the right track but definitely not done. Professor Williams agrees, giving her more detailed suggestions.

"Sabrina, what about your song? Have you been able to finish it? Do you want to play it for us?" she asks when she's done with Bela.

"Actually, I'm still working on it." It's true. I've been trying, but my head hasn't been in it, and nothing I write feels good enough. I've hit a wall, but I'm not about to say that aloud.

"It's not gonna write itself, you know." River's voice is

like a cold shower over my head. Our gazes finally meet, and he has the audacity to cross his arms across his chest and raise his eyebrows.

"I will keep that in mind. Thank you, Mr. Evans."

The classroom erupts in quiet laughter. I guess we're giving them quite the show this morning. But what the hell is his problem now? River refrains from responding, but his gaze remains fixed on me, his jaw twitching and his fingers lightly tapping an imaginary piano on his leg. So much for not losing our friendship. If I'd known this would be the result, I wouldn't have let that stupid kiss happen. As I only half listen to the next student singing her song, it occurs to me that if I knew I was going to lose him anyway, there was another way of doing things… If this was really the price to pay, I should have made that moment last as long as possible. I should have taken everything he was giving me and more.

"I still feel like I'm missing something here…" Bela whispers, leaning toward me. "Oh, wait, I got your protein bar." She takes a strawberry bar from her purse and, seeing that Professor Williams is momentarily distracted, she quickly slides it to me.

"Thanks." Shaking off my thoughts, I unwrap it, careful not to disrupt the ongoing performance, and take a bite. Luckily, Professor Williams is still busy, but I sense a pair of eyes on me. I look up, and sure enough, River is following me with his mint gaze, the green of his irises appearing slightly darker today, a tiny furrow between his eyebrows adding to his sullen expression. Determined to ignore his mood swings, I finish my bar, and as soon as the class is over, I'm the first one on my feet. Since we don't have any more lessons together today, I give Bela a hug and rush out as fast as possible.

"What has gotten into you? I would ask if you left the stove on, but that's out of the question, so…" Rodrigo's laughter echoes behind me as he struggles to match my speed.

"Nothing." I breathe out, gritting my teeth. This whole River situation is messing with my head, and that's the last thing I need right now.

"Right." He chuckles. "Does it have anything to do with Mr. Evans by any chance?"

"What?" I ask without slowing down but scanning the surroundings, making sure no one has heard him.

"I will take that as a yes." Rodrigo chuckles again but then abruptly grabs my wrist, pulling me to a halt. He looks me in the eyes. "Sabrina," he says softly. "Did anything happen between you and River Evans?"

I shake my head. "Just drop it, please. Nothing happened."

"Okay, girl. If you say so." He lets go of my wrist and gives me a quick hug instead. "Just know that I'm here if you need to talk."

"Thanks, Rodrigo." I force a smile. He's just being a good friend, but there isn't much I can tell him. I don't want to cause any trouble for River or myself, and I definitely don't want to look foolish.

"And Sabrina?" he calls after me once more before heading to his classroom. "Remember what I told you. You don't want to fall for that guy."

*

I would like to say that my anger passes as the morning goes on, but it doesn't. It simply grows stronger. Why is he acting like he's the one who gets to be angry? And what's he even angry about?

Our classes are over for today. My bookstore shift doesn't start for another three hours, and I even managed to eat some lunch. With a harmony book in hand, I pace around my dorm room, feeling, for some reason, like none of what I'm doing is enough. Self-doubt and fear of failure swirl around in my head, making it difficult to breathe. I'm not good enough. I'll never be good enough. Clutching my harmony book tightly, I press it to my chest and quicken my pace. There are so many excellent musicians already. Too many. Why am I even here? What am I trying to accomplish other than to kill myself over a stupid dream? Because maybe that's what this is. A stupid dream. And wasn't one life enough? Wasn't Alex's life enough? With each thought growing stronger, the room becomes more suffocating. Tears of frustration well up in my eyes, and I blink to hold them back.

"Hey, what are you doing? Umm, Sabrina?" I don't realize Nyra has entered the room until she's standing over me. She wears a rare expression of worry and confusion. With a slight tilt of her head, she leans over me, her long braids creating a solid curtain around her face.

"Are you crying?" she asks, frowning. At some point, I must have sunk to the floor, hands covering my face. "No, I was just... having a moment," I say, not ready to admit that I might have been on the edge of another of my panic attacks.

"Why? What's wrong?" she asks, her gaze still filled with suspicion.

My shoulders lift in a shrug. "I don't know. Nothing. Everything?" I say, attempting to laugh it off, but it's the kind of laugh that probably makes me sound unhinged— in case sitting on the floor with my face hidden in my lap wasn't enough. "Do you ever feel like you're not supposed to be here?" I whisper, unsure if she heard me, until I see her biting her lip as if contemplating my question.

"Girl, you gotta be more specific. Here on earth or here at BMC?" she asks, still looking down at me. Then she sighs and does something I wouldn't have expected her to do in my wildest dreams—she slides down and, with a little bump, sits next to me on the floor.

"Both." I snort. "But I guess I was referring to BMC, mostly."

She chuckles. "Yeah, well, anyway… I have no fucking idea if I'm supposed to be here or even on this planet." Rather than looking at me, she locks her eyes on the wall above her bed. While I only have an old picture of me and Alex on my nightstand, Nyra's wall is covered in posters of her favorite rock bands and articles from *Rolling Stone* magazine.

She shifts next to me. "But since we *are* here, I suppose it's worth trying," she adds reluctantly.

"Yeah, I guess," I answer quietly. "Maybe we can even figure out the answer to Professor Jameson's 'Why are you here?' question while we are at it." At least he was referring to BMC and our careers as musicians, not asking us to figure out our entire existence.

"I'm starting to think it's a trick question." Nyra laughs, and it's actually the first time I've heard her do that.

"We should ask one of the senior students. They definitely know the correct answer."

"Yeah, we should totally do that." My brief meltdown is over, the heavy feeling in my chest easing a little. "Thank you," I say, stealing a glance at her.

She nods, getting to her feet. "You know what I usually do when I feel this shitty?"

"What?"

"I play," she says simply, before shutting the door behind her, like it's obvious that the cause of our anxiety is also the only thing keeping us from falling apart. It takes me a few more minutes sitting on the floor to realize she's right. After that, I can't get up fast enough.

＊

My mind is spinning as I sit on the floor of the tiny practice room—God knows why I never manage to book a larger one. With crossed legs and strumming my guitar, I chase after the thoughts running through my head: the inspiring lyrics analysis we worked on earlier in class, River's painful yet true comment regarding my inability to progress with my music, the warm touch of his lips on mine—I wonder how that one got into the mix—the exhaustion and feeling of failure, the promises we make but can't keep, the things we're willing to give up to follow our dreams, and ultimately, the ones we've already given up.

*I'm sorry I couldn't keep my promise.* Alex's whisper is as clear as if he were standing right beside me. *I swear I thought I could make it work. It was supposed to be temporary. Only until we had enough money to go. The two of us together. That's what I promised you, and I let you down.*

Sucking in a breath, I realize I'm holding my guitar so tightly the strings are nearly cutting into my fingers. *You didn't let me down, Alex. You fucking killed yourself! And over what? Money?*

*That wasn't supposed to happen. I screwed up, and I know it. But you know what? I don't regret it. At least I did everything I could for my dream. Can you say the same, sis?* I can hear the hint of reproach in his voice. *Because you are alive, yet you act like you are the one who's dead.*

His words hit me, filling me with anger. *How can you say that? I'm here, and I'm trying my best!*

How can he possibly understand the struggle of coming here alone? Of leaving everything behind? Of not losing only him but also our parents?

*There's a difference between being here and actually making the most of it… You're holding back, and you know it.* His voice is softer now. *You can't change the past, sis. Let go. Promise me you will do it. Promise me you'll make sure all this wasn't for nothing.*

I stay silent, too angry to come up with the right words. But I also know he's right. I haven't been giving BMC my best efforts. I haven't been fully dedicated to my music. Finishing my song wasn't just about not being able to perform it by myself; it also meant that Alex and I would never play together again. It's a ridiculous thought, considering he's dead. The fact that we can never play together again is more than a given, but it also makes me feel guilty. Guilty for doing this without him and guilty for living the dream he can't. But what if, by wasting this opportunity, I'm only making his death be in vain? I can understand he's angry at me. Hell, I'm angry at myself. Because deep down, I know there are far worse things than failing, like not having the chance to try.

By the time I realize I need to get to the bookstore for my afternoon shift, the pages of my notebook are full of scribbles only I will ever be able to decipher, but I think I've got it. I just finished my song.

Feeling incredibly lighter, I wish I could share this moment with someone. Unfortunately, the only people who come to mind are Alex and River, which honestly sucks because one of them is dead and the other… I have no fucking clue what's going on with the other. Packing up my things, I head toward the building's main exit, the quickest route to the bookstore. Time to pay for my scholarship, as Nyra would undoubtedly remind me.

As soon as I step outside, the cold wind brushes against my face. It's ridiculous how early it's getting dark these days, but here is the thing: musicians are night creatures. There's something magical about creating in the dark when the world is fast asleep, and it's just you and your thoughts. That being said, who the hell needs the night to start at five in the afternoon? Just as I begin to put on my jacket, wrapping a long wool scarf around my neck, I feel a gentle touch on my arm, guiding me into the sleeve I was struggling to find. I don't turn around. I don't need to. His warm touch contrasts with the wintry breeze, his long fingers touching me through at least three layers of fabric but still leaving a burning sensation on my skin. The familiar smell of ginger, oranges, and something much spicier infiltrates my senses as his hot breath skates across my neck, just a little too close and yet not close enough.

"I'm sorry," he says so softly that I almost believe I have imagined it. I still don't turn around.

"What for?" I swallow, keeping my voice as low as his. Is he sorry for acting like a jerk earlier in class? Is he sorry for kissing me? He already said that much… Or does he regret giving up on our friendship? He doesn't answer. Instead, he gently grasps my waist and turns me to face him. My breath catches in my throat. For a few seconds, we remain just like that, facing each other in silence.

His eyes are filled with frustration when he finally speaks. "I'm not boyfriend material, Sabrina." There is an absent note to his voice, carrying a slight hint of sadness but also a subtle warning.

Is this what this is about? Does he think I will fall in love with him if he keeps paying attention to me? The cliché of a student developing feelings for her teacher. Anger and embarrassment bubble inside me, causing my cheeks to burn. "I didn't ask you to be one." Taking a step back, I shake off his hands, trying to collect myself. "You were the one to kiss me and then run for the hills. But you know what? It's okay. I understand." I certainly don't.

"What do you understand?" He shoves his hands in his pockets, his voice now laced with confusion.

"It's inappropriate." I look up at him.

"Inappropriate?" His eyebrows shoot up as he repeats the word as if tasting it on his tongue. "Why?"

Seriously? Why does he have to make it more difficult? Isn't this what he wanted, after all? I should focus on not being late for my shift, but I remain glued exactly where I am. For what it's worth, I decide to give him the explanation he's asking for. The one that I've been repeating to myself since the very first day we met. Since the first day I lost myself in his music and his beautiful mint-green eyes.

"Because I'm a student, and you are… you." There is defeat in my voice, and I don't try to hide it. I'm just hoping that he can read between the lines because it's not only him being my teacher but also him being River Evans that makes anything happening between us seem like the worst damn idea ever.

He doesn't say anything. Instead he gives me another puzzled look that only confirms that we aren't making much progress and this entire conversation is pretty much pointless.

"You know what?" I shrug. "Forget about it. This isn't leading anywhere. Now, if you'll excuse me, I have somewhere to be." I step aside to move on.

"Wait!" He grabs my wrist but quickly releases it when he notices my raised eyebrows and my focus on where his fingers are touching me. He shuffles from foot to foot, and if I didn't know better, I'd almost believe he's nervous. But then again, we're talking about River Evans. I have never seen the guy nervous.

"You haven't eaten again," he says.

What? Where the hell is this coming from now?

"Today, in class," he explains. "You were eating a protein bar." He frowns and looks at me again. "You said you would take care of yourself." This whole conversation is so surreal it's almost laughable. He's been avoiding me for a week, and now he's worried whether I had my breakfast? Un-fucking-believable.

Shaking my head, I'm about to make a joke, tell him he's being ridiculous, but then I remember our conversation, the little things he told me about himself, the information he trusted me with… and I sigh. "I was in a hurry this morning. I may have skipped breakfast, but I promise I had a great lunch." The lunch wasn't really that great because the campus diner is not exactly a five-star Michelin restaurant, but the tiny smile that breaks on River's lips seems worth the exaggeration.

My attempt at returning his smile ends up looking more like a scowl, I'm sure. I miss him, miss talking to him, miss sharing music with him, and I don't know where to go from here. He's driving me crazy with all his contradictions.

"I really have to go, River. I'm working at the bookstore this afternoon."

His shoulders tense, and a tiny wrinkle forms between his eyebrows again. He looks away, and when he turns back, his smile is gone. "I won't be in class next week," he says. "I'm going to New York."

Another moment of silence passes between us. I try my best to mask my disappointment at the idea of not seeing him for two weeks unless we happen to run into each other on campus.

"Okay, and why are you telling me that?" I finally ask.

I can see a slight hesitation in his eyes. "Come with me," he says. I'm not sure if it's a question or a demand.

"What? Come with you where? New York? What would I do there?" I definitely didn't see this one coming.

He nods. "I'll be recording there, and I… need an assistant."

"You need an assistant?" I repeat in disbelief, trying to choose whether to laugh or just call him out on his obvious bullshit. "You don't need an assistant, River. You have a whole damn team of assistants. Plus, even if that wasn't the case, what would I assist you with? I've never even been to a recording studio, let alone know what to do there to *assist* you." All right, so I clearly went with the latter.

He doesn't bother denying anything I said. Instead, he gives me a sheepish smile. "Well, then it could be a great experience for you, right?"

Of course it could be a great experience, and I know even Connor would tear his hair out if I told him I didn't jump at that offer right away.

"Why do you want me to come, River?" I ask again.

He angles his head, running his tongue over his teeth. "Do you always need a logical explanation for everything?"

What kind of answer is that? I'm seriously considering kicking him and leaving him standing right there, but what he just said reminds me so much of what Alex used to say. I wish I could be as spontaneous as my brother. But then again, where did that lead him other than to his ultimate freedom? On the other hand, haven't I just promised myself I would try harder to be present? A conflict rages inside me, and I bet River can see it.

"I can't just take off for New York. I have classes." It's a lame excuse.

"We'd be leaving Friday afternoon, and we'd be back on Monday. You can schedule your private lessons for another day. So technically, you'd only be missing your dance lesson or whatever it is that makes you show up to our class with wet hair and no bra." He gives me an innocent wink, and I can feel myself blushing, extremely thankful for the darkness surrounding us.

"Very professional of you, Mr. Evans," I say, aware of how much it annoys him when I address him that way. Surprisingly, this time, he only laughs.

"And, of course, you'd miss our songwriting class, but since you'll be with me, it doesn't count," he adds, flashing me a hundred-dollar smile. It seems like he's thought it all pretty much through.

"Right. And where would we stay, and how would we get there?" He must think that I don't have a spontaneous bone in my body, but the truth is there is no way I can afford a trip to New York.

"We'll go by car, and I have an apartment there." Upon seeing my expression, he chuckles, raising both of his hands. "A big apartment. With a lot of rooms. One exclusively for you."

"Do you offer to let all your assistants stay at your place?"

Against all reason, I'm actually getting excited about this trip, not that I'm telling him that. There is also this annoying, nagging feeling lingering in the back of my mind. Why doesn't he take Riley with him? It's not jealousy, though. Nope.

"Weren't you in a rush for your bookstore shift?" With a grin on his face, he turns to leave, ignoring my question completely. Seriously?

"I'll pick you up on Friday, and I'll text you the exact time."

"You don't have my number," I shout after him. Not

that I'm volunteering to give it to him, but it's the only objection I can think of right now.

He doesn't even look back, but I can hear his soft chuckle.

# Eleven

"Can someone please change the music? I swear I can't deal with any more Christmas songs," I grumble while topping the foam on one of our Christmas specials, a cinnamon-spiced holiday latte.

Rodrigo shakes his head. "Girl, I believe I've already said this, but you have no Christmas spirit."

I stick out my tongue at him. "I have plenty of Christmas spirit, but I'll go crazy if I have to listen to 'All I Want for Christmas Is You' one more time. Plus, this is a music college café, not Santa Claus's goddamn workshop."

Rodrigo shakes his head, but the corners of his mouth lift. He knows I have a point.

This week has dragged on forever, but it's finally Friday. I almost feel like a kid waking up on the day of a school field trip. If I think about it, not counting moving to Boston, the last time I did something similar was when Alex and I went to Vienna for our audition. And even knowing that my brother would want me to go and make the most of this experience, I still can't shake the guilt over feeling this excited about something. Something that he'd have loved but will never get to experience. *Survivor's guilt.* That's what my therapist calls it. God, I hate that expression.

River texted me yesterday, telling me to be ready at four o'clock. How he got my number remains a mystery. After a few morning classes, the only thing standing between me and a weekend in New York is finishing my shift at Blue Cats and surviving the third-grade interrogation conducted by both of my friends.

"So what does this assistant job exactly consist of?" Bela asks, mindlessly stirring her coffee. I feel bad about not telling her the whole story, but it's not like River ever answered my question and explained why he wants me to come with him. Maybe he was just feeling bad about what happened between us. Maybe he wants us to go back to being friends. I guess the whole assistant story just made more sense, so I went with it. Fortunately, but also strangely enough, Bela hasn't asked for any details. Something has changed this week. She doesn't seem to be herself, but I can't put my finger on the exact issue here. Other than the fact that she's not wearing any earrings today, which is odd enough.

"I'm not sure. He just said he thought it would be a great opportunity for me." I shrug.

Rodrigo is behind me, collecting empty coffee cups, and his laughter fills my ears. "I wonder why he never offered that *great opportunity* to any of us."

I frown, my stomach instantly sinking. The last thing I want is for my friends to believe I'm getting special treatment or, even worse, taking opportunities from anyone else, from them. The music industry is known for its cutthroat competition. There's not much room for friends. It's often a solitary path, but it's not one I want to take if I can help it.

"I'm just kidding." Rodrigo nudges me with his elbow. "Go have some fun! Tell us all about it when you come back."

"Deal." I grin, the weight lifting off my chest.

Bela continues to stir her coffee, but her eyes lack their usual mischievous spark. Leaning on the counter, I bring my face closer to hers and snatch the spoon from her hand. "You know you didn't put any sugar in that coffee, right? What's up with you?"

She shrugs, but her attention finally shifts to me. "Anders's girlfriend is coming to Boston this weekend," she says.

"Who?" Rodrigo and I ask in unison.

"He has a girlfriend?" My mouth opens in surprise. "Did he ever tell you that?"

Bela sighs, hesitating. "He did, actually. At the Halloween party. But then he never mentioned her again, so I thought they broke up. Which is obviously not the case, because now she's coming here. I guess the joke is on me."

"Maybe he wants to break up with her in person?" Rodrigo tries, and I'm about to dig more into that very applaudable theory, but Bela stops us before we can continue.

"Yeah, I don't know about that. He asked me to stay away from him and not to tell her anything, so…"

"What?" My jaw drops, although the story is not particularly unusual. At an international college with students coming from all over the world, it's more than likely that some may still have their high school sweethearts waiting for them back home. I'd just prefer if it didn't happen to any of my friends.

"What a jerk. Do you want me to punch him?" Rodrigo suggests, and I have to stifle a laugh. He doesn't strike me as someone who could throw a punch, but you never know.

"I can cancel my trip," I offer. It would obviously suck, but so does seeing my friend like this. I'm so used to her typically cheerful and happy self that I instantly miss it.

"What? No! Absolutely not." This seems to have awakened her. "I would never ask you to do that." She frowns. "But there is one thing, mi amor..." She glances at Rodrigo, seemingly in search of his support for what she's about to say, and then back at me. "Make sure you don't find yourself in my shoes." She smiles an unhappy smile, and I don't need her to explain any further. A jolt of pain shoots through my chest. The situation with River is much different, but the result might as well be the same. There's no high school sweetheart, as far as I know, but he has also never hidden the fact that there are other girls, numerous other girls, for that matter.

"It's not like that between us," I say, unsure of who I'm trying to convince. "River and I are friends."

Rodrigo lets out a snort as his eyes lock with Bela's, neither of them buying my bullshit. "Well, then be careful he doesn't have any other *friends* out there."

\*

That somewhat uneasy feeling is still gripping my insides when I open the door of River's car, but I decide to shove it aside for now.

"Hey. I'm sorry. Have you been waiting long?"

Rodrigo released me from my duties fifteen minutes early so I could grab my bag and take a quick shower. Of course, my hair is still wet. I did, however, throw on some light makeup, leaving it to the freezing weather to redden my cheeks. Dressed in my favorite black leggings, perfect for traveling long hours, and a blue cotton sweater hugging my upper body and keeping me warm, I think I'm all set for our little trip. I notice River has also opted for comfy clothes, sporting a pair of black sweatpants and a gray sweater with his sleeves rolled up, revealing his muscled arms. One of his hands is resting on the steering wheel while the other is typing a message. He looks up from his phone as soon as he notices me.

"Hey," he says softly, tossing the phone into the beverage holder. "No problem, I just got here." I shiver when he leans in and twists a lock of my hair around his finger. "Quick shower again?" He smirks. It's a fairly innocent gesture, but my heart races. This is going to be a painfully long ride. I should have just taken the bus. Clearing his throat, he lets go of my hair. "You shouldn't be running around with wet hair. It's too cold for that."

I shrug, not trusting myself to speak. Running around with wet hair at fourteen degrees Fahrenheit is indeed not the best idea. Hence the wool hat I just took off, but it's him switching from being so confusingly cold and distant to sweet and caring that makes me shiver.

"Where's your guitar?" He glances at the bag I tossed onto the back seat and starts the car.

"My guitar? Why would I bring my guitar? You're the one who will be playing. I'm the assistant, remember?"

He chuckles, the sound of his soft laugh echoing in the confined space of his luxury SUV.

"How long is the drive?" I ask, changing the topic.

"About four hours. We can stop somewhere once we get on the road, in case you're hungry," he says, giving me a side glance.

"River Evans, are you trying to check if I've eaten?" I raise my eyebrows, openly mocking him.

"What? Of course not." He grins before refocusing on the road ahead. "Have you, though?"

The laughter we both burst into is freeing, relieving some of the tension in the air. River turns on the radio, and we start chatting about my classes and the album he'll be recording. The conversation leads to New York and traveling in general. Although I've never been to the US before, I traveled quite a lot. When Alex and I were little, our parents would take us on trips across Europe every summer, as money was never an issue in our family.

River, on the contrary, didn't begin to travel until he became independent. The only story he shares from his childhood is about a trip to Rhode Island, which he went on with Mayra's adoptive parents, just to be returned to his foster home the following Monday. Not that he phrases it this way. It sounds like he cherished these small moments above all else. It's me who can't stop thinking about the little boy that nobody wanted enough to take him home, and it fucking breaks my heart.

A loud ringing interrupts my thoughts. I glance at River, assuming it's his phone since I rarely receive calls here, but he shakes his head. With a frown, I pull my phone from my jacket. The word 'home' flashes on the screen. So strange how the meaning of a word can completely change over time. That place certainly doesn't feel like home anymore. I decline the call and toss the phone back onto my jacket, catching River's curious gaze in the process. I know why they're calling, and I have no intention of answering.

"You don't need to take it?" he asks quietly, his expression unreadable.

"No." I turn my face away from him. Given that River is not exactly fluent in Czech, it's not like he would understand our conversation, but I don't have the energy to take the call anyway. His gaze remains fixed on the road, but he occasionally steals glances at me, lost in his own thoughts while I watch the world pass by my window. Exhaustion eventually takes over. I don't know if it's the frustration over the unwelcome call, the excitement of this trip, the proximity of the man who drives me crazy without even realizing it, or just the pressure of the entire week slowly washing over me, but my eyes start gradually closing until the landscape behind the windows becomes a blur.

When I wake up, we're not moving anymore. In fact, I'm way too comfortable to even remember I'm supposed to be in a car. And, of course, I'm not. Instead, I'm lying on a couch, covered by a warm, fluffy blanket. I sit up quickly, blinking in confusion a couple of times until my mind sharpens. How the hell did I get here? I've always been a heavy sleeper. My mom and Alex used to joke that someone could easily kill me in my sleep. I guess they were right. And it only gets worse when I'm running on borrowed energy.

I glance around, then put my shoes back on—nope, I don't want to think about that one either. The beautiful space of what appears to be a large, modern penthouse is filled with soft lights, while most of the actual light seems to be coming from outside. It's not until I reach the floor-to-ceiling windows that I discover the source of all this brightness. New York. The entire city lies right in front of me, or more exactly, below me. It's absolutely breathtaking. I've never seen anything quite like it.

"You like it?" I hear his deep, low voice and turn to see him slowly approaching from behind, holding a cup of coffee in his hands and looking like he just stepped out of a shower minutes ago. He has changed into a different pair of sweatpants and is wearing a white, short-sleeved T-shirt, and his feet are bare. This time, it's his hair that is wet, tiny drops of water still running down his temples, and I'm surprised by my strong desire to run my hand through it. The aroma of fresh coffee and his body wash, likely a combination of sandalwood and citrus, immediately engulfs me. And even though we're in a much larger space now, his presence takes up the whole of it, making it extremely hard to focus on anything else.

"It's incredible," I say, unable to believe that a view like this even exists, and I'm standing right in front of it.

He smiles. "Your room is ready if you want to take a shower or get changed. I also ordered some Chinese food because we didn't stop anywhere on the road, and I thought you would be too tired to go out tonight."

Tearing my eyes from the stunning view of New York City, I turn to the equally stunning man standing in front of me. "I'm so sorry. I didn't mean to fall asleep. I didn't realize I was so tired."

"It's okay, Violet," he says softly, not offering any details on how I got here, which I'm thankful for.

"What time is it?" I ask.

"Nine o'clock," he says, and the loud ringing of the doorbell interrupts him.

"That must be our food. I'll get it. Feel free to look around," he offers. "Your room is upstairs—the last door at the end of the hallway."

I do as he says, using the time to explore the apartment, my curiosity overtaking me. The entire first floor is essentially one enormous—and I mean enormous—living room connected to an open kitchen. One of those beautiful kitchens with a wide center island you only see in magazines and TV cooking shows. And, of course, there is a grand piano right in front of the spectacular view of the city. My fingers immediately itch to play. I can only imagine the feeling of being surrounded by the glittering lights of the city that never sleeps, lost in music.

Every corner of the penthouse exudes elegance, its walls decorated with modern art paintings. So far, I have only seen one photograph showing a teen version of River and a young girl with dark hair and gorgeous olive skin, who I assume is Mayra. I've never seen his sister, but this girl looks too young to be his girlfriend. Plus, the way he holds her around her shoulders, like a protective older brother, his lips lifted into a boyish grin, tells me it's her.

As I make my way upstairs, I can't help but wonder if River has ever brought anyone else to his place. And by anyone, I obviously mean girls. There's still so much I don't know about him, but what I do know is that despite his reputation and fame, deep down, he's a loner. And it makes me wonder why.

When I open the door to what's supposed to be my room, I'm not surprised to find all my belongings already there. The room has a nice, simple design with a comfortable-looking double bed, but it's when I see the bathroom with a large jacuzzi bathtub and a walk-in shower that I know I'll most likely cry when our brief escape comes to an end. This is every college student's dream come true. After a quick check, I discover that the other two rooms on the floor are a complete home gym and River's bedroom, which I don't enter, not wanting to abuse his hospitality. As I go back to my room, the sound of River's voice coming from downstairs cuts my exploration short.

"Violet?" he calls, and I peek my head out of the room.

"Be right there!" I shout back, hoping that there will be enough time later to indulge in the luxurious spa experience that my bathroom guarantees.

My little nap has brought me back to life, but I feel guilty for River, who must have driven for at least two hours with no one to talk to. So far, I've been the worst assistant ever. Hopefully, I can redeem myself tomorrow, even though I highly doubt my limited studio knowledge will be of any serious use to him. Too bad. I tried to tell him.

I change quickly, putting on my favorite ripped jeans and a plain white T-shirt. The apartment is heated, and I

167

can feel the warmth coming through the polished wood floor, creating an amazing sensation that makes me want to join River in going barefoot. I restrain from doing that so it doesn't look like I'm making myself too much at home. Leaving my socks on and tugging my hair back into a ponytail, I head downstairs.

A delicious aroma hits my nostrils before I even set foot in the living room, and my stomach growls loudly.

"Wow, that's a lot of food." My eyes land on the countless little paper boxes carefully arranged on the coffee table in front of the sofa.

"Umm, yeah, I didn't know what you liked, so I ordered a bit of everything," he says sheepishly, and I have to bite my lip not to laugh. A bit of everything may be an understatement. More like he ordered *everything*.

"You fine with sitting on the floor?" he asks, gesturing at a cozy nest of small floor cushions. I blink up at him. When on earth did he prepare all of this?

"Sure."

"Chopsticks?" He grins, tossing a pair of chopsticks into the air.

I catch them, sitting down and leaning my back against the sofa. He slides next to me, leaving enough space between the two of us that this could be considered a friendly dinner. And to him, it probably is. So why am I suddenly nervous? River hands me a glass of red wine, which I gladly accept, along with one of the delicious-smelling paper boxes—vegetable noodles. I dig my chopsticks into them, grateful for the distraction.

"So, do you come here a lot? To New York, I mean? Is that why you bought an apartment here?" I ask, fighting with the two pieces of wood before finally sliding a considerable chunk of noodles into my mouth. From River's amused expression, I can tell he either enjoys seeing me eat or is having fun with my lack of refined table manners.

"Yeah, I do." He nods. "Boston is my home, but New York is where I record my music. Plus, most of the business is here, so I'm in the city almost every week. I bought this place only quite recently, though. I don't like staying at hotels, and it just made more sense having my own place here." He smiles almost shyly, which makes me want to laugh.

"I admire you, you know?" I say softly.

"Admire me?" He chuckles, tilting his head. "Why?"

He probably hears it all the time, but it's the sincerity of his question that makes me want to explain. "You got where you are all by yourself. Coming from—" I pause for a moment, trying to rephrase what I was going to say.

"A foster home?" he offers. It's a matter-of-fact statement. He doesn't seem bothered by it.

"Yeah. Sorry, I meant it as a compliment. It's just… you have achieved so much, and you did all of that on your own." I glance at him as he stabs the remaining noodles with his chopsticks, not eating. I can tell his mind is spinning, and although he doesn't look up from his food, I know he can feel my gaze. "Can I ask you a question?" I whisper, and he finally looks at me. A flicker of curiosity, but also caution, flashes through his eyes.

"Shoot," he says.

I study his face for a moment, thinking about my question. The last thing I want is to make it sound like I'm comparing my situation to his. I had my parents while growing up, however misguided their actions may have been most of the time. And, most importantly, I had Alex. Every day of my life, my twin brother was right there with me. A person I could always rely on, tell my secrets to, share my dreams with. My best friend and guardian. River was alone.

"How did you do it? How did you manage not to give up when no one else believed in you?"

He shakes his head, and I see a tiny wrinkle appearing between his eyebrows. "You know the answer to that, Violet," he says softly. "You don't need anyone else to believe in you. You only need to believe in yourself. As cliché as it sounds, it's true. That being said, there's always someone who believes in you. If it's not your parents, then it's your teachers or your friends." I'm wondering which category he includes himself in because I know he believes in me. He already showed me as much. I don't ask, though, because to me, he doesn't fit into either.

"Who was it for you?" I ask instead.

"My piano teacher and Mayra. I didn't need more than that."

I smile, but it's a smile mixed with pain. Alex, of course, was the one who had the most faith in me, but he's no longer here. River must notice my thoughts have wandered to my dead brother, and he shifts uncomfortably.

"Do you want to know something?" he asks. "Something I have never told anyone?"

"Yes." I'm half expecting some kind of joke to cheer me up, which is why his words surprise me.

"I was almost adopted," he says. "When I was seven, there was this couple in their thirties that came to our foster home looking for a kid to adopt. They played with all of us, seemed quite nice. You could see they had money. It looked like they were in love." His gaze wanders around the room, and it's evident that sharing this piece of his past doesn't come easy to him. "I really wanted to be the one they chose, you know?" He laughs, the pain in his voice betraying him. I remain silent, giving him the space and the choice to continue, and after a while, he does. "They came a couple more times, and after that, I got my wish. They chose me." A look of unhappiness spreads across his face. Despite already knowing that this story doesn't have a happy ending, I can't quite imagine what happened, and my heart aches for the seven-year-old boy who only wanted to be loved. "So they took me home," he continues, his voice emotionless, but I know better. "It was amazing. Finally, I had my own room and more toys than I could have ever dreamed of. They were spending plenty of time with me. It was absolutely perfect. I thought I won the fucking lottery." He lets out a half-hearted laugh, but the tension radiating from him is clear.

"So what happened?" I whisper.

River clenches his jaw. "You know, that's the worst part. I don't know what the fuck happened. I'd been living with them for a couple of months, and the adoption was almost about to be completed, but suddenly they just… decided to return me."

"What? What do you mean to return you? Why?" My heart tightens as he offers me the missing puzzle piece. Of course he doesn't trust people. And who could blame him?

"Yeah, I mean return, as to… one day they just took me back and didn't even bother to explain why. One of my caregivers at the foster home told me, though. Apparently, they realized it was too much work. I was too much work, and they weren't ready for it."

"Are you kidding me?"

He laughs at my reaction, and this time, it's an actual, genuine laugh, the one I enjoy hearing so much. Except I'm just too angry to appreciate it right now. Leaning toward me, he takes the empty paper box from my hand and sets it down on the table, making me look at him. "It's okay, Violet. It was a long time ago."

I can't believe he is soothing *me*, but he is. I shake my head. It's not okay. "You know what? It's their loss. And I don't mean it only because you are River Evans, the famous musician making millions of dollars per year—" I have no idea how much he actually makes, but I'm happy to see him laugh. "I mean it because you grew up into this wonderful person anybody would be incredibly proud of. You are driven. You love what you do and are the best at it. You can't stand seeing someone struggling and not help. Despite everything you went through, you have this bright energy around you that makes people feel like anything is possible, makes *me* feel like anything is possible. So when you ask me why I admire you, I ask you how could I not? There's not a thing I don't love about you," I say, and it's true. His hard work. His determination. His creativity. His energy. *Him*. Fuck.

River's eyes widen at my confession. It probably came out wrong. I'm freaking him out. I sound like a stupid groupie or, even worse… someone who has fallen for him.

Have I? The weight of my confession hangs in the air, and I can't help but think that I've crossed a line.

"Sorry. I didn't mean it like that." I shut my eyes and then open them again, trying to regain some calm. My heart races, pounding against my chest as a wave of embarrassment rushes through my body.

"Like what?" he asks. His voice is soft and gentle, and I notice he's inching closer, his eyes not leaving mine.

"Let it go, River," I whisper with a shake of my head. Of course, it sounded all wrong because *I am* falling for him. It'd be impossible not to, but it'd also be incredibly foolish to expect this to end in any other way than with my heart shattered into a million tiny pieces.

"What if I don't want to let it go?" His hand lifts, and he touches my chin, tilting my face toward him. He pulls me closer, and suddenly, his arms are around me, his lips crashing against mine. *This is such a bad idea*, but I'm unable to resist. My head is swirling, my heart pounding against his chest. His lips are soft and warm, but his kiss is filled with tension, and I answer with an urgency of my own, our tongues tangling and dancing in sync. His hands travel to my waist, and his grip on me tightens. He is breathing fast, and so am I. Everything around us vanishes—River's beautiful penthouse, the whole city of New York with its brilliant lights and sounds, the uncertainty of it all, and the painful memories of our past. The only thing that exists is the two of us, gasping for air and desperately holding on to each other. Without taking his lips from mine, he pulls me onto his lap so I'm straddling him. I wrap my arms around his neck and move slowly, feeling the sizeable bulge in his pants digging into me. He is hard. *So* hard. I know this is a dangerous game we are playing, but I can't stop. I don't want it to stop. I want him.

# Twelve

"Fuck, Violet." His hands grip my waist, holding me to him. "If you keep moving like that…" His voice is low and husky, and I can sense he's losing control. "Maybe you should… you should stop if you don't want this to go any further," he whispers, his breathing heavy.

I slow down, but despite his words, he doesn't lose his grip on my hips. Running my lips along his neck, I feel his veins pulsing. I want him. I need him inside me, and I may regret it later, but right now, I don't care about the consequences.

"What if I don't want to stop?" I whisper back. He freezes briefly, allowing me to see the turmoil within him. "What are you afraid of?" I ask softly. We've stopped moving, both catching our breath. I know he wants me. I can feel him shifting uncomfortably beneath me, his eyes clouded with desire. "Is this about you being my teacher?" I probably shouldn't be asking. It's painfully obvious that this situation is far from ideal, but I also don't know what the actual policy is in this case. He isn't exactly my teacher, after all. He's a visiting artist, and the semester is almost over. And then there's the fact that I don't care, even though I probably should.

He runs his fingers along my bare arm, his touch leaving goosebumps on my skin. "It was never about me being your teacher, Violet, but you are young, and I... I don't think I can give you what you want. I don't do relationships, and I don't want to hurt you. You deserve better. You deserve someone who can give you all of that and more." He shakes his head, as if trying to convince himself of what he just said, yet his hands continue to touch me, almost as if they have a mind of their own. The hard bulge in his pants presses against me, but I can tell he's trying his best to remain still.

*I don't want anyone else.* Placing my hand on his chest, I feel the frantic beating of his heart. "I don't want anything from you. I just want this. You." I'm not sure where the words come from, and unfortunately, I do know that they're not entirely true, but if heartbreak is the price for getting closer to him, even if it's just this one time, it's a price I'm willing to pay. It's foolish and reckless. It's something I have never done before. I'm not a one-night stand kind of girl, but sometimes one night is all we have.

River swallows. His eyes bore into mine, looking for any sign of uncertainty in my expression. There is none.

"Are you sure this is what you want, Violet?" he asks, wrapping a strand of my hair around his finger. "I don't want you to regret it tomorrow."

I don't answer. Instead, I take his lower lip between my teeth and gently tug on it, letting him know that this is what I want. He is what I want. The only question is if

I will be able to walk away from this unshattered once it's over. I really fucking hope so.

River makes a low humming sound as his mouth searches mine, this time claiming me unapologetically. His hands wander under my T-shirt, caressing my naked skin, igniting me from the inside. He runs his finger along the edge of my bra and then softly palms my breasts. I gasp and raise my arms, allowing him to remove my shirt.

"Fuck, you are so beautiful, even more incredible than I imagined," he murmurs, unclipping my bra, showering me with kisses, then taking one of my nipples into his mouth, gently biting. "You're driving me wild, Violet. I've never wanted anyone this much before."

I moan, basking in his words and resisting the urge to cover myself. My breasts are in no way big, more like a handful, but River doesn't seem to mind. His erection is almost painfully digging into me, pleading to be set free. I reach for the hem of his shirt and lift, making a conscious effort not to ogle him as I do so. He is perfect. Breathtakingly perfect, like he has just stepped out of a freaking *GQ* cover, which is actually not very far-fetched because he *was* on a *GQ* cover only a couple of months ago. His arms and chest are strong and perfectly sculpted, with broad shoulders and praiseworthy abs leading to a defined V disappearing under the waistband of his sweatpants. The black ink of his tattoo runs across his chest, creating a set of six numbers, and I wish I knew their significance. It doesn't look like a date, so maybe some kind of coordinates? I'm suddenly not sure I want to know to where or to whom.

He's every girl's dream, but it's not only his body. It's him as a whole. His beautiful low, deep voice singing haunting melodies, his long fingers dancing over the keys with such ease, his mysterious aura, the way he speaks, his charming accent included, the confidence with which he carries himself. And, to me, the way his eyes brighten whenever he's reminded of a beautiful memory of his otherwise fucked-up childhood, the tiny frown lines that appear between his eyebrows when he realizes I haven't eaten, and the sound of his steady heartbeat that has repeatedly managed to anchor me whenever I needed it the most.

"Tell me you're sure you won't regret it," he insists again, pressing his forehead against mine. "Tell me you don't want me to stop."

I lock my eyes with his so he knows I mean it. "I won't. Don't stop."

He exhales heavily into my mouth, his eyes growing darker. "Take off your jeans, Violet," he orders, and I comply without second-guessing my decision. Removing my pants and socks, I'm left almost fully exposed except for my tiny black panties, which are barely covering anything and completely soaked. I'm almost ashamed of how much I want him. Almost. He eases me to the floor, arranging a cushion under my head and another one supporting my back, and his eyes fill with such hunger that I have to close mine to lessen some of the intensity that comes with his heated gaze and touch.

"Open your legs for me," he whispers, running his nose along my neck and nipping at my sensitive skin. I'm surprised to realize I'm pressing my legs together, trying to find some relief. I do as I'm told, feeling his hand slowly move to my thighs. His fingers trace the thin material of my panties, pushing them aside as he sinks his index finger into me. I moan loudly, not quite ready for such an intense feeling.

"Fuck, Violet, you're gonna make me lose it," he murmurs, using his other hand to stroke himself. "And trust me, it has been a really long time since that happened to me." He chuckles, but nothing about his expression suggests that he is joking. His sweatpants are still on, but I can tell he is beyond hard now. My hand is throbbing with the sudden need to touch him. I run my palm across his muscular chest, tracing the lines of his tattoo, but before I can continue any further, I feel him adding his middle finger. His rhythm quickens, his thumb tracing circles on my clit, bringing me to the edge of ecstasy.

"River, please," I whisper. I'm not even sure what I'm asking for, but the feeling is just too much.

"It's okay, Violet, let go. Open your eyes," he urges softly.

I bite my lip hard, taking pleasure in the pain that shoots through me, and look right at him. His eyes seem on fire, which is exactly how I feel. Once he's certain he has my full attention, he slides down his sweatpants, his hard cock springing free. No boxers, of course. The thought of him going commando under his pants the entire evening while we were talking and having dinner turns me on even more, if that is humanly possible. I want to touch him. Taste him. I want him inside me. I want so many things, and I know he can see it in my eyes.

He kneels in front of me, completely comfortable in his nakedness, which, of course, doesn't surprise me. As he allows me to take him in, he runs his hand lazily up and down his shaft, a playful expression on his face. He knows how perfect he is and probably has much more experience than I do. Hell, I haven't really had much. Three lovers in total, and until now, I thought I knew how good sex could feel. Turns out I had no idea, and he's not even inside me yet. He doesn't have to be. Everything about River Evans screams pleasure. Like the way the muscles in his arms and chest flex as he fingers me with the same fingers that can play alluring melodies and dance over the piano keys with unique precision.

"Ahh, River." I moan his name, arching my back and pulling his hair, drawing him closer. Not that he needs more encouragement. His fingers are replaced by his tongue moving expertly inside me, and I can't hold myself anymore. "River, I—I'm going to… Fuck—" I can't even get out the right words.

"Yes, that's it, Violet. You taste so good." He's breathing heavily now, his mouth still between my legs, while his free hand alternates between playing with my overly sensitive nipples and stroking himself. It's all too much. Pleasure explodes inside me, and I cry out, going completely numb in his arms.

"You are so perfect. So fucking beautiful," he whispers, showering my thighs with light kisses, making his way up to my mouth. I taste myself on his tongue when he kisses me. It's the strangest sensation, but it's also an incredible turn-on. I run my hand across his chest, down to his perfect abs, making him hiss as I wrap my hand firmly around his cock and stroke up and down. His head tips back, and his mouth opens, lips slightly parted.

"I need to be inside you," he pleads, his voice filled with lust. I know that if I teased him a little faster and took him into my mouth, I could make him lose it, but God, I need him inside me, too. "Umm, fuck. I have to find… I wasn't expecting this. I'm sorry. Give me a second," he says, breathing more heavily now. I can tell that it's costing him a lot to restrain himself.

"I'm on the pill, and I'm clean," I say softly, blood rushing to my cheeks, the implication of what I'm telling him clear. I don't know if I'm making a mistake. He's the one who has been changing partners, as far as I've heard, but for some reason, I trust him completely. His eyes, clouded with desire, widen slightly in surprise.

"I'm clean too. I've never… I promise, Violet, but you know you can still stop this, right? And it wouldn't stop me from making you come again," he whispers, lowering himself to me slowly, kissing the corner of my mouth, my neck, my breasts, taking my nipples in his mouth one by one, biting me a little harder. My body is trembling, and I feel the building sensation between my legs. Stopping is the last thing I want. And yes, he'll most likely make me come again if he continues just a little longer. "I don't want to stop."

His gaze lingers on me for a split second before his resolution snaps, and he swiftly removes my panties, sliding inside me immediately. He is big. So big, and I haven't been with anyone in a while. The sensation is overwhelming, even though he's making an effort to go slowly. I wrap my arms around his neck and try to breathe.

"Fuck. Jesus, you are so tight. You feel amazing." He groans into my neck, and I feel him getting harder inside me.

I want him to go faster. To take me completely. Slowly, I begin to move my hips. River hisses and sucks in a sharp breath.

"Is this what you want, Violet?" His voice remains low and deep, but now it carries a much darker tone, filled with unspoken promises. I don't answer, instead I wrap my legs around him, my eyes locked with his.

"Hmm, I see." He groans and thrusts into me. I let out a loud moan, relieved that there are no neighbors around. There is no way I could control myself. His thrusts are fast and deep. So deep that they are hitting just the perfect spot. I don't doubt for a minute that River knows all too well how to reach it. His every movement is charged with electricity, his breath skating over my neck. He locks my wrists above my head with one of his hands and uses the other to rub my clit. Damn it. I've never reached a climax with a guy inside me, but I already feel like I'm about to burst. He isn't holding back anymore, and I know he's as close as I am.

"River?" I breathe out, squeezing him tight.

"Come on, Violet, don't hold it. Come for me."

And I do, even before he finishes his sentence. He doesn't slow down. Instead, he keeps thrusting into me until his own release starts running down my thighs.

We stay like that for a moment, neither of us moving nor speaking. He surprises me by holding me tightly to him when he finally slides out and helps me clean up myself. Rather than protest, I nestle in his arms and listen to his heart, which is gradually regaining its normal rhythm.

"Sing for me?" I whisper the exact words he once whispered to me, and I feel him smile against my cheek.

With a soft chuckle, he begins to hum one of his songs in my ear. I close my eyes, tired but strangely happy. There is a voice somewhere in my head warning me that this is a dangerous happiness, one that won't last, but I choose to ignore it.

Drifting into a dream, I hear River singing words of a song I don't recognize. "I'm fucking falling for you, and I wish I knew how to stop it."

Except it doesn't seem like he's singing, more like whispering. But that's the thing about dreams—you don't know what's real and what's not, but you want to hold on to that feeling for as long as you can.

# Thirteen

When I wake up, I'm no longer curled on the heated floor of River's living room. At first, I assume I'm in the guest room. That's until I notice River's shirt hanging on an armchair in front of the cozy king bed I'm lying on. His bed. Memories from last night flood my mind. His lips on mine, his hands and his tongue exploring every part of my body. His strong arms wrapped around me, holding me throughout the night. His morning erection digging into me—did I dream that one? Definitely not… but that must have been at least an hour ago. Did he carry me to his room? Did he sleep next to me? The sound of water I haven't paid attention to until now suddenly ceases. The shower. Of course. Damn it. I have no clue about the proper morning etiquette in this situation. I know I promised I wouldn't regret last night, and I don't, but the reality of what we did yesterday and the fact that it might only further complicate things between us slowly seep in.

Suddenly filled with self-consciousness as last night's bravery abandons me, I get out of the bed. I'm relieved to find my clothes hanging on the same armchair. At least I don't have to do the whole walk of shame naked. That would have been pretty bad, even though it's just the two of us here. Hurriedly, I slip into my underwear and jeans, but as I'm halfway into my T-shirt, I hear footsteps.

"You're awake." It's a simple statement that doesn't reveal much, but his voice is soft, and when I finally manage to free myself of the shirt covering my eyes, I notice a smile on his lips.

He's standing in front of me in nothing but a towel, said towel hanging extremely low on his hips. Shit. I clear my throat, tearing my eyes away from his lower body and mustering the courage to meet his gaze. His expression is amused, to say the least.

"Did you sleep well?" he asks with a twinkle in his eyes. And, God, I really do try to focus on those, not on his flawless, muscled body covered in tiny drops of water. Why is he being so cocky about this? I'd have thought he'd be freaking out, too, but instead he's grinning at me.

"I did, but you should really stop carrying me around like that. It's kind of becoming a thing," I say, frowning a little. I can't deny that I enjoy it, but it's a bit worrying that this is the third time I haven't noticed him moving me like I'm nothing but a feather in his arms.

His laugh fills my ears. "I haven't noticed it becoming *a thing*, but if that's the case, I'd say it's a nice *thing*. Wouldn't you?"

I shake my head. It's not going to become a thing, because what happened yesterday is just not going to happen again. River doesn't want a relationship, and I don't want more complications in my life. And what I definitely don't want is to lose him again. So, if ignoring this… attraction between us is what it takes for us to be friends, then so be it.

He laughs again, amused by my sullen expression.

"Come on, Violet, we don't have much time. We gotta leave for the studio in half an hour. Take a shower if you need. I'll make you some coffee."

Opening the closet, he drops his towel. My mouth falls open, and I scramble backward, nearly tripping over myself in my haste to reach the door.

"Right, I'll see you downstairs, then," I blurt out, unable to ignore the alluring smirk on his face and the faint chuckle that follows me. Damn him.

✳

It takes a little longer than planned because, as I already suspected, the shower in my guest room should have a special place in heaven. And if I didn't fear River personally coming to get me out, I may have stayed there the entire morning. Which, on second thought, may not have been a bad idea at all. Ugh, I really have to stop thinking about last night. Once I finish brushing my teeth, I put on some quick makeup and tie my hair in a messy, half-wet bun. Opting for a comfortable pair of black leggings, I match them with white leg warmers, a plain undershirt, and a tight turtleneck sweater in the same color. New York is not supposed to be colder than Boston, and since it hasn't snowed yet, I'm hoping this outfit, combined with winter boots and a warm jacket, will be enough to save me from potentially freezing to death.

As I walk down the stairs, I run through scenarios in my head about the best way to handle this whole situation, coming to the inevitable conclusion that we should just talk about what happened yesterday. Clear the air… so to speak.

With his coffee in hand, River stands in the kitchen, looking as beautiful as ever in black fade-out jeans and a dark blue hoodie. God, it's unfair how incredibly attracted I am to this guy.

I get straight to the point. "Listen, about what happened last night, I think it's better if it doesn't happen again—"

"What happened last night?"

I glance to the side and meet another pair of eyes looking at me with unmasked interest. These eyes are piercing blue, though, obviously not belonging to River but to a tall, blond guy standing next to him. Shit.

He chuckles and offers me his hand. "I'm Noah."

River clears his throat. "Sabrina, this is Noah, my manager. This asshole also happens to be my best friend. He came to pick us up and brought us breakfast," he says, cocking his eyebrow and sending his friend the shut-the-fuck-up-right-now-or-I-will-kill-you look. Noah doesn't seem to mind, his smile growing even wider.

"Right, sorry about that. Nice to meet you, Noah." I shake his hand, noticing that the guy is quite handsome. Nowhere near as handsome as River, but still. The grin hasn't left Noah's face.

"I'm sorry, Violet, but you'll have to take your breakfast on the road. We're already late." River gestures for the door, saving me from further embarrassment.

I nod, hiding my heated face behind the paper coffee cup. Noah heads out the kitchen door, still laughing under his breath, while River and I follow a few steps behind him. As we enter the elevator, I take a bite out of the offered croissant, finally satisfying my growling stomach. The feeling of River's lips nearly touching my ear almost makes me jump out of my skin. "Violet?" he whispers, I suppose so Noah can't hear him, but his friend's attention is firmly fixed on his phone, sending voice messages and trying to work out the last details of today's session. "About what happened yesterday…" he continues, and I brace myself for what's coming. I wanted to be the one to tell him that this was a one-time thing, just to save us the awkwardness and show that I don't care, an obvious lie but one I can live with. I refuse to be *that* girl. The rejected girl begging for scraps and crumbs of River Evan's attention. Nope. I still have some pride.

"It *is* happening again," he purrs in my ear, his lips ever slightly touching my cheek.

What? His deep voice resonates within me, causing a shiver to run through my body. The elevator door opens, and River steps out as if nothing just happened, not even waiting for my response, not that I have one. I'm pretty much speechless, trying to get my legs to move so I can follow both men to the car that's already waiting for us. I guess today is going to be even more interesting than I thought.

*

By the time we get to the studio, River is all business. He moves quickly, with determination and purpose, issuing commands and checking that everything is ready and to his liking. His face is fixed with concentration, and his voice leaves no room for debate. I count nine people in the studio, Noah included, and they all run around River like the star he is. It's almost funny to see him like this now that I know there's a hidden, much softer side to him. What I'm still not sure about is my role in all of this. He obviously doesn't need me as an assistant because apart from Noah, Sean, the sound engineer, and Connor, the photographer, all the remaining people are assistants. Actual assistants. There are three guys and three girls, all taking care of literally everything one could think of, from getting River the special microphone he requested, changing the piano bench he didn't like—apparently it couldn't be adjusted properly—to bringing him coffee and fresh water. This last task is carried out by one of his female assistants, who happens to be stunning, with long blonde hair, green eyes, and flawless porcelain skin. She's wearing tight leather pants, a crop top, and cowboy boots, showcasing her long legs. She's beautiful, but seriously, who dresses like that for a studio session? Unless you're the recording artist, of course. It still probably wouldn't be my first choice, but I can imagine Bela pulling off a similar outfit and completely rocking it. River declines the coffee but takes the water, and it's impossible not to notice how her fingers brush against his. This girl has a very obvious crush on River Evans.

"Mia, this is Sabrina." River's voice interrupts my thoughts, making both of us look at him. "Sabrina is here with me. Make sure she has everything she needs, please," he says matter-of-factly before dismissing her.

Her jaw drops. "Of course, Mr. Evans." She nods dutifully and turns to leave, but not before scowling in my direction. Nice, I'm already making friends here. Still, I can't hide my smile. *Sabrina is here with me.*

It's only when she leaves that I turn to River. The studio is being prepared with the changes he requested, and everyone disappears to carry out their assigned tasks. We're standing in a small kitchen connected to a spacious relaxation area, complete with cozy couches, armchairs, a large TV, a cabinet full of vinyl records, and even a billiard and foosball table. Signed black-and-white photographs of musicians who recorded in this studio decorate the walls, including every famous musician I can think of and all the bands I listened to growing up. I may as well be in heaven, and I haven't even stepped into the actual recording room yet.

"You enjoying yourself?" River asks, smiling knowingly.

"You know I am. This is amazing." I shake my head. "But…"

"But?" He raises his eyebrows, tilting his head to me.

"But I thought *I* was supposed to be your assistant. There's nothing I can help you with here." I shrug, looking at my feet. I don't want to sound ungrateful. Any of my classmates would kill for this opportunity, but that's the thing. I want to feel like I've worked for my opportunities, not like they were handed to me for reasons I don't even know. Of course, explaining all of that to River would probably make me sound like a pouty child. He's gazing at me with a curious, half-amused, half-questioning expression. I'm definitely being ungrateful here.

"River! Come on, man! We're ready for you." The door of the control room opens, and I see Noah waving at us.

"Yeah, I'm coming!" River shouts back, maintaining his gaze on me.

I shake my head again. "I'm sorry. You don't have time for this right now. I just meant that if you need my help, even though I'm nowhere near as qualified as your *actual* assistants, I'm here." I finally look him in the eyes, flashing him my best carefree smile.

I'm about to turn away when he seizes my wrist and swiftly spins me back around, leaving me no choice but to look into his mint-green eyes. "Don't worry, Violet, there's a reason you are here. You'll know soon enough. For now, I need you to go to the control room with Noah and Sean and tell me how everything is sounding. Can you help me with that?" he asks softly, his eyes lingering on my lips. Once again, memories from last night flood my mind, and I try to swallow past the knot forming in my throat. How am I supposed to pretend nothing happened, like I don't crave to relive the sensation of feeling his lips on mine?

"Sure. I can help you with that."

*

God, I wish Alex were here. He would have loved this, since he was the one who used to record all our songs, even though our basic home setup was a far cry from a professional studio. All we had were a couple of cheap mics and an old MacBook Pro loaded with a pirated copy of Pro Tools. Still, those moments were always my favorite. The anticipation of waiting to be able to finally hear the song that had been stuck in our heads for weeks, sometimes months. There is no better feeling than that. No better feeling than creating something out of nothing.

Turning a knob on the mixing board, Sean speaks into the microphone. "River, that sounded amazing, man. I think we've got this one. Do you wanna keep the last version?"

"What do you think, Violet?" The speakers reverberate with River's deep voice. We've been recording for a couple of hours now, and the whole time, I couldn't take my eyes off the glass in front of us. Or, to be precise, off the man behind that glass. Seeing him here, singing and playing so beautifully, so completely in his element, has been the most utterly breathtaking spectacle. There's something about River that not every musician possesses – a special aura, a magnetism that makes everyone hold their breath whenever he starts playing. Because when he plays, he doesn't play with his fingers and sing with his voice; he does it with his whole being. It's electrifying. Intoxicating. And it's simply fucking hot.

Seated at the Steinway grand piano, he takes off his hoodie, revealing a black shirt that exposes the sculpted lines of his muscles. The vein on his neck is perfectly clear as he drinks from his bottle of water, patiently waiting for my answer, and, for some reason, I can't stop thinking that I had this man in my bed yesterday. Well, in *his* bed, but the point remains the same. Hell, what am I doing? I have to stop this. I'm way over my head here, headed toward nothing but heartbreak. The unfortunate reality is that it might be too late. He's everything I've ever imagined in a man I might potentially fall in love with. Except emotionally available, of course. Nothing is ever perfect, right?

I clear my throat. I don't know why he wants my opinion, and I'm not sure if Sean and Noah appreciate me giving input on a recording where thousands of dollars are involved, but I feel like it's something I can honestly answer. "I think the first take was the best."

Both Sean and Noah turn their heads to me before returning their attention to the glass.

"Yeah, I agree. Thanks, Violet." River grins. "The first take it is. Let's move on to the next one, guys!"

Feeling all nine remaining pairs of eyes on me, I plaster a confident smile on my face and pretend that my heart isn't on the verge of failing. When River starts playing again, Noah brings his chair closer to me, his knee almost touching mine. He leans toward me, preventing any prying ears from listening. There is only Sean with us and a couple of assistants in the back of the room. The rest must have vanished into the lounge area. "I've known River for over ten years, did you know that?" Noah says, whispering.

"No, sorry, can't say I did."

He nods, like that's the answer he expected. "River has never brought a girl to a recording before." He pauses for a moment, studying me. "I didn't think he was being serious when he told me about you, but I guess I was wrong."

Told him about me when? I'm not sure how to react to that statement. It doesn't sound like he's saying he believes I shouldn't be here, but more like he's honestly surprised by my presence. *Makes two of us, buddy.*

"Anyway, I just wanted to say it's nice to see him like this for a change."

"Like what?" I ask with a certain level of hesitancy.

"Happy. More relaxed..." Noah shrugs and looks at me again. "I certainly never fucking expected to see him with a girlfriend. Plus"—he looks me up and down, his voice filled with curiosity and a hint of amusement—"you look quite young, but hey, if that's what works for him."

"I'm not... We are not together. I'm his—" I'm not sure what I am. Friend? Student? Mentee? And why do I even care about this guy's opinion? *Probably because he's River's best friend*, my inner voice points out helpfully. Right. The age comment definitely sucked, though. I'm still frowning when I notice that the music sounding from the control room speakers has suddenly stopped.

"This song isn't working. I don't like it." River's voice fills the room again, and I turn back to the glass, considering it the end of my awkward conversation with Noah. I can feel River's gaze on us, and when I look at him, his eyes are, in fact, studying me, but his expression is unreadable.

"What don't you like about it? Everything sounds good here, man," Sean tries.

"I think it needs a second voice," River says after a brief pause.

"Second voice? Like a chorus?" Sean sounds confused by the unexpected suggestion. Given that this is the first time I'm even hearing these new songs, I have no intention of getting involved in the conversation. I believe River's voice alone sounds perfect, but if he feels a second voice could improve it, he probably knows best.

"Violet?" River's voice echoes around the room again. I find it funny that he introduced me as Sabrina but keeps calling me Violet. Surprisingly enough, no one has asked about it, but then again, it looks like no one's really used to questioning him, anyway.

"Yeah?" I answer, hoping that he's not about to ask my opinion on this one.

"Get your ass in here, please."

What? I look at Sean and Noah as if they could help me understand better, but they seem equally startled by River's request. He wants me to join him in the recording room? I know I theoretically offered my help with whatever he needed, but I certainly didn't expect him to put me on the spot like this. Damn it. What if he asks me to assist with something I don't know how to do? Noah, who already seems amused enough by this whole situation, would have a fucking Christmas morning if I messed something up. Sean, on the other hand, is a complete professional. He hadn't even blinked when River introduced me and announced I was to stay in the control room with them. Now, he seems equally confused as the rest of us, but somehow still manages to keep his calm.

"River, man, just tell us what you need, and we'll get it for you, but I don't think getting another singer here today is an option, and this is the last song. Let's just try once more, and we can wrap it up for today."

River shakes his head and abruptly stands up from the piano, taking off his headphones as he strides for the adjoining door. Everyone inside, me included, goes silent. The first one to speak before River reaches us is Noah.

"What the fuck is he doing?" He throws his hands in the air, looking at Sean with a mix of confusion and desperation. I would guess that he's used to working with River, so not much should catch him off guard. That, however, doesn't seem to be the case. The door opens, and River struts inside, chased by his puzzled assistants. I bet Mia is regretting her uncomfortable-looking outfit right now. The line between her eyebrows has deepened significantly as she remains in the doorway, rocking on the balls of her feet, unsure of the sudden turn this session seems to have taken.

"I don't need you to get me another singer, Sean. Violet can do it." River folds his arms across his chest and throws a suggestive look toward me, adopting a try-to-convince-me-otherwise expression.

"What?" The question comes at River from all existing angles, but he remains completely unfazed. I'm too shocked to even speak. He wants *me* to sing with him? On his album? Is he crazy? My heart pounds in my chest, threatening to burst through my ribcage. This album is going to be distributed by Sony Music, for God's sake. This is not some stupid class exercise. I'm nowhere near ready for this. I can feel everyone's eyes on me, and I already hate it. River knows how badly my skin crawls under this kind of attention. Why would he do this to me? I must admit, though, I'm flattered by the trust he clearly has in me. Much more than I have in myself. Still, I can feel beads of cold sweat forming on my forehead.

"River, I don't wanna be disrespectful here, man, but do you really think this is a good idea?" Noah looks at me, and I can see the doubt written all over his face. "I mean, no offense, Sabrina. I'm sure your voice is great and all, but the label might not be happy about this." He looks back at River, whose calm expression seems to have changed now. He's clenching his jaw, and his eyes are narrowed, his gaze angrily traveling from Noah to Sean. I'm sensing a coming storm, and judging from the slumped posture of River's assistants attempting to hide in the back of the room, so do they.

Noah, however, still decides to finish his thought. "I just think that if you really need a second voice here, it would be better to call a *professional* singer, right? Sean, man, feel free to fucking help me out here." Noah runs an anxious hand through his hair and glances at his colleague.

Sean and I open our mouths at the same time. I don't know what he's about to say, whether he would risk going against the wishes of his boss or if he is willing to humor him, leaving his personal opinion aside. There's definitely one opinion here that should be heard, though, and that is mine, which is funny because no one has even thought to ask me how I feel about this. Of course, River has no intention of asking me because he already knows there is no chance I'd ever say yes to this crazy idea. He already figured out that the only way of making me act is by cornering me. I can't decide if I should feel flattered that he took the time to learn to read me so well or if I should be downright angry at him because he is, once again, using it against me. The weight of all eyes on me makes my muscles tense. Yes, he definitely set me up. There's no way I'm ready for this.

River shakes his head, pinching the bridge of his nose before raising his right hand. All the murmuring and whispering immediately stop, and the room becomes completely silent again. It's definitely not the time to admire how fucking beautiful and imposing he is, standing completely straight, rubbing at his soft stubble, his mint-green eyes drifting over the room, and yet here I am, silently drooling over the man.

"Have I ever let you down?" he asks calmly, looking at Noah and Sean. "Have I ever made a decision that would in any way jeopardize the quality of my music?" Keeping his voice soft makes him sound so much more intimidating than if he were screaming at the top of his lungs. Both guys shake their heads, looking at their feet. The rest of the room stays silent. "Then trust my decision. If I invite her to sing on my album, it's because she can fucking sing. And if she says yes, I will be the one winning the lottery here, not her, because it's not every day you hear a voice that grips you by your throat so fucking tight that you can't breathe. So, no, I'm not asking for your permission here. I'm telling you this is happening, and I'm asking for your help to make it fucking happen."

I have never heard River swear so much, but that's not the reason I'm left with my mouth open. It's my throat that feels too tight to breathe right now. Is that what he thinks of me? Could it really be what he feels when I sing? Because I know that feeling all too well. My body reacts in the craziest way whenever I hear *him* play. It's *his* songs that make my heart beat in sync, allowing me to feel every note and word, tapping into the innermost places within me that nothing else and no one else can reach.

"All right, man. No problem. Let's get the show going." Sean is the first of us to find his words. He utters a couple of quick commands, and everyone starts moving. Everyone except me, that is. River holds out his hand to me.

"Ready?" he asks. His expression has shifted completely, and he's grinning widely now.

A knot forms in the pit of my stomach, churning with a mix of excitement and fear. I get up, stepping closer to him, making sure only he can hear me.

"You're going to pay for this one, River Evans."

He bursts out laughing, his eyes shining with amusement. "I don't doubt that for a minute."

# Fourteen

Turns out I wasn't really paying attention before, focusing on what Noah was telling me instead of listening to the song in question. River plays it for me a couple of times, and I'm at a loss for words. How have I not heard this? It's beautiful. And, of course, I think it's already perfect with River's voice only, but I admit it's true that the lyrics and the structure seem to be screaming for a second, feminine voice. Huh, interesting.

"Did you write this?" I ask, still reading the lyric sheet spread in front of me with the name of the song written in bold, 'Cutting the Road to Disappointment,' while unconsciously biting the pencil in my hand, underlining the parts where I'm supposed to be joining him.

River frowns at me from his piano. I'm pretty sure the guys in the control room are listening to us, although they act like they have their hands full with checking the sound of the mic Mia has graciously prepared for me, all the while bending as low as possible to give River a perfect view of her ass in those tight leather pants. And while not even I could *not* look, his eyes stayed on me. I would like to think it has something to do with what happened between us last night. I can feel that something has changed, but I'm also smarter than to think too much of it. He's just being professional. That's what he is the best at, after all.

"I don't know whether to be offended here." He laughs. "Who else do you think wrote it?"

I roll my eyes, keeping myself from smiling like an idiot, but I can't help it; I love the sound of his laugh. "Don't be ridiculous. There are a lot of musicians who have their music written by someone else. In fact, I'll have you know that there's an entire career for songwriting only."

He snorts, laughing more loudly this time. "Good to know. Even better knowing that we won't need their help." He winks, and I shake my head.

"Whatever. I just meant to say that it's... nice." The song is not *nice*, it's fucking perfect, but he doesn't need me inflating his ego any further. Still, he gives me another wink, like he knows what I'm thinking.

"Everything's ready, guys! Sabrina, put on your headphones, please, and try the mic."

I blink rapidly, feeling my heartbeat quicken. Sean is all business, while I couldn't be more nervous. Alex would have loved this. He'd have loved seeing me here. I tighten the grip on the pencil in my hand, almost snapping it in half as an unexpected wave of anger washes over me.

This is so close to what we dreamed of. Except he'll never get to experience it. I walk to the other side of the room, suddenly needing space to breathe so I don't start screaming or break into tears. Grief has the strangest way of showing itself sometimes. There's the most obvious one—sadness and tears—but there is also anger. The kind of anger that grabs you so tight you want to scream until your throat hurts, break everything and anything you can get your hands on, run until you can't catch your breath. That kind of grief is darkness, a dangerous pitch-black hole that can easily swallow you up if you let it. When Alex died, anger was the only emotion I could feel. Anger at him for leaving me behind. Anger at my parents for letting it happen. Anger at myself for not seeing what was right in front of my eyes all that time. And then there is the anger I feel at music. Is that even possible? To feel angry at the mere concept of something? I guess it is. Music got us into the whole mess in the first place, but music was also the only thing that could ever get us out.

*What would you give to wake up every fucking morning excited and looking forward to every minute of the day?* There isn't a moment I don't remember Alex's words, and sometimes I still wonder if we pushed too hard. But he always believed that a life without pursuing one's dreams was merely surviving, not truly living. *Wasn't surviving better than being dead?* A question that I can't ask anymore, but I know all too well what would have been my brother's answer. My heart still races, but I force myself to take a deep breath and calm down.

"Violet, hey, where did you go? Are you okay?" I hadn't even noticed River standing right next to me. I glance at him, unable to hide the pain of everything going on in my head.

"Forget about them. Just sing for me," he says, but it's the whispered words that follow that break through the cloud of emotions that engulfed me, giving me the much-needed confidence instead. "Remember, your voice is my favorite sound." He smiles, and it's the kind of secret smile filled with the unspoken memories of all the moments we've shared together. The moments that I'll always cherish, no matter how badly this ends.

Of course, he may be lying, trying to calm my nerves, but for once, I choose to believe that maybe it's true. There is nothing I'll accomplish by underestimating myself. I'm already here, for God's sake, in this amazing recording studio that must have cost millions of dollars, with one of the best singer-songwriters of our time and a professional crew any aspiring artist could only dream of. A crew that looks quite annoyed at the moment, waiting for me to make up my freaking mind.

Glancing at River, I turn back to the microphone. Here goes nothing. "Sean, I'm ready to try."

✴

The first couple of takes are not great, even though River seems happy enough and, surprisingly, so do Sean and Noah, who are giving us an enthusiastic thumbs-up from behind the glass.

It's only during the third take I've loudly requested, despite the tired faces of River's assistants, that I manage to completely forget about our surroundings. Everything else vanishes, just like the first time we played together, allowing me to finally truly look at the man next to me. His long fingers are stroking the keys with lightness and precision, and his eyes are fixed on me. The muscles under his shirt move effortlessly, making it appear like he's one with the beautiful instrument in front of him. A few unruly strands of hair fall on his forehead as his lips open, and his low, deep voice hits my eardrums, making its way into every cell of my body. This time, I don't even think about it when I join him.

Cutting the Road to Disappointment

One time should have been enough
But you might be the best thing that's ever happened
    to me
No, you wouldn't understand if I told you
I wish it made me feel better, cutting the road to
    disappointment
Please, don't make me lie to you

Fearing to be who you need me to
Giving up all my control, just for you
Hurt subscription on auto-renewal
Is that the only way?

Both: Cut the road to disappointment
Forget how perfectly you fit against me
And then maybe one day we will ask ourselves
Did we miss our chance?

S: I tried to stay away
Close that door
Say "This is not my place."
It's not like you haven't warned me

Both: We might agree that this is for the best
And maybe we should let go
Please, don't make me lie to you
Doesn't matter that I'm already lying to myself

Both: Cut the road to disappointment
Forget how perfectly you fit against me
And then one day we will ask ourselves
Did we miss our chance?
Did we miss our chance? (Only it's too late)
Did we miss our chance? (Only it's too late)

When the last note fades away, both rooms fall into complete silence. The only sound is the soft buzzing from my headphones. I take them off slowly, stealing a glance at River, who is watching me with an intense expression I can't quite decipher. Gone is his playful smile from before. He almost looks like he's in pain, and for the briefest of seconds I nearly forget where we are and think about reaching out to him, smoothing away that tiny crease between his eyebrows.

"Guys, that was... damn, that was really amazing." Sean's voice cuts through the air, which is still laden with tension. River's head snaps up, his focus shifting to the glass, and just like that, I know he's back to his professional self.

"What the fuck, guys? You know what? I don't mind dealing with the record label myself." Noah dashes for the door of the recording room, only to stop right in front of me, leaving me with my mouth open when he pulls me into a tight hug. River chuckles behind us while I somewhat awkwardly pat his manager on his back.

"Glad you liked it." To say I was nervous about the team's reaction would be to play it cool. And while Sean is too polite to criticize my performance to my face, Noah wouldn't have the same problem.

"Liked it? Are you kidding me? This motherfucker was right! Your voice is… man, it's really good. And the tension between the two of you—" He releases me and turns to River, throwing his arm around his friend's shoulder. "I could definitely feel *that*!" His suggestive laugh echoes around the room.

My cheeks flush, and I wish I could hit the guy with something to shut him up. Since that's apparently not an option, I settle for a polite smile and sneak a sideways glance at River. His eyes are slightly narrowed on me, his lips half parted, almost as though he's about to say something, but then he thinks better of it, tearing his gaze off me and heading for the door. "Yeah, man, we got that one. Great job, Violet. You were amazing." His words soften at the end of the sentence, but he makes damn sure he doesn't look at me again, clearly on a mission to get out of the room as fast as possible.

Infuriating. Confusing. Frustrating.

And why does it feel like this was much more than just a song? Why does it feel like these were the words neither of us was able to get out this morning?

*We might agree that this is for the best*
*And maybe we should let go*
*Please, don't make me lie to you*
*Doesn't matter that I'm already lying to myself*

I turn off the mic and grab the loose music sheets, following closely behind both men. The entire team is already gathered in the control room, ready to listen to the final result of today's recording. There is laughter and more words of admiration and praise, obviously mostly for River but also for me, more pats on the back, jokes, and relieved sighs, but I can't pay much attention to any of it. The only thing I can think about is that I'm not letting him bail on me this easily. I don't care if he thinks we're not right for each other, because I know he is wrong. This. Us. It feels right. It's the only thing that has felt right in a long time, and I'm ready to fight for it.

✳

"She's beautiful." Bela's voice sounds defeated, completely lacking the usual happy bell chime sound I'm so used to by now. "We're talking blonde-blue-eyes-tall-and-skinny beautiful." She huffs. "*Mierda*! Just… *mierda*!"

Bela swearing in Spanish is never a good sign, and not being able to comfort her with a hug makes me feel helpless.

We've just gotten back from today's recording session. River has been strangely quiet, and when we walked in the door, he disappeared into his room like there was a fire burning at his feet. He only mentioned a dinner tonight and told me to be ready. Given more than enough time to do so, I decided to give a quick call to Bela and get her up to date with everything going on. Well… almost everything. I told her about River asking me to sing on his album, but I may have conveniently left out what happened between us last night. It's not something I feel comfortable explaining over the phone, or in general, I guess. In fact, if anyone could explain it to *me*, I'd definitely appreciate it.

"I'm sorry." It's the only thing I can think of saying, even though I know it won't make my friend feel any better. "You know you could always tell her what happened, right?" I suggest, putting the phone on speaker so I can apply some makeup while giving Bela my full moral support.

"Yeah, sure, but… Would *you* do that, mi amor?"

I think about her question for a moment. It's a tricky situation, blurring the line between right and wrong. Bela shouldn't have simply assumed Anders left his girlfriend after getting involved with her, but I know that if she had known the truth, she would have never pursued the relationship. She isn't one to share or to accept second place, but she's also not one to purposely hurt another person. Anders, on the other hand, apparently had no issue playing a double game. Would the *actual* girlfriend even believe Bela if she told her?

"I don't know. Fuck. I guess not," I admit reluctantly. "It's probably better if you just stay away from him. Because you know what? He isn't worth a minute more of your attention, anyway. And I'm sure his girlfriend will discover it, too, sooner or later." It's a terrible pep talk, I'm well aware. I suck at this. My past relationships have been quite short-lived, and when they ended, let's just say I didn't lose much sleep over it. I guess I haven't yet found that epic love people rave about—that one person who completely messes with your head.

My thoughts automatically travel to the man in the other room, who's certainly driving me crazy enough with his mood swings. Could it be that he is *that* person for me? No, absolutely not. Yes, I want to fight for him to give us a chance, but just because… because… a surprisingly long list of very clear reasons floods my mind. He has a way of making me laugh, gives me the confidence to believe I can do anything, constantly pushes me to be better, makes me feel safe… *Okay, stop.* I cringe at myself in the mirror and shake my head like it can actually make these dangerous thoughts go away. They don't. I suspect they have already made themselves too much at home.

"Sabrina? Are you still there?" Bela's voice brings me back to reality.

"Sorry. I'm listening," I assure her, a bit too quickly. "I'm just getting ready for tonight."

"Right, tonight…" Her voice trails off before she continues, "I was asking how things are between you and a certain very hot, very famous musician."

I let out a laugh, glad she's making jokes again. "Yeah, they're good. He's being really nice, very… professional." As soon as I add the last part, I roll my eyes at myself, almost stabbing one of them with the black eyeliner in my hand.

"Of course. Professional." Bela chuckles, confirming that she isn't easily fooled. She doesn't push it, though, and I love her even more for it. "I'm glad you're having a good time, mi amor. Just remember to be careful, all right?" she says softly before saying goodbye and hanging up.

Motionless, I gaze at myself in the mirror for an extra couple of minutes, as though my reflection could give me some kind of answer. It never crossed my mind that River might have feelings for someone. I feel my heart leap. Yes, I'm not blind or stupid, and I've seen pictures of him with other women. He's handsome, an extraordinary musician, and enjoys a life of fame and luxury. It's not like he struggles for attention, but what if Bela has a point? What if the reason he has been trying to keep me at arm's length is because he's already taken? He said he doesn't do relationships, but there is a woman he's been seen with repeatedly. One I have already met and could never compete with. What if she's the one who already owns his heart?

I finish getting ready, not quite able to shake off the intrusive thoughts messing with my head. We've never brought up the night at the jazz club when we both showed up in the company of someone else. Yes, I was there with Connor, but I made sure to remind him repeatedly that it wasn't a date, and I didn't even let him kiss me good night. Probably because I could still see River's eyes burning holes into me when I suggested he should go back to his girlfriend and left him standing at the bar. *Are you jealous, Violet?* That was the only thing he said.

I frown again, my mood getting darker as I slip into a black miniskirt and a tight white sweater, fixing my hair into a high ponytail. This will have to do. River hasn't told me where exactly we're going for dinner, but he said it was casual rather than elegant, which is fine by me. Stepping out of the bathroom, I zip up my leather knee-high boots, ready to face the cold of New York's winter night. What I'm not so ready to face is River.

When I get downstairs, he is standing by the window. His back is turned to me, and his gaze is focused on the thousands of tiny flickering lights, his thoughts lost somewhere in the distance. For a moment, I quietly stand behind him, taking the opportunity to observe him. He stands tall, his head slightly tilted, hands in his jeans pockets, wearing a fitted, dark blue T-shirt that showcases the perfection of his defined muscles. His thick dark hair is messy, as if he recently ran his hand through it, but somehow he still looks flawless, almost unreal. He breathes out, tensing a little, and I know he is aware of my presence. Turning slowly, he silently examines me. "You look beautiful," he finally says. His soft, almost whisper-like voice contrasts with his intense gaze, sending shivers down my spine.

I make an effort to curve my lips into a light, carefree smile. "Thank you." Bela's words from earlier keep replaying in my head, causing me to question everything. To question *us*. What are we doing? Why am I here? River never needed an assistant, and even if he wanted to have me sing on his album, he could have just asked me, simply giving me the address of the studio, not driving me to New York, having me stay at his apartment, taking me out for dinners... *kissing me, holding me in his arms after making me come.* Because isn't this what couples do? This is all part of what River is so sure of not wanting for himself.

"Violet? Is everything okay?" he asks, almost as if he can see into my head, but then again, he has always been so strangely attuned to me that his question doesn't even surprise me.

"Sure, all good. Should we go?" I swallow, pushing the thoughts out of my mind. He stares at me for a moment but then nods, motioning toward the door. "Right. Let's do it."

# Fifteen

"This doesn't look like a restaurant."

River chuckles, overlooking my skepticism as he places his hand on the small of my back, directing me toward what looks like a back entrance to somewhere strange, perhaps a garage or a storage room. Definitely not what I imagined, but I'm not complaining as long as they serve food. I would take a simple place over a luxury restaurant anytime. There is no sign on the outside of the building, and even though we are in Midtown Manhattan, the street we are on looks shady, to say the least.

"Do you trust me, Violet?" he murmurs in my ear while opening the heavy black door in front of us. His words, or maybe it's his lips hovering over the shell of my ear, cause my stomach to flutter. Do I trust him? Yes. The answer is simple. He's earned my trust repeatedly. And that's more than can be said about most people in my life. Before I can answer, we step into a red curtain, and when River shoves the velvet material aside, I'm left with my mouth hanging open.

"What is this place?" I breathe slowly, trying to take it all in. It looks like I was wrong, or at least partially. This *is* a restaurant, but far from a traditional one. The medium-sized room allows for a maximum of around twenty tables. Simple as it may be, the decoration is both beautiful and dark. The walls are painted black, and so is the ceiling. Soft lighting radiates from wall lamps strategically placed to illuminate every table. There must be dozens of mirrors on the walls, each one unique and framed in gold. It's the most bizarre thing I've ever seen. Not the mirrors themselves but the reflection of the people in them, with their eyes blindfolded by a piece of black cloth tied around their heads. "I thought you may like to try something different for your first time in New York." He flashes me one of his very rare grins.

*Something different.* I cast another glance around. "This isn't something…"

River cocks his head to the side, the look in his eyes equally amused and intrigued. "Something what?"

"Something… kinky?" My embarrassment is at its highest point, but I still manage to squeeze the words out while keeping my voice as quiet as possible.

River's eyes widen for a moment, and then he snorts out a laugh, shaking his head. "You're something else, Violet."

I frown, still contemplating his reaction when he leans closer to me. "It's nothing kinky. Not because I wouldn't like that with you, but because I'm a selfish man when it comes to you. I don't want to share with anyone," he whispers, leaving the words to linger in the air between us. My cheeks grow warm. Luckily, the host arrives, and

I don't have time to think about the implications of his confession.

"I'm sorry for keeping you waiting, Mr. Evans. Your table is ready." A tall, dark-haired waiter dressed in an elegant suit materializes in front of us, two pieces of black cloth hanging in his hand. River nods, and the next thing I know, we're being led to the only empty table across the room, and our eyes are being covered by soft pieces of fabric. Nothing but pure darkness. I admit I thought for a moment or two that I might be able to cheat my way out of this. Perhaps the waiter would leave the cloth a bit looser, or the material was see-through. Maybe the light above our table could help me see something, but no. I can't see a single thing.

"This is… wow." I let out a nervous laugh when I finally believe we are alone, still half whispering, just in case.

River chuckles, his laugh vibrating through me with much more intensity than usual. There is definitely something to be said about the blindfolds, but the verdict is still pending. "You don't have to whisper," he says. "This place is soundproofed; the sound doesn't travel from one table to the other. The owner is a musician, a producer, actually."

Huh, all right, that explains some of it. "Is that how you know this place? Have you been here before?" I ask, and there's a small part somewhere in me that's afraid of the answer. *Have you ever been here with someone else?*

"Yeah, he's been inviting me forever, but I've never been here, so I gave him a call the other day… when you agreed to come to New York with me." Adding that last part almost shyly, he rushes to explain, "Almost no one knows about this place, but it's always packed, and there's an impossible waiting list if you don't know the right people."

*He prepared this. He thought of me. He chose to take me.* My inner voice is shouting with joy, but I don't want to hold on to that treacherous feeling for too long. *Calm the fuck down, it's just a dinner.* "So I understand this is like a secret place for a select crowd, but why the blindfolds?" I ask, still not sure I'm correctly grasping the whole concept of this peculiar restaurant.

"Well, for one, there's the fact that no one recognizes you, which gives you a little privacy," he says, making me realize I haven't even thought of that. No matter where he goes, River's always bombarded with requests for pictures and autographs. Does it ever get tiring? Though he may come across as distant, he's always kind to his fans. I've seen it continuously. One of my favorite things about him is his humility and gratitude for everything he has, not taking his fame and success for granted. Oh, wait a minute… fuck. Do I actually have a my-favorite-things-about-River-Evans list? That can't be good. Fortunately, he continues with his explanation, and I manage to focus back on his voice. Another favorite thing of mine. Nope, not going there.

"And then there is the actual idea of dining in the dark; the concept being that if you remove one sense, which is vision in this case, the rest of your senses automatically intensify." I feel him leaning a little closer. "Your taste, smell, and touch will heighten, amplifying your pleasure while eating, and you will rely on hearing as your only means of sensing what's happening around you. You see?

Nothing kinky going on here." His breath tickles my lips, my mind picturing his mischievous smile.

"Hmm, interesting."

"Although…" He suddenly pauses.

"Although what?" I ask a little too eagerly. He doesn't answer right away. Instead, I hear him uttering a quiet "thank you," and it's only then I feel the presence of someone else hovering over our table. It's a strange sensation. I try to stay as still as I can, making sure I don't tip over whatever is being put in front of us.

"This is our finest wine, Mr. Evans. Mr. Williams called personally to ensure we serve it for you and your lovely companion tonight." The words circle around us, along with the sound of liquid being poured into a glass.

"And right in front of you is your starter. Please use the smaller fork on your left." As we listen to additional instructions, my nose is hit with a wave of incredible scents that makes my taste buds tingle with anticipation. Huh, I'm starting to warm up to this whole experience thing. That's not to say it doesn't feel a bit overwhelming. After a few nervous bounces in my chair, I realize that sudden movements may not be the best idea.

"Try your wine, Violet." River directs me softly as soon as we are alone again. How is it possible that even blindfolded, he can still sense my distress?

Following his instructions, I carefully grasp the wineglass stem, hesitating before taking a sip. I've never been one to know how to taste wine. I know nothing about it, so smelling it and moving it around in my glass would be quite pointless, but this is different. The smell is the first thing I notice. While a wine expert would be able to make a much more accurate list of ingredients, the ones I'm quite sure of are white peach and strawberry, and since I've already figured out that our starter is made of seafood, I know it's a white wine before even tasting it. Holding it briefly in my mouth, I then swallow it, releasing a satisfied moan. "It's perfect." River hums in agreement, sounding like he's also sipping from his glass. I'm about to start a similar testing process with my food when I remember... "Wait a moment," I say, putting my glass down. "You were telling me something before." Right before we were interrupted by our waiter, I might add, but instead, I surprise myself by giving him a clearer hint at what I'm talking about. "Something related to the slight kinkiness of this place," I say with a quiet laugh.

River doesn't laugh. "Hmmm. I think I would much rather show you." I almost jump out of my skin when I feel his fingers slightly brushing along my arm, raising goose bumps on my skin. "The thing about not being able to see is that it works in other *fields* just as well." He lets out a soft chuckle this time, but his voice remains deep and husky. I don't move. My body feels like it's been paralyzed. River's fingers travel along my right arm, all the way up to my collarbone and neck. By the time he reaches my lips, I'm not breathing, and my heart is desperately drumming in my ears.

"It's *everything* that feels more intense," he whispers, brushing his index finger over my lower lip. My lips part of their own accord, and the need to take his finger into my mouth is so strong that I'm taken aback by the sensation. Damn it. Where's this coming from? "Tell me one thing, Violet," he continues, and I can tell by how breathy his voice has become that I'm not the only one affected by this little game. Suddenly, his touch is gone, and I instantly sense its absence, using the opportunity to slowly breathe out. The air gets stuck in the middle of my lungs when I feel his fingers again, but this time on my knee, slowly moving up to the hemline of my skirt. He stops there, drawing small circles on my leg, and even though I'm wearing tights, the thin material does nothing to protect my skin from the burning sensation of his touch.

"If I were to check," he murmurs, trailing his fingers a little closer to the inside of my thigh, "just how wet you are… what do you think I would find? Would I find that you understand perfectly what I'm talking about, or would I find that you need me to explain it to you some more?"

Fuck. I impulsively push my legs together and hear the deep groan that leaves his throat when I trap his hand between my legs. As much as I'm aching for his touch, I don't think I could bear it right now. If he really were to check, what he would learn is that I certainly don't need a further explanation. And if he were to continue for a couple of minutes longer, I would come undone right here in the middle of the fucking restaurant. How is that possible, for God's sake? How is it fair? He's not even properly touching me.

*Get a grip on yourself, Sabrina*, I order myself with little to no conviction. Do you want him to see what he does to you?

"Relax, Violet," he says. "I'm not gonna do it. Not right now." He adds the last words in a whisper, and it sounds like a promise. I slowly loosen the pressure of my thighs, slightly mortified to realize that I hadn't let him go, and he hadn't tried to free himself either. He chuckles, but it sounds different this time, almost painful. "You are killing me, Sabrina." He uses my real name, leaving me surprised once more. "Come on, let's eat, because otherwise, I don't think I'm gonna be able to fucking stop myself."

We start eating, and it's only after a little while, when I feel I can trust myself to speak again, that I break the silence. "Thank you for today," I say. It's not only today I should be thanking him for. I could say at least a dozen thank-yous when it comes to this man. *Thank you for helping me to find my voice. Thank you for teaching me to trust in myself. Thank you for showing me I can still enjoy music. Thank you for worrying about me. Thank you for taking me to New York for the first time. Thank you for making me feel again.* "For inviting me to record with you" is the only one I say aloud.

"You have nothing to thank me for, Violet. Having you on my album is a win for me, trust me," he says, similar to what he said in the studio. I bite back a smile, shaking my head even though he can't see me.

"I'm not going to fight you on this one, but you and I both know that you could have anyone singing on your album. Anyway, tell me more about your Christmas tour." It's not something we've discussed much, but I've been hearing a lot about his upcoming tour from pretty much everywhere—the press, social media, my teachers, and classmates. Rodrigo has even bought a ticket for River's New York concert as he will be spending Christmas there. I don't want to think about the festivities themselves, nor about the fact that River only has one month before he'll be leaving campus, but I do want to know more about his tour, know more about him.

"My Christmas tour," he repeats, and I feel our waiter approaching with more food, taking care of our empty plates. This time, River doesn't seem to mind that we're not alone. "It starts in a month, and it's only the US. I'll be going to Europe in the summer."

"That must be amazing, all that traveling, I mean." Having seen the program, I know the tour kicks off in Boston—sadly enough, the only concert I'll be able to attend—and then continues across the whole country, all the way to Los Angeles, San Francisco, and Seattle for the final shows.

"It is, but all that time on the road can be exhausting sometimes," he admits.

"Yeah, I get that." I definitely do, but I don't tell River that I would gladly trade hours of sleep and whatever else for the experience. That was our dream, Alex's and mine. Before everything fell apart, we used to talk for hours about renting a car and traveling along the coast, visiting all the cities we'd heard about. We had it all planned out. Coming to BMC, becoming professional musicians, traveling around the world, living the life we wanted. Reminding myself I can't go there, I take a deep breath and shift my attention back to the food. It kills me knowing that this, whatever it is, has a clear expiration date. I have no idea what will happen once we leave New York. Do we go back to being friends? Were we ever? A professor and a student? Or do we continue like this, somewhere in between: two lovers too afraid to love, too haunted by their pasts, until River leaves campus and goes on his tour, forgetting all about me?

"So you're not going back to Prague for Christmas?"

he asks quietly, his question catching me off guard. He asked me that the day after we finished busking at the metro station during our awkward ride back to campus. I mentioned my plan to take extra courses over Christmas, but I didn't think he would remember.

"No, I'll be staying in Boston."

"Alone? During Christmas? Why?"

"This food is really good, by the way. What is it? Some kind of pasta?" I ask, hoping my attempt at steering the conversation somewhere else is not too blatant.

"Violet," he murmurs.

"Yeah?" I shovel the food down my throat, using it as an excuse to keep my answers short.

"Don't do that with me." Busted.

"Do what?" I still try, keeping my voice emotionless, thankful he can't see into my eyes.

"Trying to act like you're okay when you're not," he points out, his voice calm and maybe a little frustrated. Who can blame him?

The thing is… he has no business worrying about me, same as I have no business worrying about him and missing him already. So why is it I still feel like I owe him an answer? He doesn't have a family to spend the holidays with. His tour is likely a welcome distraction for him, and I don't know how to explain that I'd rather be anywhere but home for Christmas. Home. Even the word sounds strange. Because Prague doesn't feel like home to me anymore. "Things are not good at home. Plus, going back to Prague costs a lot of money that I don't really have right now," I say, hoping he will leave it at that. I feel bad about throwing in the money argument. It's only part of the truth, because my parents did offer to pay for my ticket, but of course, only as a one-way journey, knowing perfectly well I would never go for that option.

There's a moment of silence, interrupted only by the clatter of our forks. I'm almost convinced River is going to let it go until his question hits the exact painful spot that I've been trying to avoid. "Is it because of your brother that things are not good at home?" he asks softly.

Putting down my fork and carefully pushing away the plate, I let out the breath I didn't realize I was holding. River knows only bits and pieces of my story. He knows that Alex died and that my relationship with my parents is broken. He knows they didn't support our dream, and I've been pretty much on my own since then, but there are still too many missing pieces in this puzzle. Pieces that I've chosen to hide. And I don't know if it's the absolute darkness or River's soothing voice, but for the first time since everything happened, I feel like there is no point in hiding them anymore.

"Have you ever done something you weren't proud of to get where you are?" I ask as I fiddle with the loose strip of cloth that's wrapped around my head.

River takes a moment to answer. "Does breaking into practice rooms after hours count?"

I chuckle. "I don't think it does."

Just thinking about telling him everything makes my stomach twist. How will he react when he learns the extent to which my brother went to support our dream? Even though I didn't know what was happening back then, and I never agreed to it, I was still equally responsible. Because I should have known. I should have stopped Alex. And, more importantly, we should have never made that damn deal.

"Do you remember I told you about the deal Alex and I made?"

"The one where you would find a way to pursue your dream if your parents refused to help you?" he asks, his voice soft. The fact that he remembers that conversation so well warms something inside me.

"Yeah." I clear my throat. "Well, Alex found it, or so he thought."

River, too, has stopped eating now, and if it weren't for his breathing, I wouldn't be able to tell he's still there. Letting air into my lungs, I gather the courage to continue. "When our parents told us they wouldn't help, I applied for a music education career in Prague." My mind fills with memories of Alex's eyes brimming with disappointment when I told him. *So you will just do what they want you to do? Is that it? You give up? I thought you wanted to be a musician, not a goddamn teacher.* "It wasn't the career I wanted, and I was still hoping we could find a way to attend BMC, but I didn't want to lose an entire year. I guess it also had a lot to do with my parents pressuring me every day. Especially Mom. She was obsessed with me becoming a teacher." I cringe, my nose pressing against the cloth over my eyes, as I remember her endless reminders about what a respectable career it was.

"Did you like teaching?" River asks, and I can't help but smile at his question.

"Not everybody can be such a wonderful teacher as you are," I say, enjoying his soft laugh. "It wasn't that I didn't like teaching, but I wanted to play and work on our music." That possibility was simply nonexistent in a music education career. The focus wasn't on becoming an artist. "I used to give music lessons to our neighbors' kids, and I liked it, but it just didn't feel—"

"Fulfilling enough?" he offers.

"Yeah, something like that." I nod to myself. "I thought it would help me save money, so I started taking more teaching jobs while studying, but turns out teaching is not the most lucrative job. My savings were still ridiculously low, even months later." A quiet laugh tinged with self-deprecation leaves me just as his hand covers mine on the table. I had stopped fidgeting with my cloth only to occupy my hand with a dessert spoon. River's gentle touch soothes me, and I release my grip on the silverware, allowing it to slip from my hand.

"So Alex didn't start college with you?" he asks.

"Oh no. Alex absolutely refused to start a career he didn't want to pursue," I say, recalling my brother's exact words: *I'm so fucking tired of being who they want me to be. Aren't you?* "He took a year off and started working at this gaming place. It was an arcade bar, a really cool one, but the money wasn't much. Plus, since he wasn't studying anymore, Dad told him he needed to pay rent if he wanted to stay at the house." It was foolish to think we would have ever been able to save enough money to cover one entire tuition and living expenses. We were so damn naïve.

"I knew Alex wasn't happy," I whisper, feeling River's thumb slowly caressing my open palm. "Neither of us was, but we didn't know what to do. We stopped playing. No more gigs at bars and metro stations, and no more writing our songs, either. Between school and work, I didn't have time for much else, and Alex slowly lost interest." Using my free hand, I reach for my glass of water and relish the sensation of the chilled liquid flowing down my throat, calming my nerves.

"It wasn't until after Christmas that Alex started to act strangely."

"Strangely how?" River's thumb is now tracing small circles from the base of my palm to the tips of my fingers, making it much easier to let my mind go back to those dark memories.

"He was coming home late every night," I say. "I knew that his shift typically ended around ten in the evening, but sometimes he wouldn't return home until early in the morning, and sometimes he would even stay out until the following day."

"Did you ask him about it?"

A sharp pain rushes through me. Of course I did, but I should have done much more. I shouldn't have let him convince me so easily that everything was all right. It was what I wanted to believe at the time. So I did. "I asked him, but he said nothing was going on. And I believed him, at least until I found the money."

"Money?" I can hear the surprise in River's voice. I suppose it's too late to change my mind about telling him. The dread of his judgment makes my throat tighten, and I swallow before I can continue.

"I was looking for some spare guitar strings one day. Alex wasn't home, and I knew he used to keep an extra pack in his guitar case," I say, remembering my shock when I retrieved the case from under his bed and reached into the little pouch inside it. There were no strings. "I found this envelope. It was full of money. Around five thousand dollars' worth of crowns. I knew Alex couldn't have made that amount of money at the arcade bar." It was just a regular gaming bar, not a goddamn casino. That's when I knew. But it was already too late.

"Where did it come from?" River asks, his thumb stopping its calming movements. The loss of his touch causes my heart to race, but there is no turning back now.

"Selling drugs," I whisper. "That's what the police told us when they came for Alex a couple of days later."

"How did he get himself into drugs?" There's no judgment in River's voice when he asks, only a hint of sadness.

I let out a sigh and attempt to pull my hand away, but he stops me, intertwining his fingers with mine instead. Calmness sets in almost instantly.

"Apparently it was a client from the arcade bar who approached him with an opportunity to earn some fast cash," I continue. "The police had been after him for a while, and they only arrested Alex to help them find him. They released him the following day, hoping he would lead them to him."

"And did he?" River asks, sounding like he's holding his breath.

"Ultimately, he did," I say. "But a lot of things could have gone differently if Dad hadn't kicked him out of the house after learning about his activities." The memory of that day is still painfully fresh in my mind, with Mom crying just as hard as I was, yet refusing to utter a single word to change Dad's mind.

Suddenly, I sense the waiter's presence as he lingers

over our table, exchanging our empty dishes for what's most likely our dessert. I pause for a moment, knowing this is as far as I can go without breaking down, but not before finally telling River the reason I can't go back home. "What Dad did was a death sentence."

# Sixteen

It's likely a chocolate mousse with little slices of orange and papaya on top, but I think we're both too distracted to fully appreciate the incredible burst of flavors on our tongues. In fact, I'm not even sure River's eating. In the past hour and a half, I've trained my ears to detect the sound of silverware hitting against the plates, but it's only my spoon filling the silence.

River's been patiently listening to me without interruption, and while I thought I could bring myself to tell him the whole story, I stopped as soon as the dark mood settled over our table like a heavy fog, making my stomach sink.

"I'm sorry," I whisper into the dark. "I didn't mean to ruin the night. This dinner… it's been amazing," I say. And it's true. I had a great time, and even though going through the memories of Alex was painful, I felt like I could finally breathe and think about that day without descending into a panic attack. And I know it's because of him. River brings a sense of calm and peace to the chaos in my life.

"You didn't ruin anything, Violet," he says softly, "but I think it's time to go home."

I sigh, nodding, even though he can't see me. As much as the word 'home' quickens my heartbeat, I know that all this is just a bubble we've hidden ourselves in. And as all bubbles do, this one, too, will burst soon enough. Hell, I've probably just sped up the process. Maybe this is for the best in the end.

"Sure," I answer. "I'm sorry I wasn't the best company tonight. You were supposed to be celebrating your album, and I… fuck, sorry. You should have just gone out with the guys."

"Violet." I feel River's hand on mine. His voice is soothing, his touch light and gentle. "I wanna go home because I really need to feel you in my arms right now," he says slowly, taking my hand in his and entwining his long fingers with mine. "And I want to look at you while I do that. Is that okay with you?"

My heart pounds against my rib cage with such force that I'm sure he must be able to hear it. "I would like that," I whisper, astonished by his words. Why does he always manage to say the right thing? And how much easier would it be if he didn't?

*

We hand in our blindfolds and leave the restaurant, mostly in silence. I suddenly feel exposed. Saying certain things is easier when surrounded by blissful darkness. It all changes when there's a set of eyes carefully following you, which is what River's been doing since we stepped into the freezing New York night. The bitter cold makes it difficult to breathe, but the burning sensation in my lungs is oddly comforting, making me feel alive.

"You said you had never been to New York before?" River breaks the silence that hangs between us.

I shake my head. "It's always been our dream to come here. We wanted to travel all across the States." I chuckle. "Not that we had the money to actually do that, but still… New York was at the top of our list. Especially because of the M&M's store." I point across the square at the famous M&M's empire, my eyes still adjusting to the light coming out of the streetlamps and endless billboards. It's a shame it's closed at this hour.

"Really? That was your reason for coming to New York?" River grins, curving his lips into one of those rare smiles I don't see enough on him. I save it to my memory among the dozens of other things I've been placing in the things-that-make-me-happy box.

Laughing, I shrug. "I know, it's stupid. We saw it on TV one day—on one of those travel programs—and we became obsessed with it. Have you been there? It's insane. Or so it looks on the screen." I make a mental note to visit the store tomorrow. While there are likely more interesting things to see in New York, they'll have to wait.

"Yeah, I've been inside a couple of times. Anyway, I was thinking that maybe tomorrow I could show you around the city." He seems almost nervous, picking at his gloves and glancing at me. "I'm not a New Yorker, but this place is my second home, so I know it pretty well." He gives me another hesitant glance, breathing out a puff of air. The winter hat is covering his unruly hair, and his red nose looks adorable. In the night, his mint-green eyes take on a darker shade, resembling the color of forest green, framed by his long, enviable eyelashes. God, he is beautiful. Probably too beautiful for his own good. Fortunately, the darkness combined with the winter hat and the fact that it's too fucking cold to even bother to look at other people serve as a perfect disguise, and I have him for myself. For how long, though?

"I thought you were busy tomorrow." While I'd love nothing more than to explore the city with River, I recall him mentioning an interview he had before we head home on Monday, which is why I assumed I'd do some touristy stuff by myself. I've already made a note of the most important things I want to see, knowing that I'll have to cut them down since there is no way to fit all of them into just one day. Hopefully, this isn't my last time in New York. I'll manage to come back someday.

"Only in the morning," he says. "It's just a magazine interview, so it shouldn't take more than a couple of hours. Since it's nearby, maybe you can explore the area, and we can meet up later?"

"Sure." I nod. "If you don't have anything more important to do tomorrow, I mean. I don't want you to feel like you have to babysit me or something."

His laughter mixes with the incessant New York noise.

"Babysit you?" He raises his eyebrow playfully. "You are pretty young, but I don't think you need much babysitting." Even after I jab my elbow into his side, he's still laughing.

"Stop it with the 'you are too young' crap, would you?" I scoff.

He shakes his head, grinning at me. "Well, you're only twenty-one, after all."

"Twenty-two," I correct him automatically.

"Twenty-two," he repeats. "Wait. When did that happen?" A look of surprise flashes across his face as his brows knit together.

"Umm…" I glance down at the tips of my boots.

"Violet?" he asks again. "You said you were twenty-one at the Halloween party."

I sigh, looking at him. "Why does it matter if I'm twenty-one or twenty-two? Does it change anything for you?" I challenge. This conversation is heading dangerously close to something I've been trying to forget about the entire week.

He frowns. "No, it doesn't," he says quietly.

Just as I'm about to apologize for snapping at him, he abruptly halts his steps.

"Jesus Christ, River! I swear… What now?" I turn to see him just standing there in the middle of Times Square, his eyes narrowing at me.

"Show me your driver's license," he demands.

"What?" Has he suddenly gone crazy? "I don't have my driver's license on me. Just forget about it and walk, please. I'm fucking freezing," I try, but he doesn't budge.

"Your student ID will do." He stretches out his hand to me, his eyebrows shooting up. Apparently, he knows that while most students' IDs don't show the date of birth, the international students at BMC have an ID that includes a lot more information than necessary. Damn it. Why is he suddenly so freaking difficult?

We both pause, staring at each other. I'm freezing,

and I bet he isn't feeling much warmer. As something cold brushes against my cheek, I realize it's starting to snow. River blinks a few times, his sullen expression remaining as little snowflakes cover his long eyelashes. He's beautiful but stubborn as a mule.

Reluctantly, I dip my hand into the pocket of my jacket and pull out my student ID. Closing the gap between us, I hand it to him, turning it upside down. He takes it from me, flipping it without a word, his eyes quickly finding the desired information. Snowflakes are swirling around as people quicken their steps, likely heading home to find warmth. I dare to look up at him, only to find him still staring at the piece of plastic in his hand. "Your birthday is tomorrow," he murmurs softly. "Why didn't you say something?" There's confusion and disappointment on his face, almost as if it were his birthday I was trying to forget about. But no, I've saved that date in my head, thanks to Wikipedia. It's still more than four months ahead. I wonder if he'll even be in Boston then.

"I don't celebrate it," I say, hoping we can leave it at that.

"You don't celebrate it," he repeats, and I can see the wheels turning in his head. "Why?"

I sigh. "Because. I just don't, okay?" I take my ID from him. "Can we go home now? We're going to catch cold here, and you have an interview in the morning," I say softly, and, to my absolute relief, he nods. We resume our walk in silence until he looks at me, his eyes widening. "Fuck. I'm so sorry, Violet. I'm such an idiot!" I shake my head. "It's Alex's birthday, too," he whispers, more to himself than to me.

"It is. Don't worry about it. I just don't want to celebrate it, okay?"

He wraps his arm around me, drawing me so near I can feel the warmth of his body. "No celebrating. Got it."

*

The loud ringing echoing through the room is like an explosion. I groan, pulling myself up and rubbing my eyes. The first thing I notice is that the spot next to me is empty. When did he get up?

Of course I never made it to my bed yesterday. Just as he promised, River took me into his arms as soon as we got back from our dinner and wouldn't let go of me for the entire night. Nothing happened between us, though, and I would never admit this out loud, but I was dying for him to touch me. Feeling him so close and warm, his intoxicating smell, his long, gentle fingers drawing delicate circles on my bare arms and thighs, his beautiful voice quietly humming to me... all of that left me more torn and unsettled, unable to drift off to sleep. At some point, though, I must have given in to my exhaustion.

I'm finally able to locate the source of the annoying noise. My phone is in the pocket of my jacket, where it's been for the past twenty-four hours. I'd hoped that my parents would get tired of calling, pretending they want to celebrate my birthday any more than I do. But when I look at the screen, it's not my mom's picture that I see but Bela's. Without hesitation, I press the green icon and put my friend on speaker while I get out of bed and head to my room, determined to get dressed and find River.

He wouldn't have left for his interview without saying goodbye to me, would he?

"Hey! What's up?" I ask. "Isn't it a little early for social calls?" Bela isn't a morning person, especially on Sundays, so there must be a reason for her early call.

"*Cumpleaaaaños feliz, cumpleaños feeeeliz, te deseamos tooodos—*" The speakers of my phone almost burst under the unexpectedly loud interpretation of what I only imagine must be the Spanish version of 'Happy Birthday' presented by my friends. And what's Rodrigo doing there? Are they both at Blue Cats? I haven't told anybody about my birthday, not even Bela, and certainly not Rodrigo, so this surprise catches me off guard, my eyes immediately stinging with tears. God, I miss Alex. I miss him so much that any reminder of the fact that today is the day we should be celebrating together hurts too fucking much.

"Umm, that is… thank you, guys."

"Are you okay, mi amor? Are you crying?" Bela's high-pitched voice cuts through the phone.

"Why would she be crying?" Rodrigo asks, confused.

I take a deep breath. "What? Of course not. I just woke up, and this was quite a surprise. A really *great* surprise! Thank you, guys." I'm a terrible friend and an even worse liar. Luckily, they don't seem to notice.

"Of course it was a surprise," Bela says, her voice sounding slightly annoyed. "And you know why it was a surprise? Because you didn't tell us about your birthday. So if it wasn't for Rodrigo here, who hired you, and therefore has access to all your secrets—"

"Sorry, Sabrina!" Rodrigo's voice, muffled by the noise

of a working coffee machine, comes from somewhere in the background.

"I'm sorry, guys," I mutter. "I don't really celebrate my birthday, but I appreciate this. I do."

"You don't celebrate your birthday? Are you serious?" Bela squeals. "Yeah, that's not happening. We're celebrating when you come back. And you, mi amor, are giving me all the details—"

"Okay." I know what she's about to say, and I don't feel like diving into that conversation with her again right now. Not when there's nothing new I can tell her. I still don't know how River feels about me. How can he say he doesn't want a relationship yet hold me tightly all night as if he was afraid I might suddenly disappear?

Bela continues for another five minutes, telling me about our roommate, who apparently didn't spend the night in her bed—good for her—and then makes me promise I'll let her take me for pizza tomorrow after class. And since saying no to free pizza is not something I would ever do, I agree, and it's only then I'm finally released.

I wash my face, getting rid of any remaining tears and applying light makeup—River won't catch me crying today. Since I showered last night, I simply pull my hair back into a ponytail and finish getting dressed, finally heading downstairs, wearing my favorite ripped jeans and a white cotton sweater hanging off one shoulder. By now, I'm pretty sure that River must have already left, but it's the delicious smell that hits my nose when I reach the open kitchen-living room space that tells me I'm wrong. Pancakes? My stomach growls. Slipping my phone into the pocket of my jeans, I glance around, my eyes widening at the sight of the kitchen island covered with what looks like a full continental breakfast for at least ten people. What on earth? Is this what he's been up to?

I can feel his presence behind me and smell the woody ginger aroma of his shower gel I've been secretly stealing from him these days, even though I brought my own vanilla one. If he's noticed, he hasn't said anything.

"Good morning," he whispers.

I slowly turn to face him, my mouth falling open once more. Damn. He's already dressed for his interview, wearing black dress pants combined with a navy blue shirt, its sleeves rolled up and the top buttons undone, revealing the set of intriguing numbers on his chest.

"Good morning." I smile back. A sexy, knowing smirk crosses his face. Of course he knows what's going on in my head. I've been staring at him for way too long, openly checking him out. Clearing my throat, I hop onto one of the barstools. "Are Noah and Sean coming over?" I ask.

"Noah and Sean?" He sounds genuinely confused.

I wave my hand at the ridiculous amount of food in front of us. "I just thought… This is a lot of food." Again.

"Is it?" He slides past me, handing me a glass of orange juice and a plate with three huge pancakes, one on top of the other, topped with berries, sliced banana, and peanut butter. "Coffee?" he asks innocently. I may not have known him for a long time, but I recognize the mischief in his eyes when I see it. My gaze darts suspiciously between my pancakes and the beautiful man standing in front of me.

"River Evans!"

I see him winking at my use of his full name.

"What's going on here?" I ask, frowning. It'd probably be much more convincing if I could resist the temptation of taking a bite of what I've now determined is the most delicious breakfast I've ever tasted. The moan that escapes me is perhaps not helping either.

He angles his head, studying me for a moment, and then shrugs. "Nothing. It's… Sunday," he says.

"Sunday," I repeat.

"Yep. That's what we do in the US. Sundays are pancake days." He leans forward, taking a bite from my plate. "Come on, Violet, eat your breakfast."

I shake my head at him but do as he says, unable to resist. "When is your interview?" I ask, my mouth full.

He looks at his left wrist. "In forty-five minutes."

"What? Aren't you going to be late?" I know his interview is in the area, but still, this is New York and it can take forever to drive through the crowded city streets.

"I'll be fine. I have a car waiting for me downstairs."

"Oh, okay. Good." I can't help but feel disappointed at the prospect of him leaving so soon. *He waited for you to wake up. He made you breakfast. He should have left a while ago.* Of course, I know all that, but this being our last day together, something inside me urges me to hold on to it before it ends. *To hold on to him.* It's for the best, though. I wouldn't be much fun to be around today. Plus, I already know just the place to go.

"I'll be done by noon, and then I'm yours for the rest of the day." He grins, and even though I know that isn't what he meant, it hits me that's exactly what it is. He's going to be mine for the rest of the day, and then tomorrow morning, we'll head back to Boston, acting like none of this ever happened. As if this trip hasn't changed everything. *For you or for him?* I must have winced because River's face is marked with a frown as he looks at me.

I force my mouth into a smile, meeting his gaze. "Sounds great."

He just nods, as if unable to decide if I'm telling the truth. Then, without a word, he leans forward, planting a soft kiss in my hair. "Be careful if you go out exploring. New York is a wild city."

# Seventeen

New York is a wild city indeed, and Times Square is the wildest place of them all. I pull the long scarf tighter around my neck, trying to breathe through it. The snow that fell last night hasn't melted yet. New York has awoken under its light blanket, and it's freezing yet stunningly beautiful. The ground beneath me is crunchy and slippery, making me take cautious baby steps to avoid falling on my face, which is almost exactly what I do when I look up and see River. He's looking down at me from a massive, vibrant digital display situated right beside the newest Netflix and flashy Apple iMac ads. *River Evans's Christmas Tour: Speaking Through the Silence.* Fuck. I lose track of my surroundings, standing there, oblivious to people bumping into me, my focus on the promo of River's tour. The one he'll be going on in three weeks.

A mix of sadness and immense pride overwhelms me. He deserves this and so much more. This is the guy who grew up in foster homes, never being loved enough by someone to be chosen and shown that love is worth fighting for. He's worth fighting for. And yet, he made it. And although he made it seem effortless, I know it was anything but. It occurs to me that, in the end, even though River has accomplished all his dreams, he is still that broken little boy. A boy who is now celebrated by millions but continues to wander the world alone.

The ad promotes his new album, which shares the same name as his tour and will be released just in time for Christmas. The album I'm apparently singing on. Oh, my God. The moment I realize that, I almost wish I could die, considering the terrifying number of people who will listen to it. Will they like it? Will they hate it? I'm sure they won't hate it since River is the one who wrote it, and my part in it isn't that important, but the idea of people actually listening to it makes me queasy. I can almost hear Alex laugh at me, and the sudden thought of him makes me smile. So does the idea that there's still one surprise I've been holding on to for River. I know he'll love it, and I can only hope that he'll be as proud of me as I am of him. After fishing out my phone, I take a picture of the ad that will always remind me of the man I've fallen in love with. There is no point in lying to myself anymore because, unfortunately, that's exactly what has happened. I've set myself up for one hell of a heartbreak, and I only have myself to blame for that.

*

A huge, yellow, egg-shaped M&M with one of its arms raised is smiling at the entrance, welcoming the crowds of tourists entering the famous candy shop. I manage to snap a couple of pictures before heading inside, shaking my head at the number of people taking turns hugging and kissing the somewhat already beaten, life-sized candy—no doubt for Instagram pics.

If only Alex were here. I can hear my brother's voice filled with jokes, laughing as we explore the endless gifts, from T-shirts and mugs to blankets and fluffy slippers. He'd have loved this place. After examining both floors, I find myself back in front of the pile of blankets. This place is a Disneyland, and just as expensive, which is why I'm not buying anything, as much as I would like to. There are currently three hundred bucks in my account, so there's no way I'm spending over thirty dollars on a souvenir. I notice a little girl standing next to me. She can't be more than seven or eight years old. With her tiny hands, she's pulling at the blanket, clearly trying to send a message to her mom, a tall blonde woman in her forties, who appears to be occupied with a phone call. The little girl pouts, moving her hands to her hips, and a slight, adorable frown crosses her face as she realizes her efforts are in vain.

"You like this one?" I ask her. She doesn't answer. Instead, she silently studies me. "I'm Sabrina," I tell her. "What's your name?"

She blinks a few times, seemingly unsure if she should be talking to a stranger. Her gaze briefly shifts toward her mom, who's still on the phone but not too far away, and then back to me.

"Juliette," she introduces herself, finally wrestling the blanket free and hugging it to her chest. "Mommy is gonna buy it for me." She seems more confident now. I feel myself smiling.

"Juliette, come on, we gotta go." When I turn, I see a little blond boy taking Juliette's hand. He must be her age or maybe just a year or two older. My heart tightens, and a sharp stabbing pain shoots through my rib cage. I envy them. I envy them with all my heart because they still have each other. They walk away, oblivious to just how lucky they are, but Juliette abruptly stops and, shaking off her brother's hand, runs back to me. She halts in front of me, looking up and handing me her blanket. "You should have it," she says, and not waiting for my answer, she sprints back to her mom and her brother.

I smile. I don't know how long I stand there, staring after her long, wavy blonde hair getting lost in the crowd, hugging the blanket to my chest, just as she did only minutes ago. I'm sure Juliette saw that there were at least ten other identical blankets, but that's not what she was trying to give me. She was trying to make me smile, and she succeeded. I leave the shop with a much lighter heart. If only I could buy that blanket and keep smiling every time I look at it, but I know it wouldn't be a wise choice. I think of River making me promise I won't skip any more meals, and I know he's right. I do, however, treat myself to a cup of coffee, and, with a few hours remaining, I retrieve my list of must-see places, putting on my headphones and immersing myself in River's soothing voice, instantly feeling a little less lonely.

*

When I receive River's message, it's almost two in the afternoon. He asks me to meet him at home, so he can change into something more comfortable for our city exploration. Huh. I wasn't sure he was serious, but apparently he hasn't forgotten about showing me around. I head back to the apartment, searching in my bag for the extra set of keys he left me this morning.

"River?" Even though I was temporarily given a set of keys, it doesn't feel quite right to just walk into his place without announcing my presence. There's no answer, though, so I stop being ridiculous and step inside, closing the door behind me. He's nowhere to be seen, but I can hear a series of noises coming from upstairs.

"I'll be down in a second!" he shouts.

Since I don't need to get changed, I decide to wait downstairs, checking my phone in the meantime. There are another three missed calls from home since I silenced their number this morning, hoping for a peaceful start to the day. But one can't pretend forever. I sigh, deciding it's better to rip off the bandage. It's already quite late in Prague, and if I don't call now, we won't be able to talk today. Not that I would mind.

The call only rings once. "Sabrina!" Mom answers breathlessly. "I've been trying to call you for a couple of days," she says, not hiding the accusatory tone in her voice.

"I know." I'm sure she noticed I've been purposely screening her calls, and I don't feel like denying it.

"Have you thought about coming home?" she asks quietly. And we're back to that. She isn't talking about Christmas, we both know it.

"No," I say, anger bubbling inside me. "Have you and Dad thought about coming to see me?"

Mom sighs. All our conversations are the same. I'd love

to tell her about New York, about my first recording in a professional studio, about finishing my new song, about River… but I can't tell her any of that. My parents want me to be the perfect daughter they dreamed of, the one I never was and never will be. They want their son back, but Alex is gone.

Our breathing is the only sound punctuating the long silence that has settled between us.

"Where is Dad?" I finally ask.

"At work," she says. It's not lost on me that he hasn't tried to call me once. Not even today.

"Okay," I whisper, hearing River's footsteps. "I have to go, Mom."

"Okay," she answers, and right as I'm about to hang up, I hear her voice once again. Except it's much softer now. "Happy birthday, darling."

I shove the phone back into the pocket of my jacket like it's burning, doing my best not to burst into tears, given that River is standing right in front of me now, his head cocked to the side like he's trying to understand what made me so upset. Fortunately, he couldn't have understood our conversation, but I think he can probably tell a lot more by my face than I'm giving him credit for. I lift my lips into what I hope looks like a smile. "Hey, how was your interview?" He's dressed much more casually now, in dark jeans and a hoodie, his 'blend-in uniform,' so he can move around the city without people stopping him on every corner.

"Good." He grins. "How was your day so far?"

"Great." I nod. He doesn't look like he believes me, but he knows me well enough not to push.

"Have you eaten anything yet?" he asks instead, and it's his expression that makes me laugh. He's trying to sound indifferent, but I know exactly what he's doing. Of course I haven't eaten. After the breakfast he prepared this morning, I could keep going for at least another couple of hours.

"Are you checking on me, River Evans?"

"No." He frowns. "I just thought we could grab a bite on our way out."

"What? They didn't give you anything to eat at *GQ*?" I chuckle, mocking him. He didn't mention which magazine he was interviewing for, but I did read articles about him in both *GQ* and *Esquire* recently. I'm definitely not admitting that, though.

An amused smirk crosses his face. "Are you making fun of me?"

"Never." I shrug innocently.

Laughing, he wraps his arm around me and guides me out the door. "All right, let's get you something to eat. You are mean when you are hungry."

*

We get takeout from Subway and eat it on our way to Liberty Island. I discover River isn't only an amazing musician, but he knows a great deal about history, too. Listening to him talking about how New Amsterdam became New York and how it turned into the cultural melting pot we know today is fascinating, and it helps me forget about everything else. Time flies while we explore the city, and I only realize it's almost seven when River's phone rings.

It's been dark outside for a while now, and I'm enthralled by the countless Christmas lights surrounding us. With all the pictures I've taken on my phone, I could potentially convince Rodrigo that I actually don't hate Christmas. Not as much as he thinks, at least. I only hate Christmas without Alex in it.

River is talking to someone, and even though I try to respect his privacy, I can't help but catch parts of his conversation.

"You're in New York?" I can hear the surprise in his voice. "Why haven't you told me? Where are you staying?" He listens for a moment, frowning and shooting quick glances at me. "When? Now? Yeah, I don't think—"

It's a woman's voice I'm hearing, and he sounds genuinely happy to be talking to her. Is it Riley? It must be.

"I'm kind of busy now," he says. I feel the hesitation in his voice, though, and that's enough for me. Our eyes meet, and I'm the first one to look away.

"Hey, do you mind if I call you back later?" he asks her. "I really wanna hear everything," he adds softly, and I hate myself at that moment. I hate myself because I shouldn't feel jealous, but I do. He hasn't promised me anything, after all.

I only notice he's hung up his call when his body shifts to me. I make an effort to keep my focus on my feet, doing my very best not to look at him. We walk in silence until I can't do it anymore.

"You can go if you want to, you know?" I say. I still don't look at him, trying to sound as nonchalant as possible.

"Oh." He shrugs. "It's fine. I can see her another day. I just didn't know she was in New York." He gives me a half smile and keeps walking. What the hell? It's one thing he hasn't promised me anything and another thing to act like a jerk. I slow down, almost stopping, and finally look at him. "Because if you did, you wouldn't have asked me to come?"

The words have somehow slipped out of my mouth, and now it's too late to take them back. River seems genuinely confused. Or hurt. I don't even know anymore. I just know I'm acting like an idiot. A *jealous* idiot. *Way to go, Sabrina.*

"No," he says slowly. "If I did, I'd have let her know earlier to meet us somewhere for a coffee or something."

What? Can he really be this oblivious? "You would want us to meet? Why?" It's not like we haven't met already, because we did—that night at the jazz club where River introduced me as his student. I wonder how he would introduce me now.

We're walking slowly again, but I keep my eyes on him this time, hoping for a more elaborate explanation.

He sighs, shaking his head as though unable to understand what has gotten into me. "Because I'm pretty sure you and Mayra would understand each other quite well."

"Mayra?" Wait a minute. My brain slowly catches up with the information. Oh, my God. Did I just make a complete idiot of myself? "Your sister was the one you were talking to?"

He scowls. "Yeah. Who did you think I was talking to?"

Just as I'm about to come up with an excuse I haven't quite figured out yet, my feet slip on the icy ground inconspicuously covered by a layer of peaceful-looking snow. I immediately lose my balance and, trying to save myself, I grab River's arm. Before he can register what's happening, we're both flying in the air and falling onto our asses.

"Fuck," he cries. "Are you all right?" His hands shoot to me, traveling up and down my face and body, making sure that I'm in one piece. Seeing his panicked face and looking at us both still half sitting, half lying on the ground, I can't help myself; I burst into laughter. River looks startled for a moment, but it doesn't take long and we're both laughing, drawing curious glances from those around us. Some people are suppressing laughter, while others remain indifferent, quickly passing us on their way to the warmth of their homes. This is New York, after all. Nothing is that surprising. Luckily, River, wearing a winter coat and a hat, is almost unrecognizable from afar. I can't imagine Noah would be thrilled if he saw us pulling these stunts in the middle of the city. River's image is typically serious, but I can't help but wonder how his fans would react to seeing this funny, carefree side of their idol. And how selfish is it of me to want to keep it to myself a little longer?

"I'm so sorry." I look at him.

He nods, a smile breaking on his face as he offers me his hand to get up. A silent understanding passes between us. I'm not only apologizing for taking him down with me but also for the way I acted earlier. He doesn't ask any more questions and doesn't let go of my hand either. Whether he knows what was going through my head or not, it looks like we both prefer not to talk about it. Meeting Riley doesn't sound at all appealing to me, but I'd like to meet the girl River calls his sister, knowing Mayra is a huge part of his past. The past he mostly keeps to himself. Perhaps meeting her might actually shed some light on all the things I still don't understand about the man who has so effortlessly managed to steal my heart.

"Umm, so, you said Mayra is here?" I ask, trying not to focus on his fingers still interlaced with mine. Even with gloves on, I can feel the warmth of his skin, and it's almost surprising how good and natural it feels. *Don't get used to it. He isn't yours.*

River glances at me and then nods. "Yeah. Looks like she came here to visit a friend or something."

I inhale, the freezing air traveling through my lungs. "We could still meet her for a cup of coffee if you want."

His eyes study me for a moment. "You would like that?"

"Sure. Why not?"

"I don't know." He shrugs, but I clearly feel that there is something behind his hesitation.

"Spill it." I give his arm a tug and see a hint of a smile on his lips.

"You're annoying, you know that?" His eyes meet mine, and I know he's joking. "I just wanted today to be special for you," he finally says, kicking the snow at his feet.

"What? Why?" I frown, looking up at him.

"Because it's your—" He freezes abruptly. My eyes narrow at him. "First time in New York," he finishes, with a sheepish look on his face that contrasts highly with his usual self-assured expression.

I bite back my smile. "Call your sister, River."

# Eighteen

Mayra is a force of nature. She arrives at the nearby Starbucks, talking on her phone, laughing loudly, and shaking tiny snowflakes from her red winter coat. In one swift motion, she shoves her phone into her pocket and scans her surroundings. As soon as she spots us, her face brightens, and she starts making her way through the room. I find myself liking her right away. Her short black hair cascades down to her shoulders, complemented by her dark eyes, olive skin, and full red lips. She's beautiful. Her adoptive parents may be American, but there's something striking and unfamiliar about Mayra's looks. I wonder if she knows what her exact origins are. When River introduces me, her left eyebrow raises in a questioning smile, revealing a tiny scar. She wraps her arms around us both, planting a kiss on River's cheek and giving me a tight squeeze. River introduces me simply as Sabrina, but his hand doesn't leave the small of my back until we sit down again.

"Glad you were able to fit me into your busy schedule, Riv." Removing her coat, she teasingly pokes him. It must have started snowing again because her hair is filled with slowly melting snowflakes. Tying it into a bun and lifting her lips into another wide smile, she turns her full attention to me. "So, Sabrina, are you also a musician?"

"I'm working on it." I nod.

River shakes his head, not satisfied with my answer. "Sabrina is an amazing singer-songwriter." I stifle the urge to correct him. Yes, I've been enjoying singing much more lately, and, most importantly, I was finally able to perform my own song, the one I wrote for Alex. So what if the audience consisted of my fifteen classmates? What if River is right, and I could actually do this?

"Oh, wow, really?" Mayra's eyes move from her brother to me. "So, are you guys playing together *or something*? Is that how you know each other?"

River chuckles, seemingly unfazed by Mayra's nosy questions. "You could say that. Sabrina recorded a song with me. We know each other from BMC." *Huh, nice way out.*

Mayra raises her eyebrows again, her tiny scar almost reaching her forehead. "So you teach there too?" she asks. I'm fairly certain she can tell there is an age difference between River and me. Most teachers at BMC are over forty years old. The visiting artists are often younger, as is River, but even he's obviously among the youngest ones.

"No, I'm a student," I say. Mayra's surprised expression doesn't seem to affect River, but it makes me shift uncomfortably in my chair.

"If you are done with the interrogation, you can tell us what *you* are doing in New York," River suggests with an eye roll, but a smile plays on his lips.

"Why don't you get me a cup of coffee first?" she throws back at him, making me realize she hasn't ordered yet, while we are already sipping from our cappuccinos. River gets to his feet, murmuring under his breath something about a long line and self-service, and Mayra laughs.

"You want something else, Violet?" he asks with a brief touch on my shoulder.

"No thanks, I'm good." I shake my head.

Mayra tries to hand River her credit card, slipping it back into her pocket when he rolls his eyes at her, but not before my eyes catch the tattoo that expands across her right wrist. A set of six numbers. By now I have memorized the numbers on River's chest, so I know they are not the same, but it does look like the same tattoo. Coordinates to different locations, maybe?

"Violet, huh?" Mayra grins, turning to me once River's tall frame vanishes among the crowded tables. I don't bother with an explanation. Damn him with his little nickname. *Like you don't like it.* Despite his disguise, River must have been recognized because he's quickly surrounded by a group of teenagers thrusting their phones at him. He poses for a few photos, his smile seeming genuine, and signs what appears to be a napkin.

"Yeah, well, that's kind of a long story."

"We've got some time." She grins again.

Reaching across the table, I grab her hand and gently turn her wrist upward. "What does this tattoo mean?"

There's a brief look of discomfort that flashes across her face, but she masks it quickly. "Why?"

"River has a similar one," I admit.

"It's kind of a long story," she throws back at me.

I chuckle. "We've got some time."

Her mouth curves up, and she laughs. "All right, but you might be disappointed. It's nothing fancy, quite the opposite, actually."

"What do you mean?" I frown.

"River told you I got adopted when I was seven, while he stayed behind, right?"

I nod, waiting for her to continue.

"I've always had a hard time making friends." She sighs, her eyes instinctively searching for River across the room. He hasn't been able to escape his fans yet. "With Riv, it was easy because we were the same and understood each other, but once I was out there, in the real world, everything was different. The other kids weren't like me. They had real siblings, real families. They never had to struggle like we did. Elementary school was hard for me, but high school was pure hell at the beginning, because if little kids can be mean, teenagers are the masters of meanness. Anyway, during my first year, there was this group of girls who took me in, and we became friends. One day, we went to a party and got drunk, and I guess it must have been the alcohol, because I never used to talk about my past in foster care, but they got me talking. It felt good, you know? Thinking that my friends were actually trying to get to know me better."

I nod again, unsure where the story is going.

"There was this guy I liked, and he was hanging out with his friends too. We got a table with them and started playing this stupid teenage game where you had to either accept or decline a challenge. At first, it was small things like kissing someone or telling the truth about something, but as we kept drinking, it escalated. The guy I liked suggested I get a blind tattoo, meaning they choose the design, and I agreed. My girlfriends were the ones who were supposed to choose it, so I expected a fucking butterfly or something." She laughs, but it sounds strained. "We went to this tattoo studio that was open until late at night. The guys knew the owner, so he never even asked for our IDs, and he certainly didn't care that we were drunk. I got my tattoo and didn't even look at it until the following morning. That's when I saw the numbers," she says, her voice trailing off.

"What are they?" I ask softly.

"They're my file number from foster care."

"What?"

Mayra laughs when she sees my look of confusion. "Yeah, I told you. Nothing fancy. These are basically the numbers we were identified by when we lived in the system. I've never forgotten them, and I used to wear them engraved on a bracelet. It was a reminder, albeit morbid, of my roots. Riv never liked that bracelet, and he tried to make me throw it away, but I couldn't bring myself to do it. That night, I had told my girlfriends what it meant and that I was trying to get rid of that bracelet… and I guess they thought it would be a good idea to carve it into my flesh instead."

My jaw drops at that cruelty. "That's—"

"Fucked up?" She chuckles. "Yeah. It is. When Riv saw it, he got incredibly mad—I've never seen him like that in my life. He dragged me into the nearest tattoo studio, and I thought it was to have it removed, but that would have been impossible because it was still too fresh. Instead, he seated me in the waiting room, and in less than an hour he came back out with the same tattoo across his chest, with his own set of numbers. I've never been more thankful for having him in my life than in that moment," she finishes.

My heart squeezes. This is certainly not a story I've ever expected, but it doesn't surprise me in the slightest. It only makes me fall in love with the man even further.

"He likes you," Mayra says suddenly.

"What?" I blink at her.

"I've never seen him like this," she continues, ignoring my question.

"Like what?"

"Happy," she offers. "He may not be my real brother, but to me, Riv is family. I've known him forever. He has never shown up to any of our meetings with a girl before." She winks at me.

"Yeah, well, I might have been the one who told him to call you back, so it probably doesn't count," I say, glancing at the counter. River has managed to free himself and is waiting for his order.

Mayra laughs, but her expression turns serious quickly. "Listen, I know how guarded and stubborn he can be, but I can tell he cares about you."

I respond with a shrug. *But that's not enough, is it?*

"Don't let him push you away," she says, almost as if she could read my mind.

"I don't think that's up to me." What does she want me to do? Tie him up? Kidnap him and lock us both in his New York apartment? We have lives we need to get back to. Our little bubble will burst after tonight, and there is nothing I can do about it. He made his choice, and I made mine, knowing perfectly well he didn't want a relationship and still going for it.

"This is what he does," Mayra says. "He pushes away the people he cares about because he's afraid they will leave him eventually. It's his way of protecting himself from getting hurt. He sabotages his own happiness, and I don't think he even realizes it. And, you know, I understand it. When you grow up like we did, relationships become much more complicated. You don't trust people. I was lucky enough to escape the system quickly, and I don't have that many memories, but he does. He never had the opportunity to have a family, and except for me, he had no one to care for him. Trust me." She grimaces. "That kind of stuff can seriously fuck you up."

"I know," I whisper. It's understandable that he struggles with trust, but is that why he keeps pushing me away? Or is it simply because relationships don't fit into his celebrity lifestyle? *You know that's not true*, the subconscious voice in my head tells me. *That's not who he is.*

"There you go." River places a cappuccino in front of Mayra and then hands me a brown paper bag as he sits back in his chair.

I eye the bag suspiciously, giving it a light shake. "What is it?"

He shrugs. "It's a muffin. I thought you may want something sweet with your coffee." I've come to accept that River will always try to feed me, and I've learned to secretly enjoy it, but Mayra's amused 'I told you so' look still finds me. *Not what you think.* I shake my head at her.

We talk for another hour, and it's nice. Comfortable even. I make a conscious effort to push Mayra's words out of my mind. She's the one who does most of the talking, telling us about her new boyfriend, whose parents live in New York—apparently the reason she's in the city this weekend. The information, of course, triggers an avalanche of protective, older-brother questions from River and makes me smile. I love their relationship, and I'm glad River has at least some sense of family in his life. Mayra may not be his real sister, but she has always been there for him, and they stuck together even after Mayra got adopted. River could have easily been jealous, but he decided to be happy for the little girl who, just like him, was abandoned by her parents. And that says a lot about a person.

After that, we talk mostly about BMC. Mayra asks about my experience so far and tells me she wants to study music therapy. According to her, River is the superstar, while she prefers to use music to help people. River argues that helping people is the ultimate goal of *any* good artist, and I'm transported back to Professor Jameson's class. Of course, this is the answer to his question! I smile to myself. Music shouldn't be about the artist; it should be about what the artist can offer to the world. Just as we dive deeper into a discussion about music and art, Mayra's phone lights up with messages. "I gotta go," she says, smiling at the lit screen and quickly typing back. I can easily tell who the recipient of her messages is just by looking at her beaming face, and so can River.

We get to our feet, collecting our empty cups and putting on our coats. "It was great meeting you, Sabrina," she says. "Don't forget what we talked about." River's gaze flickers my way, and I shake my head. *You'll have to take this one up with your sister.* She chuckles, kissing him on the cheek as she whispers something into his ear. His jaw tightens, and then he nods, ruffling her hair with affection.

We're alone once again. I wish I could stop counting down the hours we have left.

"You feel like going home now?" he asks softly.

Our walk home is silent as we both get lost in our thoughts, walking at a slow pace. At some point, River reaches for my hand, lacing our fingers together. Even though the night is cold and it's still snowing, we don't put our gloves on this time. Feeling each other's warmth, we don't even notice the cold.

He breaks the silence first. "Thank you for wanting to meet Mayra today."

"Are you kidding? I loved her. Thank you for introducing us and for... everything else."

He glances at me, and there is something in his eyes I can't quite decipher. "I already told you, you have nothing to thank me for."

But I do. And while our story may end here, I'll never forget everything he did for me. I will never forget him.

"I finished the song," I whisper, hot air coming out of my mouth, creating little steam clouds.

Surprise flashes across River's beautiful face. "Your song?" he asks. "You finished it? When?"

"After you chewed me out in class," I admit, laughing.

He chuckles, but his expression quickly turns serious. "Listen, Violet, I'm sorry about that... I was—"

"Don't be, you were right," I cut him off. We both know that him chewing me out in class had nothing to do with my music and everything to do with what happened between us, but truth be told, without River motivating me to push harder, I don't think I would have ever been able to finish it. I was so comfortable with the arrangement Alex and I had. He was the one who loved the spotlight. I never did. I've always been more of a behind-the-scenes girl, confident in my writing skills but lacking confidence as a performer. The decision to come to Boston had been a difficult one, not only because of the financial struggle and the need to stand up to our parents in order to follow our… *my* dream, but also because coming to BMC meant putting myself out there. And that is the most difficult thing an artist can do. I know I still have so much to learn, but for the first time ever, I don't doubt that I'm on the right path. I just wish I wasn't about to lose the only person who makes me feel like I can take the whole world on.

"Will you play it for me?" he asks quietly.

Once upon a time, I may have needed much more convincing, but today, I'm actually glad he asked. He deserves to be the first one to hear it.

"I would love to." I smile.

\*

Silence fills the elevator, and the tension is palpable, making it hard to breathe. I wish River would say something to ease the tension, but he stays quiet. Instead, he observes me, his pensive eyes scanning my face and lingering on my lips. The moment the elevator doors open, I swiftly make my way out, feeling a wave of relief.

"I'll order pizza," he calls after me.

"Right. I'm going to take a shower if you don't mind." Yes, a shower is exactly what I need right now. Possibly a cold one, despite the freezing temperatures.

He nods, and I head upstairs, quickly reaching the bathroom. It's not until I'm under a hot stream of water—a cold shower wasn't an option after all—that I manage to calm my nerves a little. Getting out, I run a brush through my wet hair and then wrap myself in a towel before returning to my room to get dressed. It would probably be odd to dress up for a pizza night, but I still don't want to show up in my pajamas. Not that River hadn't seen me in them already. Since the heat is on and the temperature inside is perfect, I decide to go with jeans and a basic top.

Just as I'm about to drop my towel on the bed, I spot a medium-sized box sitting there. It looks like a storage box, the kind you'd use to store sweaters and coats in after winter. Weird. Is it River's? And how did it get here? I'm pretty sure it wasn't here this morning. Yet it's sitting on my bed. I frown, my curiosity getting the best of me. It's my room, after all. Well, not really, but right now, it still is. Holding my towel with one hand, I reach for the suspicious box with the other. It's not sealed, so it opens right away, and it's only when I peek inside that I'm hit with even greater confusion.

The first thing I fish out is a T-shirt. It's a size small and obviously a girl's shirt, so it couldn't possibly be River's. A green M&M shirt. What's going on here? I sit on the bed, bringing the box onto my lap, and stick my arm inside again, pulling out item after item: a blue M&M mug with a smiling face, three tubes of the colorful candies, a key chain, a red stuffed M&M with its eyes rolled—that one makes me smile in particular. My heart tightens as I swallow the immense lump that has formed in my throat, and I reach in and take out the last item. My eyes overflow with tears, even though I am trying so hard to keep them at bay. The blanket. Just like the one Juliette handed to me at the store this morning. River couldn't have possibly known that, though. My tears flow in a full stream as I notice him standing in the doorway.

"Hey, what's wrong?" He's next to me in a matter of seconds, pushing a strand of hair out of my face.

"You... you... Is this for me?" I finally manage to get out, the words catching slightly in my throat.

He frowns a little but then nods. "I'm sorry, I just... I thought you would be happy. It's not a birthday present, you see?" he says, nervously tapping at the not at all birthday-like box containing the very birthday-like presents.

I smile through my tears. He's right. I don't want it to be my birthday present. Hell, I don't want it to be my birthday, but he went to all this trouble because he must have remembered me telling him how important the store was to me because of my memories with Alex. Did he go there after his interview? Is that why he told me he needed to go home to get changed?

"It's not a birthday present," I repeat, "but it's still a present."

"Is that why you're crying?" He smiles as his fingers gently touch my cheek, wiping up the remaining tears.

"No."

"Okay," he answers quietly. He doesn't ask why I'm crying then, and I love him for it. I love him for that and for much more, and I wish I could tell him, but everything he does is just becoming more and more confusing. It seems like he just now realizes how close he's sitting to me while I'm still wrapped in my towel that is dangerously slipping off my breasts. His eyes linger there for a moment, and I can feel him tensing. He shifts nervously next to me, clearing his throat. "You should dry your hair," he whispers, his hand brushing back my wet hair. It only lasts a second, but I wish he wouldn't stop. I need him. I want him to touch me.

"River," I murmur.

His breathing is quick, but I know he's trying to restrain himself. "You're killing me, Violet," he whispers back.

"Why?" I could tell him he's killing me too. He's killing me with all these mixed signals. He's killing me by being so close and so far away at the same time, but none of that matters right now. All I want is to feel him as close as possible once more.

"Because I can't have you," he says softly, his lips now only a couple of inches from mine.

"Why?" I repeat.

He runs his tongue over his teeth. "Because this won't end well for either of us." But his arms are already around me, and his lips crash hard on mine. His mouth feels warm, and he kisses me like he has been starving for it. So have I. I moan into his mouth, and his restraint disappears. "Come here," he orders and helps me to get on his lap so I'm straddling him. He's fully dressed, but I'm completely naked under my towel, making it much easier to feel how hard he is for me. His touch glides over the towel, his breath hot against my ear. "You really are killing me, you know that? I need to touch you. I need to touch you so fucking bad."

Instead of answering, I begin to move on his lap, seeking that incredible and agonizing friction. He groans, running his hand over my breast, which has peeked out of the towel that is no longer hiding much. I'm only seconds from coming, and I know River lost his control long ago. That's when the bell rings. The stupid pizzas.

"Fuck," River curses. "Fuck." He runs his hand through his thick, messy hair, trying to compose himself. "I'm sorry," he whispers. I'm not sure what he's apologizing for.

I turn away, readjusting my towel. "It's okay." I smile. "I'll see you downstairs."

River nods as he rearranges his pants, trying to hide the obvious bulge. "Yeah." He swallows hard. "I will see you downstairs."

It's only when he's gone that I allow myself to close my eyes, breathing out evenly. Maybe the interruption was for the best. Maybe this shouldn't happen again, because it only complicates things further. But even knowing all that, I would have still gone through with it without a moment's hesitation.

✳

Of course, at this point, I've decided to change my dinner outfit. It now consists of the same pair of jeans I chose earlier and my new green M&M shirt tied in a knot under my breasts. I don't bother with a bra since this shirt is clearly not see-through. I'm pretty sure green isn't my color, but I love it.

The genuine smile that breaks on River's face as I enter the living room confirms my choice and clears the loaded air between us.

"It suits you," he says.

"Thanks." I smile back and grab myself a chair, seeing that our pizza is already set on the table.

"I didn't know which pizza you liked."

I notice he ordered one that looks completely vegetarian and another one with prosciutto.

"I'm surprised you haven't ordered all of them." I smirk at him.

"Can't say I wasn't about to."

We both burst into laughter, and I'm relieved we're back to talking normally.

"So you're still not going home for Christmas?" he asks.

"No, I'm not." I shake my head, placing a piece of pizza on my plate. "Anyway, it's been a while since we celebrated Christmas." *Since Alex died.* The look in River's eyes tells me he knows the reason.

"You miss him," he says softly.

"I do." Every single day. "I just wish he had the chance to come here like I did."

River nods, contemplating, before glancing back at me. "You still haven't told me what happened," he whispers.

I look up from my pizza, suddenly losing my appetite.

His gaze is fixed on me, but his expression is gentle and patient. I've only told him I held our parents responsible for what happened to Alex, but that's not entirely true. I hold all of us responsible. Myself included because I should have known. I should have stopped him.

"He ODed," I say, and the words hang heavily between us. A look of confusion fills River's eyes as he stops eating. I shake my head, my voice cracking ever so slightly when

I continue. "He wasn't a drug addict. And I don't believe he did it intentionally. But… After he got kicked out of the house, I guess he was looking for some form of relief, or maybe he did it to spite our parents. I don't know. The drugs he took… it was supposed to be coke, but the police said it must have been mixed with fentanyl."

"And you think he wouldn't have done it if your dad hadn't kicked him out of the house?" River asks carefully. It's a question that has been on my mind for a long time.

"Honestly? I don't know," I admit, "but I think they should have talked to him. They should have listened."

I know Alex wasn't a drug addict. He became a drug dealer, though, and the very substance he thought would secure his future ended up destroying him, robbing him of all his dreams, *our* dreams.

Yet, I probably wouldn't be here if it wasn't for him. I admit I was losing hope and trying to convince myself that our parents might be right after all. I was going to stay in Prague and follow the path they chose for us. Alex was not. He fought for our dreams, but he chose the worst possible way to do so.

"They should have listened," River agrees.

"And I should have known," I whisper.

"Violet." He looks at me with such gentleness in his eyes that I have to look away. "This is not your fault. You can't go there, or you will drive yourself mad," he says, and I know he's right. I only wish it was that easy. "The best thing you can do to honor your brother's memory is to become the amazing musician he saw in you."

"Yeah, I really hope he won't be disappointed." I laugh, but it's a mixture of laughter and tears. After Alex died, I left my studies and spent two years in treatment for severe depression. My therapist used to say it wasn't depression; it was just grief, and only time was going to solve that. I can't say I haven't thought of solving it myself, but I couldn't do it. I know Alex would have never forgiven me. After all, I love life, but the idea of life without him was a difficult one. It was the letter from BMC that broke through the darkness I had surrounded myself with. The letter said they couldn't keep my acceptance and my scholarship on hold anymore, making this my last chance to come to Boston. So I did. There was no other possible decision.

"I don't think he could ever be disappointed in you, Violet." River smiles softly. "Why don't you play that song for me?"

# Nineteen

Choosing one of his guitars, I sit on the floor, crossing my legs. River situates himself right in front, his eyes fixed firmly on me. I don't need him to close them this time. Quite the contrary, I have learned to find comfort in the way he looks at me.

Like I can do anything. Like he is already loving the song I'm going to sing even though he hasn't heard it yet.

I shift, adjusting the guitar in my lap once more, and with my eyes not leaving his, I hit the chords.

Why wouldn't you listen?
Keep going, there is nothing we can't do
And I believed you, always so damn sure
Was it me who didn't see the storm coming?
Was it you?

You left me alone
Surrounded by those I don't even know
You asked me to keep smiling
But my heart doesn't hold

They say if you don't decide who you are
The world will tell you
But do they know?
Did you?

Why wouldn't you listen?
Keep going, there is nothing we can't do
And I believed you, always so damn sure
Was it me who didn't see the storm coming?
Was it you?

So tell me it was all worth it in the end
You say "yes of course it was"
And I wish I could say the same
But there is nothing left but silence

Oh, there is nothing left but silence
Nothing left but silence

With the last note fading, my heart leaps, and a strange sense of happiness washes over me. I started writing this song a few months after Alex's death, but back then, I couldn't bring myself to finish it. I couldn't get past the silence that had embedded itself so deep in my heart that it was the only thing I could hear. Not music. Only silence. The silence of a life without my brother in it. River broke that silence, reminding me that there is nothing more comforting than losing yourself in music.

There is a warm glint in River's eyes as he looks at me. "I wish we'd recorded this song at the studio," he says.

I carefully place the guitar on the coffee table. We

remain seated, facing each other on the floor, with River's legs gently brushing against mine.

"Does that mean you like it?" I ask, not trying to hide the eagerness in my voice. "I can still work on it some more." By now, he must know that I admire him not only as a person but as a musician, and since he isn't exactly known for giving compliments freely, his words mean that much more to me.

"Yes, it means I like it. A lot." His grin makes the lump in my throat dissolve.

"Really?" I can't help but smile. "You aren't just saying it because…" My voice trails off. Because you like me? Because we slept together? Because—

"Because I don't want to hurt you?" he offers.

I nod.

"No." He shakes his head. "You know I'd never lie to you." Our eyes lock, and I see the seriousness in his expression.

"But I really don't want to hurt you, either, Violet," he whispers, the weight of his words settling heavily in my chest. I'm pretty sure we aren't talking about music anymore.

"Why would you?" I ask, my voice barely above a whisper.

He looks away, raking his hand through his hair. There is a trace of emptiness in his voice when he speaks again. "Because that's what would happen." No explanation. How can he be so sure of it? He's already said it all, though. He doesn't do relationships. And Mayra said the rest—he pushes away the people he cares about. The protective walls he constructed around himself have become so thick that not even he can see beyond them. Or perhaps I'm just imagining things, and he doesn't actually care about me.

"Does this have anything to do with Riley?" I ask, even though I have no business asking. He never said he had feelings for me, but he also never talked about *her*, and the not knowing is killing me. So is the pretending that I don't care about him.

"Riley?" There's a hint of surprise in his voice as his eyes find mine again. "Why would you ask that?"

I shift uncomfortably under his gaze. I'm not about to admit that after seeing them together on TV and meeting her in person, my detective instinct kicked in. Or should I just say my jealousy instinct? Googling River's name, there were dozens of pictures of beautiful girls appearing on his arm—and I hated every single one of them—but Riley was the only one who kept reappearing in different photos. Plus, I saw the way she looked at him. I think she's just as in love with him as I am.

He sighs but doesn't break our gaze. "Riley and I are not together."

"Did she want to be?" I ask, surprising myself. I must like suffering. There is no other explanation.

He cocks his head to the side, probably trying to understand where all these questions are coming from. "Yes, she did," he finally says. His voice is quiet as he waits for my reaction. I don't give him any, so he continues. "We kept seeing each other for a while, but it wasn't working. I couldn't give her what she wanted." *I couldn't give her what she wanted.* His words echo in my ears, causing my chest to tighten. *I don't think I can give you what you want from me.* Those were the exact same words he said to *me*, not so long ago.

Something inside me finally snaps. Maybe this is the reaction he was looking for. Well, I'm tired of not telling him how I feel. If he can't take it, that's on him. It's funny how we always believe we have enough time for everything. We convince ourselves that there will be another day, another opportunity to pursue our passions. Another opportunity to express our love to someone. We hold on to our comfort zones, taking all those precious moments for granted until... someone we love is taken from us. It's only then we realize that time isn't always on our side, and if we miss saying or doing what we really feel, we may never get the chance again.

"The same as you can't give *me* what I want from you?" I ask. I say it without looking at him, but I can see from the corner of my eye the recognition that dawns on his face.

He shakes his head furiously. "Violet." He mutters my name softly, almost as a subtle warning.

"What?" I challenge.

"Don't compare yourself to Riley."

"Why?"

The tension around us is so thick that a knife wouldn't be able to cut through it. I'm furious. Furious at him for not talking to me. Furious at him for being there for me. And most of all, I'm furious at him for letting me fall in love with him.

Taking a deep breath, he runs his fingers through his hair. "Because she has nothing to do with you. Nothing to do with us. What we have is different."

A mixture of pain and laughter surges through me. "Different how?"

He inches a little closer, a strand of hair falling into his eyes. "Just… different."

I hold his gaze, not moving. "But still not enough?"

"I didn't say that," he murmurs.

"So what are you saying?"

"I…" He looks away.

"Right." I smile, but it's tinged with sadness. River is just like me; he would rather write thousands of songs than talk about his feelings, but I want the next song I write to be a happy one. "That's what I thought."

Without realizing it, I'm on my feet. The look on River's face mirrors the same confusion and turmoil bubbling inside me.

Well, at least I said it, right? *You didn't tell him you love him.* No, of course I didn't. Because he doesn't want to hear that.

He's next to me in a split second. "What are you doing?"

Good question. I have no idea what I am doing, but I need some space to think. "I'm going to my room."

"Please don't," he whispers, and there's so much vulnerability in his voice, it's almost painful to hear.

My heart jumps into my throat, and so many different emotions surge inside me, tangled and impossible to sort out. He rests his forehead against mine, his warm breath tickling my lips and the vein on his neck frantically pulsing. We've solved nothing, but there's another way to tell him how I feel about him. How I feel about us.

"Kiss me," I say. It's not a question.

"Violet," he warns again, but this time I don't let him think about it. I bring my lips to his, daring him to respond. And he does. Groaning into my mouth, he closes his strong arms around me. "Not here," he whispers. "I want you in my bed."

He takes my hand and silently leads me up the stairs to his bedroom, and I'm suddenly overcome with nervousness. This is not our first time. We've already seen each other naked. He's already been inside me. That's what I keep telling myself, but there's something different about this moment. Maybe it's the way his eyes are studying me. The time he's taking to remove my shirt and jeans. The way he's caressing and kissing every little piece of my skin like he wants to engrave it into his memory for eternity. And so do I. Realizing I'm not wearing a bra, he groans deeply before taking one of my nipples into his mouth and kicking my clothes away. The only fabric left on me is my black lace panties until he moves them aside and inserts his finger into me. I moan, steadying myself on his shoulders.

"So damn wet." He hums in my ear.

"Hmmm." Words escape me as I shamelessly push back against his hand.

"Show me what you need, Violet." His voice comes out raspy, and I respond with a loud moan when he adds his middle finger.

"River." His name leaves my lips as he spins me around, pressing my back to his chest. With one arm, he supports me as his other hand skillfully moves inside me, maintaining a perfect rhythm. My legs are wobbly, and if it wasn't for his arm wrapped strongly around me, I wouldn't be able to maintain myself on my feet.

"Please," I moan.

"Please what, Violet?" he asks softly, but his fingers keep moving and curling inside me, creating an overwhelming sensation. Is it supposed to feel so intense? But everything with River feels like that.

"You want me to stop?" he whispers, his lips grazing my neck, fully aware of the effect his touch is having on me. "Or do you want me to make you come? Tell me, Violet," he urges, thrusting his hips against me. The hard bulge in his pants is pressed against my ass, but he's still fully dressed. I want him naked. He is so fucking perfect, his muscles flexing under his shirt, his strong arms holding me in place, his long fingers so masterful at both playing the piano and giving me pleasure, as if they were made specifically for those two purposes.

Continuing to hold me against his chest, he shifts us both slightly to the side. "Tell me," he repeats.

"I want you to make me come." I breathe out just as his thumb starts playing with my clit. Only now do I realize why he moved us around the room. The tall mirror next to his bed is now directly in front of us. My eyes widen at the image of his fingers sliding in and out of me. His eyes burn with intensity, and his every move is filled with raw desire. "You like what you see?"

I can feel my heart thumping against my rib cage. "I do," I whisper. Knowing exactly what I crave, he removes his shirt, briefly pulling his hand away from my wet center. I immediately notice its absence, but I'm relieved he didn't use the arm that supports me, because my body is too weak. I've given myself to him completely, and he knows it. Whimpering lightly, I arch my back, pushing my ass against him. He makes a low humming sound as he removes his pants, his boxers following quickly and his cock springing free. If there was any doubt about whether he was as turned on as me, it's gone.

"So impatient," he whispers in my ear.

Hell yes, I'm impatient. Everything about this man is addictive, and if he doesn't touch me, I might just come from simply looking at him in the mirror. He palms himself twice, and then his hand returns between my legs. I'm completely fascinated by our reflection, unable to tear my eyes away from the mirror.

"Fuck, Violet," he groans. "Seeing you exposed like this is torture. All ready and open for me… I want to keep you like this forever. I want to save this image and replay it a thousand times when I'm alone. You want to know how fucking fast I come *every time* I think of you?" As his hand travels to my breasts, playing with my nipples, I feel an urgent pressure building within me. It's all too much; his fingers delicately twisting my nipples, his other hand between my legs touching just the right spot, quickly moving in and out, completely soaked in my wetness.

"River!" I cry out. "I can't—" I don't even have the time to finish the sentence or to think about everything he just said, although the image of him getting off all by himself while thinking of me is now strongly embedded in my mind, and I don't think I will be getting it out any time soon. The wave of orgasm that rolls through me is so strong that it almost tears me apart. I've never felt anything like it. I've never come so hard in my life. River's grip on me tightens.

"Shh, it's okay, let go. I've got you," he whispers in my ear.

I do as he says, and my body loosens completely in his arms. He withdraws his hand from between my legs and showers my neck with gentle kisses. "I've got you," he whispers again, then slowly spins me around so we are facing each other.

"I thought you wanted me in your bed," I murmur.

He chuckles, and I can feel how hard he is, his erection standing heavy and prodding at my entrance. "If you know exactly what I want and *where* I want you, what are you still waiting for?" he asks, arching his eyebrow and looking pointedly at the king-size bed behind us.

I smile. It's my time to have some fun. I take a few steps back and he follows, a predatory look in his eyes as he slowly palms himself with his right hand. Reaching the bed, I sit down, patiently waiting for him to get closer.

"Lay down," he says, his voice coming out hoarse.

I love the sound of it. I shake my head slowly, and he gives me a look of surprise.

"You want me to stop, Violet?" he asks carefully, his expression filled with worry.

"No, I want to taste you," I admit out loud. I don't wait for his reaction. This has already cost me enough courage. Instead, I reach for him, wrapping my fingers firmly around his hard erection, and take him into my mouth.

"Fuck," he cries. He hardens in my mouth, all words abandoning him. "You don't have to—" But I'm already taking him deeper, as deep as I can. He's big, but I do my best and notice his body tensing, instantly responding to me. As he gives up trying to stop me, his fingers tangle in my hair, and he starts thrusting in slowly.

"Look at me," he whispers, and I do. He runs his index finger along my cheeks and hooks it under my chin, directing my gaze back to the mirror. The image I see takes my breath away. River stands between my open legs, the muscles in his chest and legs working as he pumps in and out of my mouth, groaning loudly. I'm sitting on the bed, blood rushing to my cheeks, my nipples erect, and my hand wrapped around his cock. The taste of him is pure ecstasy. He sucks in a sharp breath and pulls out of me.

"I can't take it any longer, Violet. I need to be inside you."

The palpable need in his voice sends shivers down my spine. I nod, opening my legs wider, letting him know I want him just as much. He pushes inside me, carefully shifting me under his body until we both lie on his bed.

"I finally have you where I want," he murmurs softly, moving inside me.

"You do," I whisper back. The smile that flashes across his face is filled with tenderness and affection, and I wish I could ask him to put it into words. I know he wouldn't, though, and in the end, I realize it doesn't really matter. River has countless ways of expressing himself, and I've become attuned to him beyond words. I know he cares. I just wish he cared enough to fight for us.

I wind my arms around his neck, my breath coming out in short gasps. River quickens his pace as the pressure builds between my legs.

"Fuck, Violet, I'm coming," he chokes out, burying his face in my neck as we both come together, panting hard and holding tightly on to each other.

We stay silent as I nestle into his arms and close my eyes. I want to live here, enveloped in all that is River. But knowing what I have to do, sleep is the last thing on my mind. I just wish I didn't have to do it now. I wish I could stay in his embrace forever. Unfortunately, forever isn't an option for us as long as River keeps pushing me away. His breathing is slowly returning to normal.

"Happy birthday, Violet," I hear him whisper into my ear, planting a small kiss in my hair, fully convinced that I'm asleep and can't hear him anymore. I swallow hard, trying not to choke on the lump that has formed in my throat, and wait until he falls asleep.

It's only then that I reluctantly untangle myself from his arms and get dressed.

If I stay, I know exactly what will happen. In the morning, he would be sweet and attentive because that's simply the way he is. He will prepare breakfast for me and make sure that I finish it. He will even tell me he had a great time this weekend. After that, he will drive me back to campus, trying to come up with the best way to tell me that despite everything that happened between us, it doesn't change what he said. He doesn't want a relationship. And love is not something that can or should be forced.

Perhaps it's because I'm just not strong enough to face another rejection, but I'd much rather hold on to the memories of this weekend. Yes, I'll probably have to see him at least once more in class, but other than that, we don't have to see each other anymore. We tried to be friends once already, and it didn't work.

He doesn't owe me anything.

And I owe him so much.

He helped me find myself, but he also took something from me along the way.

A heavy pit forms in my stomach as I grant myself one last glimpse of him. He looks so peaceful, with his eyes concealed beneath his long lashes and his lips slightly parted.

I don't leave a note. What would I say anyway? *I made the mistake of falling in love with you. P.S. I'm sorry*? I'm sure he knows. Too bad he doesn't feel the same.

The idea of losing him hurts much more than I ever imagined, but it brings me comfort to know that I wouldn't have done anything differently. I tell myself that I'm not running away, because I did try, but it would be a lie if I said it makes me feel any better. Nothing about losing River could ever make me feel better.

# Twenty

It's still dark outside, the cold seeping under my skin and making me shiver. "The Port Authority Bus Terminal, please," I tell the cab driver as I turn off my phone.

At almost seven in the morning, the bus is still filling up, but luckily, the seat next to me remains empty. For nearly two hours, I've been waiting at the station. I'm cold and tired and must look like hell, not that I care. My tears continue to spill as I curl up in my window seat and close my eyes tight, waiting for our departure. I'm thinking about calling Bela, but it's way too early, and I don't want to turn on my phone. Feeling bad for not leaving a note, I sent River a brief message on my way to the station, telling him I would take the bus back home and he didn't have to worry. It seemed like the right thing to do. He never lied to me, so he didn't deserve to feel worried or guilty. Is he already awake? Has he tried to call me? Perhaps he woke up and realized I was gone and thought it was for the best. This way, he doesn't have to tell me again, doesn't have to remind me that there is no place for me in his life. I think of what Alex would say, but I can't come up with anything. He would want me to be happy. And he would be proud of me. I know as much now. He would be proud of how far I've come. Leaving home. Performing without him. Writing my first solo song. Recording at a professional studio. Almost finishing my first semester at BMC. Falling in love… And even though that part didn't turn out well, it still left me with much more than I came here with. It left me with hope.

I drift off, lulled by the rhythmic vibrations of the idling bus motor and the heat slowly warming my exhausted body, when I'm startled by the commotion coming from the door. Have we not left yet?

"Sir, you can't get on! You don't have a ticket." The driver raises his voice, trying to get rid of whoever thought he could get on without paying. I feel for the guy. The price of the ticket is plain robbery.

"Come on, man, I'll pay for the stupid ticket. I just need to talk to someone."

My eyes open as my heart threatens to jump out of my rib cage. It can't be. But it is. I would recognize that voice anywhere. Our eyes meet, and I see the hurt and anger in his face. He tosses a couple of bills at the bus driver, not bothering to wait for his change, his expression changing into determination. "Get off the bus, *Sabrina*." He stops in front of me. His voice is gentle but uncompromising. I silently shake my head. He isn't supposed to be here. What does he want, for God's sake? To make things even harder?

"Look, I don't know what's going on here or why you left, but please, just come with me." I refuse to take his outstretched hand. He sighs in frustration, as though this is the reaction he expected, and sinks into the seat next to me.

"What are you doing?" My eyes widen as I hear the bus door closing. "You have to get out of here, the bus is leaving!"

River frowns, not moving the slightest. "I'm not going anywhere without you," he says.

My mouth opens and closes in surprise. "River, please," I plead with him to regain some reason. This is ridiculous. What does he want me to do? I know it's not in his nature to let me go back to Boston by bus since he's the one who brought me here, but this is precisely what I didn't want to do. The awkward goodbye once we both arrive home.

"I don't want you telling me again," I whisper. "Just go, please."

"What?" Confusion appears on his face. "What don't you want me telling you again?" When I don't answer, he shifts his body toward me. I'm glad the seats surrounding us are almost empty, except for a teenage girl with her headphones on, listening to punk rock. The volume must be leaving her half deaf, but at least she doesn't have to listen to us. The rest of the passengers seem to be either asleep or glued to their phone screens.

"What don't you want me telling you, Violet?" he asks again. The bus begins maneuvering out of the parking lot. If he doesn't get off now, he won't be able to anymore.

"I don't want you telling me again that you don't want a relationship. I don't want you telling me that you don't feel the same as I do. I don't want you telling me that I shouldn't have fallen in love with you because I was stupid and I did... And now there is nothing I can fucking do about it! Are you happy? Now get out of here!" I blurt, and despite thinking I had no tears left, I feel them falling down my cheeks, taking away the last of my dignity. Not that it matters anymore.

"What did you say?" River's eyes widen and his teeth grit together so tight I can almost hear the noise.

"I said, 'Get out!'"

"No getting out now, folks! Better figure out your shit. You've got four hours," the bus driver calls. All right, so maybe we haven't been as quiet as I thought.

"I'm not getting out," River says firmly. I'm not sure if he is reassuring me or the driver.

"Damn it, River!"

He frowns slightly, his eyes locked on my lips. "You said... you love me?" he asks, his voice suddenly quiet and hesitant.

Perfect. We'll be stranded here for four hours and I just confessed my unreciprocated feelings. Could it get any worse?

"Just leave it alone. I don't understand why you're here, anyway. I gave you a way out. Why don't you just take it?"

"A way out?" he asks incredulously. "Is that what you think you're doing? Giving me a fucking way out?" He raises his voice again, running his hand through his messy hair. He must have left in a rush. He isn't even wearing a jacket, and his car, along with everything he brought for the weekend, has been left at his apartment. How did we find ourselves in this mess? I shift in my seat and look out the foggy, half-frozen window. He stays quiet for a while, except for his uneven breathing.

"Violet," he whispers. "What if I don't want a way out anymore?"

"You don't mean it, River. You say that now, but you're right, our lives are too different. You'll be leaving on your tour soon and—"

"Come with me."

"What?" I'm not sure I heard him correctly. "Come where?"

"On my tour," he says calmly. "It's during your winter break, and you said you weren't going home."

Has he gone crazy? "I don't think I would make a good groupie. I'm sorry." As attractive as his offer sounds, I don't think this is the right way for us.

He chuckles, giving me an amused look. "I don't doubt that you would make an amazing groupie, Violet, but that's not what I'm asking you. I want you to be my opener. And before you say no, I've already talked to Noah and sent our song to my record label. They loved it, and they're on board with you coming."

"What? I don't understand. When did you talk to them?" He must have run after me as soon as he woke up, so it couldn't have been this morning.

"I talked to Noah about it a couple of weeks ago, actually, but he thought the label wouldn't approve. That's why I had you record with me. I needed to have something to send them first. They listened to it yesterday and called us right away."

I feel my heart leap. Was he thinking about inviting me on his tour a couple of weeks ago? Is that why he kept asking if I was going home for Christmas? If that's true, this couldn't have been a hotheaded decision based on the amazing weekend we spent together.

"I know what you're thinking," he whispers.

The bus has taken the highway, and the road ahead of us seems endless. So does this conversation, since there's no way out of it anymore.

"What?" There is still a hint of pain in his eyes as our gazes meet. I hate that I'm the one who put it there.

"You think I'm offering you the spot because I have feelings for you, but that's not true." He frowns slightly as I let out a pained burst of laughter. Right. Of course, he needed to remind me.

"I know you don't have feelings for me. You've already made that clear." I shake my head. "Why are you here again?" I can't stand looking at him. It hurts too much, and I'd really like to conserve what's left of my pride. As I shift back to the window, I catch his confused look.

"I didn't… Fuck." He groans in desperation and, taking a deep breath, he starts again. "I meant it's not true that I'm offering you the spot because of that… Because I *do* have feelings for you."

I've never seen River so frustrated. He's always so calm and sure of himself. Why wouldn't he be? Seeing him like this confuses the hell out of me. Wait… what?

My eyes widen, but they stay fixed on the road, replaying his last words. Is asking him to repeat them an option?

"Did you hear me, Violet?" he says softly when he sees no reaction on my part.

"Why are you saying that?" I whisper, still not looking at him.

He slowly reaches for me, gently tilting my head toward him so I'm once again looking into his beautiful mint-green eyes.

"Because it's true. Because I want to give it a try. I know what I said. I know I insisted I didn't want a relationship. I just always thought it wasn't for me. I didn't want another person leaving me. I didn't want *you* leaving me. You are young and incredibly talented. You don't know where your dreams will take you. You're not even from here. I want you to have the chance to explore your dreams and make the best of them because you deserve that much." A look of agony crosses his face, and his jaw twitches. "I want you to have all of that, but I'm also selfish; I want to have you. I want to be there for you, seeing you rise and cheering for you every step of the way." His lips part, and he smiles.

His words cause my heart to skip several beats. "Come on the tour with me, Violet. Show the world what you can do. Show *me* what you can do. And maybe, just maybe, consider giving us a chance?" His eyes plead with me as he bites his lip, waiting for my response. "Just so you know, it's not a condition," he adds. "I want you on my tour either way because of your talent. It would fucking hurt to see you and listen to your beautiful voice every day, knowing you aren't mine, but I would still choose what's best for the show… and that's you." His look of defeat makes my resolve to pretend I'm angry at him crumble. He's serious, and it seems like he's thought this through. He wants me on his tour. He has faith in me as an artist, and, more importantly, he has faith in us, something I never thought possible given his history of being let down by those who were supposed to love and protect him.

"I won't leave you, River Evans," I whisper.

He looks at me questioningly, but there is a glint of hope in his eyes.

"You said you didn't want me leaving you," I explain, slowly turning to him. "Well, I won't. And I don't understand how someone could have ever done that, because leaving you this morning has fucking broken my heart. I'm the one who couldn't handle the thought of losing you. I don't know how many people know the real you—the one who's incredibly sweet and funny, a little too overprotective, the one who wants to take care of everyone and never would admit he needs anyone to take care of him. The one I've fallen in love with…"

I pause for a moment, and his cautious eyes study me as a tiny smile finally tugs at his mouth. "But I'm incredibly grateful that I've had the chance to do that. You saved me, River. I came to Boston broken. Broken as a musician and broken as a person, and you helped me to put the pieces back together. If you want me on your tour, I'll be there. And if you want me in your life…"

He puts his finger on my lips, not letting me finish. "I *need* you in my life, Violet. I think you still don't understand that. I fell for you a long time ago. Actually, now that I think of it, it must have been the Halloween costume."

I snort, hitting his arm. "Don't," I warn him.

He raises both his hands, laughing with me. "Now… when the fuck can we get off this bus?"

# Epilogue

I stare at the crowd and feel my heart pounding as if trying to jump out of my chest. The energy is palpable, and even though I'm nervous, I thrive on it. This, right here, is the best feeling ever, and I could never thank the universe enough for letting me experience it. Last night's performance in New York was one of the best nights I've ever had. The venue was jam-packed, and the crowd sang along with River throughout his entire performance. I couldn't have been prouder of him.

Another incredible highlight of the evening was that Rodrigo was able to join us for the show, and the three of us had dinner after that. Bela, on the other hand, came to our Boston concert, which was the very first one, and left for Spain right after. She said she needed to clear her head after what happened with Anders and wanted to spend some time with her family. I used to envy her when she talked about going home for Christmas, but now I don't. Even though the holidays haven't turned out how I expected, I'm enjoying every single moment.

It's funny because I was so anxious about telling Bela and Rodrigo about my relationship with River, but they took it in stride and seemed happy for me. What's more, there was an interesting development when Bela came to our Boston show and we introduced her to Noah. They were glued to each other the entire night. I seem to remember Noah, not that long ago, questioning how young I was compared to River, but he definitely didn't seem to have the same issue with my friend. Interesting. And that's not the only unexpected couple that appears to be forming, because right before leaving for our tour, I caught Connor and Nyra kissing at the bookstore. Wow, I really didn't see that coming, and I'm definitely not opening that storage room ever again. I suppose we have a lot to look forward to in the coming year.

I'm excited about the beginning of the new semester. It'll be a fresh start, and I can't wait for it. I'll still work at the bookstore to pay off my scholarship, but thanks to the significant amount of money I'm making on this tour, I know I'll be able to pay for my expenses and finally focus on my music. And, of course, with River no longer teaching at BMC, we don't need to hide, something neither of us was willing to do. Honestly, I was surprised how smoothly River settled into a relationship, especially after his previous hesitation, but he no longer seems like that broken boy he once was. He looks happy. We both do. It's true that healing takes time, but time alone isn't enough—to heal properly, we also need to learn to open ourselves to love and vulnerability again. And there is nothing more haunting than that.

A lump forms in my throat as I look out at the audience from backstage and scan the second row. There are two seats, right in the middle, that have remained empty. Repeatedly. Show after show. There are thousands of people in the audience, but those two empty seats send a spiral of hidden pain right through me. They haven't come.

When the Christmas tour started, River convinced me to send an open invitation to my parents so they could come to any of our shows. "They'll be proud of you, you'll see," he said. "Why don't you let them see how far you've come? Why don't you show them they were wrong not to believe in you?"

River's Christmas tour consists of fifteen shows in total, and this is the fourth one. So far, they haven't come.

"They're still your parents, Violet. They've made some really fucked-up decisions, but they've already lost one child. Maybe it's time to give yourselves another chance." I know he's right; I just don't know if it's not too late. My parents made a lot of mistakes, but so did Alex and I. The truth is that we all fucked up, and we all paid the price.

They say that a perfect family doesn't exist, and I guess it's true. I like thinking, though, that I would do things differently with my future children. River and I haven't broached the topic of kids yet; it's obviously too soon. We still have so much ahead of us, but I know he wants them, and so do I. I also know that once we have them, we'll do everything in our power to help them achieve their dreams, and, most importantly, we'll make sure they know we believe in them.

"This is for you, Alex," I whisper as I step onto the stage, catching River's encouraging smile from behind the curtain. *You have this*, I see him mouth. I smile back at him. As always, the simple sight of him anchors me. I'm where I'm supposed to be: on stage and with the man I'm madly in love with. I grin as I grab my guitar and step to the microphone. "Good evening, Atlanta. I'm Violet."

# Acknowledgements

Dear reader,

If you've made it this far, my deepest thanks go to you. I hope you enjoyed Sabrina's and River's story, and that it serves as a reminder that it's never too late to pursue your dreams, no matter how challenging they may seem.

Just like River said, you always have someone who believes in you. Sometimes it's your parents; other times it's someone more unexpected — a friend, a teacher, or a partner. But in the end, please remember that the only person who really has to believe in you is *yourself.*

That said, I want to express my gratitude to the two people who believed in me and supported me when I needed it most. *Pilar y Ricardo, muchas gracias por todo.* None of this would have been possible without you.

And of course, thank you to Ricardo Curto, my love and constant source of encouragement. Your hard work and dedication to your art inspire me every single day. *Te amo con todo mi corazón.*

A special mention goes to my little daughter, Persephone—you're still far too young to read this story, but I look forward to watching you grow and chase your own dreams. I promise I'll be there for you every step of the way.

While the story of Sabrina and River is completely fictional, it was inspired by my years of study in Boston and my career working with musicians. I am eternally grateful for the lessons I've learned from so many amazing artists every day. To all of you I have crossed paths with, thank you for letting me be a part of your dreams. There is a little piece of each of you in this story.

And of course, none of this would have been possible without the incredible work of my professional team. I want to begin by thanking Karen Grove for her patience and dedication in polishing and editing this story. I would also like to thank the fantastic Scott Editorial team, especially Emma, for her meticulous proofreading and for ensuring the story is as flawless as possible, as well as Amy, for helping me find the best house for my book. Finally, a special thank you to The Book Guild for believing in me and bringing Sabrina and River's story to life.

# About the Author

Laura Lo Sapio is a Czech-Italian author and music producer. Based in Spain, she co-founded Yamaha Music School Valencia and Sound Vanguard, a music-for-film studio behind projects for Netflix and Amazon. Her debut novel, *Nothing Left but Silence*, blends her love of music and literature. Fluent in four languages, Laura brings her international background into contemporary romance that explores trauma, healing, and the blurred lines of morality.

Did you enjoy Sabrina's and River's story? Please consider leaving a review on your preferred book platform.

Stay up to date with the latest news about Laura's books and projects by subscribing at www.lauralosapio.com and following along on social media:

Instagram: @laura_lo_sapio
TikTok: @laura.lo.sapio